D1500114

OUR
BEAUTIFUL
HEROINE

OUR
BEAUTIFUL
HEROINE

JACQUES
ROUBAUD

TRANSLATED FROM THE FRENCH BY
DAVID KORNACKER

THE OVERLOOK PRESS
WOODSTOCK, NEW YORK

First published in 1987 by
The Overlook Press
Lewis Hollow Road
Woodstock, New York, 12498

Originally published in French as *La belle Hortense* by Jacques Roubaud
copyright © Editions Ramsay, 1985

Library of Congress Cataloging-in-Publication Data

Roubaud, Jacques.   Our Beautiful Heroine.

Translation of: La belle Hortense.   I. Title.
PQ2678.O77B4513   1987   843'.914   87-5765
ISBN 0-87951-290-3

PAGES ADDED
BY THE AUTHOR
FOR REASONS OF STATE
(AT THE REQUEST OF THE PRESENT EDITION'S EDITOR
IN ORDER TO FILL UP BLANK PAGES)

OTHER BOOKS BY JACQUES ROUBAUD

DEDICATION

I dedicate this book to all my American friends, particularly Harry Mathews, Rosmarie and Keith Waldrop, Alice Notley, David Antin, Jerome Rothenberg, Ron Padgett and Paul Auster.

ACKNOWLEDGEMENTS

I would like to thank Deborah Baker and the staff at The Overlook Press who have helped to publish this translation of my work. I hope that it will be as successful as THE OVERLOOK GUIDE TO SMALLSCALE GOATKEEPING. May it be overlooked by all cat-haters.

I would also like to thank David Kornacker for his translation. My work was clearly improved by his diligence. In fact it is certainly closer to English than the original.

I would also like to thank my parents, friends, and acquaintances. Without them, if they had not been who they are, in other words, if they hadn't been my parents, friends, and acquaintances, I would not be what I am and consequently, this book would not have been written.

I also thank my characters, whose extensive support permitted me to undertake this task.

I particularly thank Alexander Vladimirovich.

EXTRACT FROM A LETTER

FROM HORTENSE TO THE
AUTHOR OF THE NOVEL
ENTITLED
OUR BEAUTIFUL HEROINE

Dear Sir,

I was especially touched by your particular attention to my feelings in your novel OUR BEAUTIFUL HEROINE, which tells of my adventures. In the French edition, Monsieur Jacques Roubaud somewhat awkwardly mentions that I am beautiful (how could he say otherwise?); he mentions the obvious somewhere else—the fact that I am also the heroine of the novel. Unfortunately, he never mentions anywhere that I am a "beautiful heroine." This is regrettable.

Yours truly,

Hortense

EUSÈBE

Eusèbe's grocery store opened at eight in summer. In winter too, for that matter. But in summer Eusèbe himself opened up: he would pull the two sections of the iron grating apart (they were never completely together), set the crates of fruits and vegetables out on the street, open them, and arrange their contents—tomatoes, oranges, peaches, lettuce, bananas—into a pleasing, businesslike display, meaning that the most visibly rotten ones were kept beneath or behind the others, those that were still presentable; then, his daily toil being thus completed to his utter satisfaction, he would take up his position on the side of the road, between the garbage cans, a few steps from the T-line bus stop (by request).

As soon as the store opened its doors, or at the very latest when he heard the rusty sound that immediately followed the grating being parted, Alexander Vladimirovich would appear and make a princely leap onto the crates, preferring to settle in among the lemons, whose health struck him as being more reliable than that of the pears or the onions. There he would wait, sphinxlike, for Madame Eusèbe to get up, and above all for her to serve him his morning milk (Gloria condensed only). The wait was never very long, as Eusèbe was totally uninterested in the store, and all responsibility thus fell to his wife. He was occupied by other matters.

We shall take advantage of this brief pause to flesh out the portrait of Eusèbe (by *we* I mean this story's narrator, or rather its narrators, since any story assumes not one but a whole host of explicit or implicit narrators, so great is the number of places and skulls in which anything important happens in any normally constructed story; only an idiot of a novelist always stays in the same spot, within himself, behind his own chin. I, Jacques Roubaud, am only the one holding the pen here, at the moment a black felt Pilot Razor Point with a fine tip—a fact indicated by a bit of yellow at the top of the cap as opposed to a white band, which means a thicker tip; the fine tip is more expensive, but too bad—that's why I say *we;* it is a plural of modesty. Furthermore, in this novel there is, as will soon be revealed to you, a Narrator, who is one of the characters. He will appear beginning with the second chapter and will say *I,* as narrators generally do in novels. I request, however, that you not confuse him with me, the Author).

We will take advantage of this brief pause to flesh out (if one may say as much) the portrait of Eusèbe: at sixty, the age he was to retain almost until his death, Eusèbe stopped being interested in the basically trivial problem of managing the store, which he left more or less entirely in Madame Eusèbe and Alexander Vladimirovich's care, and began devoting himself to an activity that was, if not more noble, then at least more exalting in his eyes.

The Eusèbe grocery store, founded half a century before by his father, Eusèbe senior, was set back from Rue des Citoyens in a recess at the corner of that tiny fragment of Rue des Milleguiettes that is then framed by Grands-Edredons Square. This stretch of Rue des Milleguiettes is very narrow, whereas the outcropping of Saint Gudule opposite appears to have widened Rue des Citoyens, which must then skirt the edge of the church to reach the most central parts of the City, something to which it has been accustomed for quite some time now. To the right or east (for the moment we are putting ourselves mentally in Eusèbe's shoes, standing at the side of the road, in front of the grocery), very nearby, just past the T-line bus stop (by request), is the intersection of Citoyens with Vieille-des-Archives. This intersection has itself become a bit more ample, not only because of the previously mentioned widening of Rue des Citoyens but also because, almost directly facing us, the house on the corner has fallen victim to old age, like a tooth uprooted by bacterial infection and spiritual apathy. Being revealed in this way, the large, bare wall of the neighboring house (supported by wainscoting and half-torched beams, which create the most marvelous old-Norman effect) is decorated with graffiti and posters locked in savage competition; among them, next to the sort of declarations one would expect ("Emilienne's a whore! We seen you Saturday in the square: Béber"), was this melancholy and somewhat enigmatic oath:

"I am quite alone in understanding Puvis de Chavannes!"

The municipality, in a momentary fit of civic horticulture, planted two pessimistic locust trees. The carbon monoxide appears to put them off, and they try to seem as though they're not there. They are dangerously successful at it: Rue des Citoyens is in fact one-way west to east, hence, for our purposes, from left to right; Rue Vieille-des-Archives runs from top to bottom (on the map of the City, but for our purposes from front to back), in the direction that must then be, if you have followed us, north to south. So the cars, separated from one another by the locust trees, confidently drive up to the intersection, each sure of its own right of way. The absence of a traffic light, combined with the efforts of the locust trees, produces a set of collisions that are noisy, shrill, and frequent—particularly in the wee hours of the morning—and provoke a rash of cops, ambulances, and bitchiness nasty enough to warm the heart of Madame Croche, the concierge of 53. These upheavals left Eusèbe cold.

It must be said that Rue des Citoyens—in and of itself utterly devoid of historical or any other sort of interest, a characteristic it shares with its rival and cross street, Rue Vieille-des-Archives—

links two parts of the City that are highly attractive to tourists: the first, to the east, because of its ancient buildings from ancient centuries, its ancient streets with renovated facades (Rue Olenix-de-Mont-Sacre, Rue Péréfixe-de-Beaumont "clerk of courts and writer," Rue Péan-de-la-Croulardière "judicial counselor," Rue Emile-Zola "novelist with materialist ideas," Rue Eléazar-de-Bro-court-Sercilly, sire of Chandeville, and now let's move on), its old studios belonging to famous old masters, its posh tea gardens and lawns done up in autumn leaves; the second, to the west, on account of its jangling and centrally located modernity, its galleries offering New York–style paintings by all the Bronx's unsold artists along the lanes of the pedestrian zone, its bums invited by the city council (fifty percent bum-narcs, fifty percent undercover-cop-fake-bums), its mock poets who spew their verses from the tops of fountains, and its young musicians, both male and female, with their little recorders and their large viola da gambas, who practice on passing ears headed for an evening of Marin Marais. The guides suggest that one visit the old quarter in the morning and the modern one at night; hence, from morning till night, a powerful convection current develops between the two, and the tourists circulate, most often on foot. When, for example, they reach the intersection, they hesitate, take maps from their purses, backpacks, or pockets, and flag down taxis, passers-by, cars, or the T-line bus to inquire in various foreign tongues: "Poudipon, donde?" "Giougo, wo?" and then set out again, filled with wonder, before disappearing behind Saint Gudule or perhaps turning down Rue des Millequiettes, into Grands-Edredons Square.

From Eusèbe's point of view, the one we are adopting in this chapter, tourists could be strictly divided into two categories (once certain odd or borderline cases had been discarded—Scotsmen and the like); category I was made up of men, category II of women. Category I held no interest. In category II (women), he once again drew a distinction between two subcategories ("It's kind of like canned vegetables," he would explain to Madame Eusèbe. "You have your green beans and you have your peas; now you take your peas, you have your fine and you have your extrafine; and if you take the extrafine, you have your cooked and you have your uncooked, get it?" he would say to Madame Eusèbe; but she would have already fallen asleep). In category II, women, there were thus the Interesting (A) on the one hand and the Uninteresting (B) on the other. The subcategory made up of the Uninteresting (IIB) interested him no more than the one made up of men (I). He was only interested in the Interesting (IIA), from among which, moreover, he constructed, after mature reflection, a special sub-subcategory: that of the Not-Uninteresting, an idea inspired by Old Man Sinouls, a great admirer of Nicolas de Cuse, who, he said, gave him "a good laugh"; we shall note it as IIA*.

Fine, fine, you will tell us that it still remains to be seen how, by what properties, Eusèbe recognized the interesting specimens within the category women (by "You" we are designating, naturally and for the rest of the novel, the Reader, whose portrait— generic or robotic—adorns the office of our publisher's sales director; we address our reader with capitalized formality, out of respect). The answer is simple: by age, which had to be at least equal to a minimum fixed, for reasons of biology and prudence, at 15, and less than a maximum, set for him at 59—that is to say, at 60 minus 1, 60 being, as we have already said, the age Eusèbe himself internally maintained. Madame Eusèbe was then 59 years old, which may be expressed as 60 minus 1, if our calculations are correct, meaning that she was just coming to the end of her time among the Interesting (and anyway it was the era of the coming of Alexander Vladimirovich, onto whom was transferred from then on all the affection of which Madame Eusèbe was capable); but, since she herself had very visibly continued to age, she was at the same time obviously one of the Uninteresting, which meant that, being at the same time in some sense historically Interesting and contemporaneously (if one may say as much) Uninteresting, she was, so to speak, out of the running, which was ethically satisfactory for Eusèbe.

So from 15 to 59 every woman was Interesting; but Eusèbe had immediately added a second criterion that introduced a supplementary restriction: that of Touristhood. Only Tourists could be Interesting. Let us specify that certain of the neighborhood's appropriate-aged female inhabitants entered, very much in spite of themselves, the critical category, IIA (IIA*, to be precise), having been in some sense assimilated into the class "Tourists," or even having become honorary Tourists. To penetrate further into this system of classification, whose interest will escape no one, we must ask ourselves *in what way* a woman, a Tourist at that, could be interesting. For this reason, we are going to accompany Eusèbe on his examination of candidates, whom he subjected to a constant ranking.

Whenever a tourist appeared at the intersection, she entered Eusèbe's field of vision, and his eyes would follow her, keeping her under observation, until she disappeared. If she was walking down the facing sidewalk, he would examine her in profile. If she crossed in front of him to the other sidewalk (the sidewalk facing the facing sidewalk), he would face her directly. (To keep her from crossing too soon and walking behind him, forcing him to turn around, he had arranged garbage cans and old crates on that side of the grocery in a way that discouraged such behavior.) Finally, when she had passed him, and especially if she left by way of Rue des Milleguiettes, he would examine her very carefully from behind. Standing, he would hold his position, with his feet slightly apart, his gray pants with the nebulous knees practically covering his shoes, his green jersey—the one covered with food stains—stuffed haphazardly into his pants, and his gray Retired Gas and Electric Workers of France cap sitting askew.

His body would stay almost perfectly still, with the exception of his head, which would turn on its axis (we call it the neck) to accompany his eyes, and, on his head, relative to it, his extremely protruding and pointed and ill-shaven jaw, which would rise and fall rhythmically with a most amazing gurgling sound built upon an indistinct murmur-groan (a phrase, learned from his grandfather, the meaning of which he had never understood and which he intoned purely for his own benefit, as a sort of slogan, exhortation, or commentary: "It turns me on, it's taking a turn for the better!"); he would not look at face or feet; or neck or shoulder either, and just barely at knees (and only if they were bare). He followed the movement of the intervening parts exclusively—the thighs, stomach, chest, and back—seeking, like a true researcher, to deduce from the visible the (more or less) well-hidden invisible, attentive to meaningful pubic bulges, the blessed absence of bras, certain fabrics that a favorable combination of the physical laws of motion and friction sometimes caused to ride up noticeably until they were caught between the buttocks, provided but that these be sufficiently endowed with flesh, firmness, purity of form, and smartness of movement (the use of the phrase "but that these be" is imposed upon us for reason of musicality despite its somewhat antiquated ring). He would never omit the detection of lines and marks at the edges of panties and bikini briefs, made perceptible by localized linear swelling that set them off in relief. He watched most particularly, one might say slaveringly, for climactic events: sidelong revelations due to undone blouse buttons; the color of a "fleece" revealed by a miniskirt with nothing under it (and especially in the case of a possible contradiction with hair color [only then would his gaze venture as high as the chin]); and rear specifications, acquired upon someone's bending over to pick up a dropped object, made him quiver. On these rare and blessed occasions he reached a sort of ecstatic state from which he would only emerge at the sight of a new apparition, bearer of new hopes.

It can easily be seen why he preferred summer, and why he limited himself to tourists. Summer, quite simply, because during that season (along with spring and some bits of fall), so long as there was enough sun, the overall quantity of clothing diminished, as well as the weight of each piece, which favored the appearance of wide-open spaces and improved the chances for transparency and even for those moist secretions that so stirred his gaze. His exclusive preference—at first spontaneous, then thought out and even made statutory (according to his own internal code)—for tourists had a more complicated origin. His was not an aesthetic undertaking, so it was not because he found tourists more beautiful that he reserved all his attention for them. His goal was knowledge—that is to say, classification. Now, the natives, hardened since adolescence by Eusebian, neo-Eusebian, or para-Eusebian gazes—they are the rule because of our climate—fend them off with that armor which is the sort of beauty associated with elegance: in other words, perfection. For perfection is impenetrable. The slicker of beauty is better protection than a rain hat. Knowledge, as Eusèbe was well aware, needs imperfection to flush out nature's secrets. If a gaze wants to follow a leg under a dress up to that place where, as they say, it meets the other, could there be a better guide than a stocking with a run?

That is why the sartorial clumsiness, the naiveté, the indifference, or the plain simple innocence of tourists, especially those from countries where men's glances never confront them directly, gave Eusèbe all his opportunities: buttocks spilling out of shorts that even revealed the panties underneath; the colors of dark panties showing under thin fabrics that weren't terribly opaque; transparencies in the light disclosing a treasure of locks under nylons emerging diaphanously from beneath short skirts; such essentially different transparencies as were caused by moisture at the onset of a sudden shower, thanks to which wet dresses created a clinging relief highlighting the unpredictable uprisings due to breezes and storms. From May to October, the hordes of Swiss, German, Dutch, English, American, and even Japanese tourists offered themselves up in this manner for Eusebian investigation. They generally emerged from it rather surprised and even somewhat upset.

There was one last reason for his choosing tourists: Eusèbe, having unwittingly adopted the poet's motto, "love what you will never see twice," desired that each of his experiences be unique, an adventure that might be more or less surprising and more or less intense, a point between the irrevocably departed past and the ineffable future (repetition horrified him, except in cooking): "You never look at the same tourist twice on Rue des Citoyens," he would say to Madame Eusèbe, so as to give her philosophical instruction and prevent her becoming in any way jealous. "But you're always the same, y'old swine!" she would answer affectionately. Besides, he would have had a hard time recognizing a tourist if, by chance, she had taken it into her head to reappear before him. That is why, when he examined a native by mistake, he never identified her as such and forgot her completely from one time to the next: "You know," Yvette would say to Old Man Sinouls, "it's not so much the way he drools over my ass that bothers me—at my age that even gets to be kind of flattering—no, it's that he never recognizes me!"

2
H O R T E N S E

The morning this story begins, a warm, pretty morning in early September, I left my house a little before eight o'clock. I was rather drowsy, since my job forced me to keep hours, more variable than late, to which I was not yet accustomed (I had only started working at it recently).

First I went to Monsieur Bouelles's butcher shop. I was generally his first customer, so the shop would still be empty and fresh with some of the pleasant odors of a meat locker: that aroma of calf's head, parsley, and sawdust. I bought two half-pound pieces of tenderloin, a package of very fine frozen peas, and a vacuum-packed sack of so-called new potatoes, which were precooked and needed only be submerged for about three minutes in boiling water before being served and eaten mashed with a fork and mixed with a little virgin olive oil. In this way I made sure I would stay four meals ahead, each meal then being topped off with flavored yogurt from Madame Eusèbe's and bread and fruit I bought farther down Rue des Citoyens. I always plan my meals ahead in groups of four, each menu being determined by a circular and dietetic permutation consisting of a fixed list of factors, taped up over my refrigerator. It's very simple and keeps me from having to think, which is the most despicable of all undertakings (particularly in my business) and which, above all, takes up time. Sometimes I dine at the greasy spoon on the corner because of the salad and the celery with mustard dressing (the dessert: crème-caramel or plum pudding). Occasionally I eat Chinese because of the ginger preserves and the litchi syrup: that adds extra variety to my diet.

Monsieur Bouelles once went to the Chinese place with his wife, Madame Bouelles, on a Saturday night when he wasn't going to open Sunday morning (Veronica was with her grandparents from Thiais), and he determined that they don't really prepare meat the way we do: "Monsieur Mornacier," he said to me, "the thing for us is a nice rump roast or a tenderloin with shallots. But little bits of who knows what animal scattered everywhere—it just won't do. Not that I'm not saying they don't do it well, but all the same!" Above his stall, Monsieur Bouelles had hung a painting he had found in the attic of his in-laws' place in Yonne. "It's at least a hundred years old, this painting is!" he said proudly. It shows a human cadaver stretched out on a table, surrounded by men in old-fashioned black clothes holding sharp objects that they are using to cut into the cadaver in various places. Monsieur Bouelles adores his painting, which, according to what he's told me, no one appreciates except me. Madame Bouelles finds it "disgusting" and says it should be kept out of Veronica's sight. But Veronica, who is five years old, has quite different worries on her mind: she thinks about maintaining her usual place in the sandbox in Grands-Edredons Square and defending it against all the other little snots who covet it. But let us return to the subject at hand; otherwise the Narrator will tell us his life story.

Once I had been served, I left the butcher shop, and Monsieur Bouelles joined me at the edge of Rue Vieille-des-Archives. Together we watched a troupe of fresh young Scandinavian girls pass by on the other side of the street. They were just out of Scandinavia and were outfitted most succinctly in view of their upcoming summer adventures in the South. Had we been much older (like the Author, for example), it would have served as an emotional reminder of the first naked little Swedish breasts glimpsed on the timid screens of the fifties, those of Bibi Anderson (?) in *One Summer of Happiness,* for example. The Scandinavians had stopped in the still-mild sunshine. They chirped as they waved blue-and-green tourist guides along with red-and-brown street maps and sowed the air with Scandinavian consonants peppered by innumerable ö's and ø's. All that was rather pleasant, and we were silently contemplating them with an avuncular eye when we were most unpleasantly torn from this contemplation by the hydrochloric voice of Madame Croche, the concierge of 53, who was putting the building's garbage cans back in their places under stairways A,B,C,D,E, and F respectively now that the trash collectors had come by: "A spot of sexbeef, as the English say!" At that moment Saint Gudule's bell began to chime, and I hurried over to the grocery ("Eusebwards!" as they'd say at Oxford), since the unwitting cause of my morning awakenings was to show up at any minute now.

Eusèbe had already taken up his post in the street. In the shady part of the shop, Madame Eusèbe and Alexander Vladimirovich were chatting with Old Man Sinouls, who had come to buy fruit-flavored breakfast yogurt for his twin daughters, Armance and Julie: apricot for Armance, who was a redhead, strawberry for Julie, the blonde—a chiasmus and clash of colors that had the same strident effect on me as would have the cavity of a wrong note in the gleaming sonorous smile of the pieces their father played on Saint Gudule's organ. (In my business, one must know how to slip in a beautiful sentence; the Author never would have come up with that one!) Old Man Sinouls was in fact an organist and an atheist. Along with the yogurt, he had come to buy cheese and a quart of Valstar beer for his ten-o'clock snack; it was an occasion for one of his standard conversations with Madame Eusèbe:

"You poor dear, your Coulommiers are so chalky!"

"Ah, Monsieur Sinouls, that's the way They make them nowadays. They only send me the pasteurized kind. They keep the rest for themselves to export."

"Oh, a nice Coulommiers made properly from fresh milk, good and yellow inside, it's almost better than a Camembert, don't you think?"

"Ah, if only we still had good Maroilles, you have to go back more than thirty years for that!"

"And a Vieux-Lille!"

"And a good Puant-du-Nord!"

"You know something, the best Brebis de Corse is the kind where when you cut it open there are little worms wriggling around inside. And what about your husband, same as ever?"

"Same as ever. Look at him, the old swine!"

Alexander Vladimirovich assumed a disgusted look behind his whiskers. The conversation was marking a stopping point, a ritual pause, before getting its second wind. I could have slipped into the breach to buy my own fruit-flavored yogurt (raspberry and lemon, two of each, not black currant, whose bright red color didn't speak to me), but I wasn't in a hurry.

Old Man Sinouls put the milk, beer, and cheese in his shopping bag, wondering all the while what second topic Madame Eusèbe was going to bring up, since it was her turn. Madame Eusèbe greatly enjoyed her conversations with Old Man Sinouls. Because her imagination was stuck around 1950, she was uneasy with the subjects that aroused the passions of her younger customers: television, the Arab question, tennis . . . Old Man Sinouls was of her generation, or just about. She could choose one from among the "relaxing" subjects, which were: "today's youth!"; "what do They have in store for us?"; "those crazy drivers" (with the local variant: "what are They waiting for to put up a traffic light at the intersection? Really, tonight by one in the morning at the latest! . . ."); and then there were the controversial subjects, two in number: "the weather" and "religion." It will hardly be found surprising that the subject of God and his representatives on earth was a bone of contention between Madame Eusèbe and Old Man Sinouls, the former being a good Catholic on account of her profession, the proximity of Saint Gudule, and the cross she had worn ever since the ill-fated passion that had led her to Eusèbe; the

conversation broke off. As Hortense is the heroine of this story (its
Narrator, Monsieur Mornacier, is absolutely not the hero—we
prefer to say it right away to avoid confusion, which he would not
fail to take advantage of for personal and rather debatable ends), a
first description is in order.

The girl who, as she did every morning, and every morning for
a month independent of the day before, was triggering Eusèbe's
excitement (Eusèbe's reactions were, as we saw in Chapter 1,
essentially due to objective criteria of a purity without memory;
the striking uniformity of his salivation at the sight of Hortense
proved only the consistency of his judgment, and nothing else,
since he didn't recognize her from one day to the next), this girl, as

we were saying, who was walking down Rue des Citoyens, was about twenty-two years and six months old. She was slightly taller than average, with big, wide eyes, naive knees, and soft cheeks. The *only* things she was wearing—let us strongly stress only—were a very minimal dress, which didn't cover much but was pricey and light, and shoes perfectly unsuited for walking but adequate for Eusèbe's purposes, since they provoked so many sudden and involuntary gaps between the fabric and her body as she attempted to move rapidly down the sidewalk. That will do for now, since we shall certainly have occasion to conduct a more thorough, attentive, and unobstructed examination later on.

The reason for her haste, as well as for the (relatively exceptional) absence of panties under Hortense's dress, was that she was late. Because her head had not yet really cleared following the late and untimely intervention of her alarm clock, she had snapped up the first garment she could lay her hands on in her huge apartment and the imposing darkness of her closet, without checking either its weight on its opacity. She was entirely oblivious to the five pairs of eyes riveted on her and to the five strongly contrasting impressions she was conveying to their five brains respectively:

—Old Man Sinouls was looking at her with a gentlemanly indulgence, since she reminded him of his daughters, and especially of his daughters' little friends, a whole contingent of whom—apparently young, charming, and, to his eyes, dangerously interchangeable and scantily clad—gathered whenever possible in the hospitable Sinouls household. His quart of Valstar in hand, along with his Coulommiers and his yogurt, ready for the coolness of Saint Gudule followed by good conversation in a bistro, he imagined the rest of the morning without displeasure, and the sight of Hortense made his eyes sparkle ever so slightly behind his glasses.

—My own gaze was clearly more troubled: every morning for a month (but for strictly different reasons than Eusèbe, and knowing quite well who I was looking at), I had been arranging my schedule in such a way that no matter when I had gone to bed the night before, I too would be at the grocery early enough to catch Hortense passing by on the other side of the street, and this was the first time it had been granted me to see her in such detail.

So I was obviously upset by this vision, but even more so by the imperious necessity—to which I found myself subjected because of my particular professional projects, then approaching a crucial period—*not* to fall in love with her. It was something already decided once and for all and irrevocably (which is more sure); but it turned out that the minute of contemplating Hortense that I allowed myself every morning, far from guaranteeing me, by its fixed and limited nature, the perfect spiritual tranquillity I had expected for the remaining 23 hours 59 minutes of the day, made my resolution waver more and more. The effect of the omission of a bit of cloth, much as it would ordinarily be—as far as I could judge (maybe not with Eusèbe's accuracy and precision, but sufficiently)—minimal, as well as the hurried nature of her gate, with all of its consequences, was creating an extremely dangerous situation for my future. That's why my gaze was less serene than Old Man Sinouls's, and less open than Eusèbe's.

—Madame Eusèbe herself was completely indifferent to the whole show. She had seen the like walk by for thirty years now. One more, one less, who cared? Besides, if it made Eusèbe happy and kept him from messing up the tomatoes, rice, or milk, she was happy about it too. She merely felt that Hortense was cheeky for going out with her cheeks showing through a dress that hid just about nothing. But that didn't surprise her. Today's youth.

—As for Alexander Vladimirovich, he found Hortense's behavior morally degrading and the whole business excruciatingly boring.

Hortense disappeared down Rue des Citoyens, accompanied by five pairs of silent eyes, a conclusive clucking sound, and a sigh. Alexander Vladimirovich coughed.

3

ALEXANDER
VLADIMIROVICH

"You're coughing, Alexander Vladimirovich. That'll teach you to go out barefoot!" said Madame Eusèbe.

This reproach, made by a grocer to a cat, calls for a few remarks.

It was snowing one winter morning in the year of Our Lord 19———. Shivering, Madame Eusèbe had gone down to open the store (Eusèbe, pleading the apparently total absence of tourists, had refused to get up) when she spied a smart-looking wicker basket in front of the door, a sort of cradle richly shrouded in purple cysemus (*Cysemus:* a type of precious Poldevian velvet— *Author's note*) whose handle was decorated with a pink ribbon. Attached to this ribbon was a letter sealed with orange wax.

Blowing on her numb hands to warm them up, she opened the letter, which read:

> Here in this cradle am I, Alexander Vladimirovich, the fruit of a passionate, princely, and illicit love. My mother, a member of the retinue when the Poldevian Princes visited your city, sinned with a noble and irresistible native. The very highest diplomatic and dynastic considerations prevented her marriage. That is why you see me here, an abandoned orphan entrusted to your care, Bertrande Eusèbe. The attached purse, full of Dalmatian and Poldevian gold pieces, will provide for my keep and upbringing until the time comes for me to claim my rightful place at court. My diet shall consist of the following: milk every morning, but Gloria brand only, and in a *clean* saucer; meat, but only ground raw tenderloin; and creamed Baltic herring once a week. The rest according to my mood. You, Bertrande, to whom I have been entrusted, shall duly appreciate this honor and therefore treat me in all circumstances with the respect appropriate to my origin and future rank. Specifically, you shall address me formally. All diminutives and nicknames, be they Alex, Vladi, or Kittykins, are strictly forbidden.
>
> *Signed:* [illegible (in Poldevian)]
>
> P.S.: Add to the diet an egg on Sunday, which shall be soft-boiled and served with toast and bacon, the yolk having been kept hot and liquid in a small steamer for eggs, called an egg-coddler.

In this cradle there was in fact a little baby cat with a long nose; he was faintly exotic but noble, and his whiskers were already noble as well. He opened his eyes, looked at Madame Eusèbe, and with a quiet but authoritative meow indicated that he was hungry. Madame Eusèbe made haste.

From then on, Madame Eusèbe dedicated herself to the well-being and upbringing of Alexander Vladimirovich. She immediately converted the Poldevian gold into petrodollars that she put in the national savings bank on Rue Vieille-des-Archives so that on the day Alexander Vladimirovich was called to the Poldevian court—a day she never doubted would come—he would be in a position to live in a manner commensurate with his rank. The idea of disobeying these instructions, spelled out to the letter, never occurred to her. She kept them in the drawer of her night table, along with a portrait of her late father, her cleaning bills, and a supply of Carter's Little Liver Pills (her entire inheritance). It must be admitted that her blind obedience was due in large measure to fear.

The author of the letter had demonstrated in a truly unlikely, supernatural, perhaps even satanic way that he was aware of her guilty secret, her Sin, something she had thought erased from human memory for all time ever since the death of Saint Gudule's former priest, to whom she had admitted it in confession.

Madame Eusèbe's first name was in fact Bertrande, but *that was not the name under which she had been married* before God and man; that was Edwige, which she thought much more compatible with her true spirit and which was now her official name. By destroying her family as well as the records of both church and state in her native northern city, the bombings of World War II had rendered the substitution painless and irrevocable for the young orphan. The train having deposited her in the big city, she was placed in the household of Eusèbe senior through the good acts of Father Ancestras, in whose church she had found shelter after wandering all day, suitcase in hand, upon leaving the station.

"What is your name?" he had asked her.

And without thinking about it, she had answered on a sudden impulse that had come from the very depths of her soul and of her admiration for the actress Edwige Feuillère:

"Edwige, Father."

So it was Edwige and not Bertrande whom Eusèbe had seduced and married after his father, Eusèbe senior, had seduced but not married her. And now, after so many years of impunity, a Poldevian cat's mysterious benefactor had discovered her guilty secret. Her only hope for salvation lay in absolutely obeying the instructions she had been given. She obeyed.

Alexander Vladimirovich grew. Having learned at a very young age of the mystery surrounding his birth—Madame Eusèbe often reread the letter aloud to be sure she was in no way contravening the orders she had received—he set about turning to his advantage the mediocre place and circumstances into which fate had thrust him. He was firm and benevolent, but distant, with Madame Eusèbe. He only allowed her to pet him as much as was strictly necessary for the maintenance of his purring faculties. The moment she overstepped the bounds of decent affection, he would, without moving an inch, dip his back so sharply that the hand put forth to pet him would meet with nothing but a receding hollow line. And at the same time his green eyes would distinctly say (silently, of course):

Remember, Bertrande!

And Madame Eusèbe would pull back her hand as if she had just been given an electric shock.

Now at the end of his second summer, Alexander Vladimirovich had successfully extended his authority over all the territory he had decided to subject, territory that formed a sort of Poldevian principality or enclave in barbaric lands, encompassing the sidewalk on the Eusèbe side of Rue des Citoyens, Grands-Edredons Square, and the surrounding houses, including Saint Gudule. After several memorable battles, he had driven off the alley cats and strays; all the local barons had been subjugated, and his authority was now only very rarely put to the test by a new arrival. He had then reduced the dogs to a state of abject terror through well-prepared ambushes, thereby provoking a nervous breakdown in a Doberman, who could only be cured by means of psychoanalysis and leg of lamb. The old bulldog that belonged to the antiques dealer Monsieur Anderthal hardly dared set foot outside anymore. His effect on Old Man Sinouls's dog, Balbastre, called Babou, was particularly impressive: as soon as he caught sight of Alexander Vladimirovich, Balbastre would sit on his hind legs and start howling without pause in imitation of the organ stop called Vox Humana; the sound was so grim that after trying to cure him with kicks accompanied by insults like "son of a bitch!" Old Man Sinouls had been forced to give up dragging him to the grocery or even the square. That left the birds and the children.

Aside from a few negligible boxwoods and spindle-trees, there were two trees in the square: a linden and a Judas tree. Located above the fountain, the linden belonged to the sparrows; they held their plenary sessions there and at its foot took the summer dustbaths recommended by their doctors. As for the pigeons, they were devoted to dirtying Saint Gudule's roof and facade as much as possible, in addition to sullying the foreheads of lovers and philosophers who came to sit on the benches. For reasons of both moral and medical hygiene, this situation struck Alexander Vladimirovich as intolerable, and he set about remedying it. Fear rapidly dispersed the sparrows, who went to other squares; but the pigeons, being, as everyone knows, particularly stupid, did not understand; a few dozen pigeon corpses had to be found in the gutters before the municipal government was convinced that an epidemic of unknown origin was attacking the birds, and that they therefore posed a danger to the schoolchildren; it was decided to capture the pigeons at great expense with nets, bird lime, and tranquilized birdseed, and then to set them free at the foot of the cathedral in a neighboring capital, which never noticed this invasion. Saint Gudule was now clean, and Alexander Vladimirovich could turn his attention to the problem of the children.

Every day around noon, and again around five (and practically all day Wednesday), hordes of marauding children assaulted Grands-Edredons Square. The smallest ones took up positions in the sandbox with their pails and shovels. Under the tender eye of single parents or lenient grandparents, they peed in their pants, wiped their noses on their overalls or coats, and shoved various objects into their asses, navels, eyes, and other orifices known and unknown. The bigger ones whistled, screamed, ran, jumped, climbed onto railings and branches, played soccer with book bags, caps, or old Coke cans, pulled up their skirts, pulled down their pants, explored in their underwear. . . in other words, they gave themselves over to all the childish and educational activities for which parks were specially designed.

Alexander Vladimirovich had no intention of restricting their activities; he simply did not want them interfering with his. To make sure of that, as soon as a new child (not yet acquainted with the rules of the game) appeared in the square, Alexander Vladimirovich would approach him casually, draw him away as far as possible from the mothers' field of vision, and, just as the poor careless creature, unable to believe his eyes, was enthusiastically getting ready to pull his tail, burn or cut his whiskers, or throw sand in his eyes to prove his affection, he would settle his hash with a spectacular scratch in the calf, bottom, or thumb—places where it hurts and bleeds a lot but isn't dangerous. There was just one exception (there's always an exception): young Veronica Bouelles. She and she alone could indulge herself in petting Alexander Vladimirovich, a fact that obviously gave her great superiority over both male and female rivals in the sandbox. Had Alexander Vladimirovich been asked the reason for this favored treatment, he would doubtless have answered: "Because it was her, because it was me." But there was another reason, which will be explained at the appropriate time.

The first to leave the grocery after Hortense had passed by, Alexander Vladimirovich hesitated for a moment. He had been planning to visit the D stairway of 53's third floor to make the acquaintance of a young red-haired cat who had just moved in. But showing his curiosity so quickly was beneath him and ran the risk of giving the young girl the wrong impression. His princely bearing, his numerous and well-known victories over the other cats in the neighborhood, his thick, slightly bluish gray-black fur, his relaxed manner, his whiskers—they all combined to make his conquests innumerable, easy, and a bit tiresome. Wherever he went, he dragged the hearts of all the local ladies with him. But he visited the apartments located in his own territory not merely for amorous reasons. He wanted to know what was going on: one day, perhaps someday soon, the situation in Poldevia would make his return there desirable. He would be tracked down; someone would come from over there on a secret mission, would settle in the square—in one of the houses, no doubt—and would make discreet inquiries about him before officially introducing himself to Bertrande Eusèbe; he wanted to know about it ahead of time, since his enemies might act first. Hence the simultaneously friendly and condescending relations he maintained not only with the mistresses of the local households, but with their cooks and cleaning ladies as well. He knocked on windowpanes, opened shutters with a paw, and slipped into apartments through poorly closed doors. Furthermore, he was intrigued by something: the fourth-floor apartment on the right side of the C stairway, which had remained empty for eighteen months, had just received a new tenant a week before (unless it was the same tenant returning after more than a year's absence; he did not recall ever having seen him). There were two rooms: one, the bedroom, looked out on the square, and the other on Rue Vieille-des-Archives (53 Rue des Citoyens took up two sides of the square).

It was quarter past eight. The bedroom curtains were drawn but billowed gently in the breeze (the window was open); they allowed Alexander Vladimirovich, who had gracefully climbed up a drainpipe, to look inside while balancing lightly on the window bar between a bottle of milk and a curious clay statuette. The room had a bed and a chair. Its walls were bare, except for the back one, which was covered by a bookcase and divided by a glass door. There were packages of all different sizes wrapped in various sorts of paper piled up everywhere, as well as several suitcases and boxes; their contents were not visible. He knew (because he had been there the day before) that the other room was similarly cluttered: a table, a kitchen chair, and a refrigerator were the only evident signs of this room's different purpose. The bathroom and doglegged hallway were also filled with suitcases and boxes whose contents were not visible. Alexander Vladimirovich was quite intrigued. Most of the books whose titles his keen eyesight enabled him to make out were rare: bibliographic or bibliophilic curiosities, first editions, catalogues of sales and shows, brochures from manuscript dealers; there was no apparent organization by title, era, or subject.

The mysterious occupant (and Alexander Vladimirovich could not even be sure he was not a squatter) was sleeping. He was a young man of about twenty-three who was slightly taller than average and had light-brown hair, eyes of uncertain color since they were closed, a long, fine nose, and no distinguishing marks. A small Kintzle alarm clock was sitting next to the bed on a German beer crate that was serving as a night table. He was sleeping in the nude. Because his own life was essentially nocturnal, Alexander Vladimirovich had quickly noticed that the man went to bed very late, never got up before nine, and never received visitors or even mail. He would leave his apartment unseen late at night, always carrying one or two suitcases or packages that were not, as far as Alexander Vladimirovich could tell, necessarily the same ones each time. Alexander Vladimirovich was even more intrigued by this young man. He doubted the man was a terrorist; he didn't really believe he was an envoy of the Poldevian Princes or of their enemy, since he had not shown the slightest interest in felines and had never asked any questions about Alexander Vladimirovich or found any pretense to talk to Madame Eusèbe. Perhaps he was awaiting the appointed hour.

Alexander Vladimirovich jumped nimbly into the room and noiselessy approached one of the suitcases set against the wall facing the bed. It wasn't quite closed. He peered at such of the suitcase's contents as were visible in the opening. He understood completely. The young man hadn't moved.

4

SAINT GUDULE

Old Man Sinouls took his key out of his pocket and opened the church's little side door at 2 Rue des Milleguiettes. As on any other morning, he walked down the aisle, shopping bag in hand, on the way to his organ. On his left, a high wall separated him from the square; on his right was the Chapel of the Poldevian Princes. The chapel was extended by a long, rectangular vegetable garden, at the end of which was a chestnut tree growing up against the main body of the church.

Saint Gudule, like Sainte-Chapelle and the Pantheon, is, as everyone knows, one large chamber adorned with elements from all ages, styles, and eras. To the delight of art historians, this chronological and architectural miracle, one of the crown jewels of Gothic art, sports Roman relics above Renaissance masonry. Tombs of twelfth-century bishops are alongside catacombs with frescoes from the dawn of Christianity (contemporary, according to some, with the martyrdom of Saint Gudule, who holds a purple rose stained with her blood; according to others, with the erection of Sacre-Coeur). The church suffered affronts at the hands of the paladins; during the Empire one of Durand's pupils temporarily took on its care. In short, it has just about everything.

The Poldevian Chapel is a recent addition. Formerly located near Avenue de Chaillot, it was being threatened by renovation, annexation, and destruction in favor of an urgently needed parking lot when it was saved at the last minute by oil. In fact, it was in Poldevia, in that mountainous and autochthonous region of our terraqueous globe, home to bandits and mustaches (and often bandits *with* mustaches), that—contrary to all the proofs indicating its impossibility presented by German geologists in specialized journals (*Archiv der petroleum studies, Annalecta oilia,* etc.) not forty years ago—one of the most valuable sources of black gold was discovered during excavations for new hot springs in the capital's outskirts. The drill brought up a gusher of the precious liquid, and Poldevia entered the modern world there and then. The field was centered directly beneath Queneleieff Square, the very heart of the capital, obliging the engineers to do some fancy footwork, but no matter!

For all that, the six Poldevian Princes, though resolute supporters of Poldevia's modernization, did not simply forget about their past. The plentiful royalties they collected allowed them to finance quite easily the simultaneous transportation, brick by brick and plant by plant, of the chapel dedicated to the unfortunate Prince Luigi Voudzoï and of the attached vegetable garden, whose upkeep was entrusted to a vegetable grower from Saint-Mouëzy-sur-Eon.

The sun was slowly emerging from the morning mist and lighting up the square of dark, thriving, tender lettuce plants marking the (symbolic) location of the fatal riding accident that cut short the life of the ill-fated Luigi. The wonderful rustic scent of horse manure emanated from the freshly turned compost. The vegetable garden's lettuce plants were actually slightly exotic, since they were specially fertilized by the manure of little Poldevian mountain ponies, which was flown in weekly at great expense. Old Man Sinouls paused for a moment to drink in the evocative smell that brought forth many memories of his youth in the Gatinais. Then he entered the church.

It was empty and cool. Empty, that is, with the exception of three worshipers (two old women and one young girl, one pretender and two of the True Faithful) who were waiting with fading hope for one of the rare visits of Father Domernas, Saint Gudule's priest since Father Ancestras's retirement two years before. Because of the need for thrift imposed by the church's financial straits, Father Domernas had to look after several Houses of Worship at once; he had a very tight schedule and a bicycle. Because he felt ill at ease with the faithful, he usually managed his time so as not to run into anyone, particularly anyone of the female persuasion. Further, Saint Gudule had Old Man Sinouls, and Domernas was very much afraid of Old Man Sinouls, who, like the devil himself, was an excellent theologian.

Old Man Sinouls adored his organ, an organ the likes of which they don't make anymore. At once powerful and tasteful, it had miraculously escaped the twin scourges of aging and restoration. The great Louis Marchand was even said to have played on it. It was anachronistic and occasionally surly, but superb. Old Man Sinouls loved it.

He put his bottle of beer within easy reach and set about limbering up his fingers. For that purpose, he chose a nice piece of a rather mystical nature: Jehan Alain's "Litanies," in which a soul, having gone beyond the point of no return in the night of desolation, has no other means of escape than determined recourse to the invocation and affirmation of faith . . . or something like that. But this piece has one particular advantage to which no organist is insensitive: it makes a lot of noise. It was clear to Old Man Sinouls that an organ had to make a lot of noise. Why else would they have built churches in days gone by with such big thick stones, if not to resist the vibrations created by the Great-Stops? Any self-respecting organist's ambition (secret, of course, since it's the kind of thing that is difficult to admit before the church authorities, who might well take it amiss) is to bring a cathedral crashing down, as armies once caused bridges to fall.

Old Man Sinouls began Jehan Alain's "Litanies." Down below, the three worshipers (still the pretender along with the two True Faithful) all but fell out of their seats from fervor. Indeed, that was the piece's third virtue: it made worshipers crash ass-first to the ground from fervor. Old Man Sinouls had discovered this particular property of the "Litanies" during a journey through Scotland, thanks to an organist from Inverness who was also an alcoholic miscreant. He had taken on a mistress he didn't want to marry and had been refused a raise for this rather unpresbyterian behavior; he exacted his revenge by attempting to provoke heart attacks in the congregation. After the appropriate number of whiskies, he had confided some of the tricks of the trade to Old Man Sinouls, at that time a bachelor just starting out. They hadn't fallen on deaf ears.

Having warmed up his fingers, ears, and spirit thanks to the perfect success of what he called his "wake-up operation," Sinouls began thinking about the professional problem currently plaguing him, a problem he had to solve fairly soon. First he drank off half the beer, belched comfortably, and put the quart back down. Then he ruminated. A significant event involving Saint Gudule was about to take place: the thirty-five-foot stretch of Rue des Milleguiettes joining Rue des Citoyens to Grands-Edredons Square (the road then continued past the square toward other horizons) was going to be debaptized (if we dare express ourselves thus) and called Rue de l'Abbé-Migne from then on; this new ultrashort road would have only one address, 1, which would be affixed over the little side door through which—you haven't forgotten—Old Man Sinouls had just entered, and which allowed for direct access to the Chapel of the Poldevian Princes. This already old project had been impossible to bring off for many years because of the lay and church parties' alternate or combined opposition, depending on the particular session of the town council. It had been suddenly approved when Monsignor Fustiger had skillfully obtained both parties' consent by convincing each, through calculated indiscretions, of the other's supposedly intransigent opposition. There had been only one dissenting voice, that of an independent councilman who was outraged by this scandalous bending of the rules governing street numbers in urban areas of any importance (we only know of one other exception, that of the little town of Caunes-Minervois, famous for its pink marble, where all the buildings are numbered as if they were on one side of one single street. These numbers follow a pattern that defies any attempt at explanation). The new street's only number should have been 2, not 1, as the decree designated it. The choice of this site to honor l'Abbé Migne will be explained at the appropriate time. The abbot, as everyone knows, is the immortal author of the *Patrology,* a collection in . . . volumes of the works of the Church Fathers, Greeks as well as Romans; Old Man Sinouls was supposed to draw up a program of organ music for the dedication ceremony that would be suitable to the solemnity of the moment and to the nature of the *Patrology.* But after long and careful deliberation, he had only come up with one piece that simply had to be chosen: Johann Sebastian Bach's Prelude and Triple Fugue in B-flat. To be perfectly honest, his galling inability to see why he had been called upon kept him from concentrating. He didn't have any highly placed friends on the town council, and his superiors found his ideas scandalous, even if his private and family lives were impeccable: he had no mistresses and was never seen obviously drunk in public.

He drank down some more of the beer and decided to go have another drink at Madame Yvonne's café across the street. A great cool silence reigned over the nave. Old Man Sinouls heard the sound of a voice in the sacristy. "Well," he said to himself with surprise, "is Father Domernas here?"

Not wanting to miss the chance for a little theological debate about predestination, the Immaculate Conception, or the problem of Nuclear Weapons—three subjects about which he was sure to obtain excellent responses from the unfortunate young priest—Old Man Sinouls opened the door to the sacristy and found himself face to face with Monsignor Fustiger.

"Sinouls!"

"Fustiger!"

It had been a long, long time since they had last seen each other; not since their student days, or just about.

"So, things still shipshape?" asked Monsignor Fustiger.

"Shipshape," said Sinouls.

Monsignor Fustiger's career had progressed merely rapidly at first, before taking off when, as an apostolic nuncio in Poldevia, he had succeeded in reconverting two of the Poldevian Princes to the Catholic faith; for the Church, this reconversion represented an unexpected access to a not insignificant sum of Poldevian petrodollars. It was quite natural that upon returning to his native land and reaching an even loftier position he would do all that lay in his power to properly honor the Poldevian Chapel: the dedication of Rue l'Abbé-Migne (and the little surprise he was preparing for that occasion) came under this heading. While looking over the list of possible organists for the dedication, he came across the name of his old friend Sinouls, long out of sight but definitely not out of mind. That was why, to the surprise of the general public and the consternation of the party in question, he had indicated his preference for Sinouls.

"Shipshape!" Sinouls and Monsignor Fustiger said in unison as they warmly slapped each other on the back.

Father Domernas, his knees trembling, couldn't believe his eyes or ears. But Fustiger had things to do, and Sinouls was getting thirstier and thirstier; he rushed off on his break after giving his address and recalling two or three stories that made Father Domernas blush.

"We'll eat in style!"

Monsignor Fustiger's visit to Saint Gudule was not merely due to the necessity of preparing for the ceremony. It had to do with matters sad and serious, albeit unknown to the public: two years earlier, at the time of a visit to our country, or rather to our city, young Prince Gormanskoï (all the princes' names ended in -skoï or -dzoï, the princesses' in -grmska [pronounced "groomoorska"] or in -jrmdza [pronounced "joormoordza"]), first in the Poldevian line of succession, had *disappeared*.

The order of precedence among the Princes was modified each generation in accordance with a permutation immutably fixed since the thirteenth century, when the princes of that time put an end to their bloody disputes: the oldest son of the First Reigning Prince was moved to second place in the hierarchical order (or the oldest daughter, who then became Second Reigning Princess), the heir (or heiress) of the second moved to fourth, the third passed to sixth, the fourth to fifth, and the fifth to third. The Sixth Prince's successor (boy or girl) then found himself first; after a simple calculation, dear Reader, you can easily see for yourself that each family successively occupied each position in the hierarchy. The original order, that of the First Prince (Arnaut Danieldzoï), was reestablished after six generations, and everything remained consistent with the Poldevian emblem, the helix, and satisfactory to their sacred beast, the snail (which could never under any circumstances be hunted in the Chapel's lettuce patch). Futhermore—and this should not be dismissed lightly—all disputes over succession and all political assassinations had been avoided, as well as all abeyances in government (since, at each transfer of power, the six heirs had to take a British spouse—that is to say, Welsh, English, Scottish, Cornish, Manx, or even Northern Irish). The system had proved itself, as it had functioned for seven centuries without incident.

But Prince Gormanskoï, who was soon to become Number One in Poldevia, since the succession took place when the current Number One reached the age of 53, had disappeared. All investigations undertaken by secret police and private investigators had failed to track him down. No one even knew if he was still alive. Time was growing short. The date chosen for the dedication of Rue de l'Abbé-Migne and the consecration of the Poldevian Chapel's new site by Monsignor Fustiger was to coincide exactly with the fifty-third birthday of the current First Prince and the setting in motion, according to the ritual (including the Great Snail Race, which was said to have given Arnaut Danieldzoï the crucial idea), of the institutional succession process. The absence of the young prince might well have the most regrettable consequences for the Principality's stability and the Balance of Power at the World Level. Then new information, acquired by chance, had come to Monsignor Fustiger's attention: it was said that Prince Gormanskoï had been seen in the vicinity of none other than Saint Gudule. Monsignor Fustiger had come to ask Father Domernas to keep his eyes open, or more exactly his ears, and to pay the closest attention to the slightest clues he could gather from his parishioners' conversations, since, if the tip was accurate, it was unthinkable that something wouldn't filter down to him. His hope, which if made reality would definitively assure the future of the Apostolic, Roman Catholic Church in Poldevia at the expense of its rivals (one of the Crown Princes was an Anglican, another was Eastern Orthodox, a fifth was an agnostic, and they said the sixth was a computer hack), was to find the young prince before the fateful date, convince him to return to his native land and take on all the responsibilities attendant to his position, and then unveil him spectacularly before the assembled masses and current princes in the course of the ceremony itself. Which explains why, despite the pleasure of bringing up old memories with Old Man Sinouls, he didn't linger. He had no reason to suspect that he had just passed up a unique opportunity to draw nearer to solving the great mystery.

5

THE HARDWARE-STORE HORROR

The Gudule Bar, the café across the street from Saint Gudule and next to Grands-Edredons Square, was just about empty when I walked in: the early-morning customers had already gone off to their various jobs; the others hadn't stuck their noses outside yet. The owner, Madame Yvonne, brought me my large coffee—very light and not too hot—my two croissants, and the paper. For reasons of economy, both of paper and thought, the full name of the one newspaper was:

The Daily Worker of the News Dispatch in the Free Capital for All Times.

This title was the result of the successive takeover, by the most powerful newspaper, of each of the six other papers that had once competed for the few potential readers; the title had thus grown inordinately long through evolutionary acquisition, each paper as it was being swallowed up having obtained, in a final spasm of dignity, this last trace of its existence before disappearing for good. It was rather hard to just go up to the newsstand and ask for *"The Daily Worker of the News Dispatch in the Free Capital for All Times,* please" in one breath. To keep things short and sweet, it was also called the *Paper.*

And right there on the front page was the expected headline:
The Hardware-Store Horror Strikes Again

Beneath the headline was a completely blurred photo showing what one might have assumed to be a hardware store, but which in fact looked rather more like a tomb; perhaps it was indeed Saint Peter's Basilica in Rome—you could see next to nothing. The photo took up almost the entire front page. Beneath it was this simple caption: *Read our special correspondent's rexqwt on page 8.* I immediately turned to page 8 and found that it was devoted entirely to international news, organized in columns alphabetically by the name of the place in question: Adélie Land, Afghanistan, Alabama, Andorra, Atlantis . . . as is done nowadays in newspapers; there was nothing on this page 8 that could in any way, shape, or form be thought to have any relation to the news proclaimed by the headline on the front page. I didn't even allow myself to be distracted by an alluring subhead—*Genghis Khan's Daughter Runs Amok*—and concluded that there must have been a numbering error, that 8 should have been 6 or even 9. And indeed, there on page 4 was the article's continuation: *The Hardware-Store Horror* (cont. from p. 7):

"It was 11:59 P.M. (11:58 P.M. according to other witnesses) yesterday on the evening of September fourth [. . .], on a peaceful street [. . .] of the [. . .] neighborhood in our fair city when (see the continuation on page 3)."

On page 3 (where, miraculously, the continuation was indeed to be found), the article had cleverly been written backward from bottom to top as one long word, making me think for a moment that it had been written in Poldevian; however, my professional training regained the upper hand, and I was soon up to decoding what followed:

". . . Monsieur and Madame Lalamou-Bêlin, hardware-store proprietors, owners of the hardware store located at [. . .] on the street mentioned above, had just gone up to the bedroom of the apartment they live in above their hardware store when they were suddenly filled with abject terror by the horrifying sound emanating from the floor below.

"Madame Berthe Lalamou-Bêlin said 'My God!' and Monsieur Gustave Lalamou-Bêlin, her husband, said 'Shit!' but despite this difference of expression, they had both just had the same thought: from that moment on they were the thirty-sixth victim of the bold criminal who has been on an eighteen-month rampage in our fair city, who has foiled the colossal efforts of the police set on his tail and is now known as 'The Hardware-Store Horror.' 'No doubt about it,' Inspector Blognard told our special correspondent, 'it's him!' Inspector Blognard, who personally took over the investigation after the seventh attack a little more than a year ago (see *The Daily Worker of the News Dispatch in the Free Capital for All Times* of June 14th [. . .]), arrived on the scene less than half an hour after Monsieur Lalamou-Bêlin's anguished phone call. 'It was undoubtedly him. Same time. Some m.o.' Those were Inspector Blognard's own words, quoted exclusively for our readers [here (*Author's note*) the reference is to the *Paper*'s readers, but our own Readers may also remark this]. The Lalamou-Bêlin hardware store does in fact present the sort of sorry sight (see photo on front page) to which we have grown sadly accustomed. As usual, the evidence seems to be both overabundant and meager. . . ."

I stopped reading there. I could have finished the rest of the article with my eyes closed: like all the (35) other times, the criminal had evidently slipped into the store shortly after closing, without setting off any of the traps or alarm systems, just as Monsieur and Madame Lalamou-Bêlin were retiring to their apartment for their roast with shallots and their evening television. Proceeding in the silent and diabolical manner he had used so effectively from the outset (ever since the beginning of his rampage they had been vigilant, as had every other hardware-store owner, but there hadn't been a sound), he had been faithful to his m.o.: he had scattered all the store's cleaning products on the floor, poured scouring powder on the toilet paper, torn the bristles out of all the brooms, melted the candles, and mixed the wax, being careful, as always, to separate the different-colored products meticulously so as to create a kind of rainbow that was oriented southwest-northeast. It was only after the fourteenth attack that this troubling piece of evidence had been discovered, thanks to Inspector Blognard's phenomenal perspicacity (the Inspector had checked the color photos in the criminal records bureau to verify that it had doubtless been this way from the start). As always, the criminal had worked quickly and efficiently at his sinister task. As on every other occasion, he concluded by hanging a series of saucepans from the ceiling in what was likely a spiral. A tiny explosive, carefully set to go off just before midnight, had caused the string holding up the saucepan configuration to break, thus creating the characteristic terrifying racket that had revealed their unfortunate fate to Monsieur and Madame Lalamou-Bêlin. Apparently (and subject to inventory), nothing had been stolen.

Everyone was indulging themselves in conjecture over the criminal's identity and aim (and it wasn't even clear that it was one man acting alone and not a gang). Inspector Blognard had stated in the most definitive manner that it was one man acting alone, but no one knew what clues had led him to that conviction (which, I must say, was also my own). At first, people thought it was a protection racket, but this hypothesis was soon shown to be untenable because the profits of small hardware stores in no way justified such an effort on the part of organized crime. There was also not the slightest trace of the sort of funny business in which the members of the honorary guild of hardware-store operators with any insurance at all might have engaged. Most observers thought the culprit was a madman, a skillful, meticulous madman, but that was not the Inspector's opinion. The public was divided, and everyone followed with great curiosity the implacable struggle of uncertain outcome being waged between the unknown villain and our most celebrated detective, Inspector Blognard. The Inspector had laid his reputation on the line and brought all his great wisdom to bear on the matter. Insurance rates for hardware stores had doubled. Meanwhile, time was passing, and the police investigation was apparently at a standstill. Alas, these anti–hardware store raids took place at irregular intervals, but on the average once every two weeks. All areas of the city had been struck; in each case the store affected was on a quiet, somewhat isolated street, and no one had ever been able to give even the slightest description of a suspect. The evildoer made child's play of locks, worked noiselessly, and then disappeared like an impalpable shadow into the dark alleys of the night, his infamous mission accomplished. At one minute to midnight, the racket made by the saucepans announced that he had stopped by. Inspector Blognard would arrive with his faithful assistant, look around, clench his teeth, say a few words to the media, and keep his cool. It was obvious, however, that he was growing more and more anxious. He hadn't announced that an arrest was imminent, or even that there was a promising lead. He would come, look around, go back to his office, nervously undo the silver wrapper with diagonal black stripes on a new Callard and Bowser's, ordered specially at Fortnum and Mason's by a colleague at Scotland Yard—they were his one vice—eat it, crumple up the wrapper, toss it in the wastepaper basket (which he missed more and more often), and immerse himself in the file for the hundredth time. The country held its breath. It seemed that the flash of inspiration wasn't coming, that for the first time in his career the Inspector was, dare we say it, *unequal to the task*!

I refolded the newspaper and gave it back to Madame Yvonne. The café was starting to fill up, and naturally conversation revolved primarily around the events of the night before. I barely listened, since I was in a state of intense feverishness. It was a decisive moment for me; decisive for my career, my ambitions. I had pondered the problem, checked out certain details, made certain hypotheses and deductions, and I was pretty much sure they were right, but that of course wasn't good enough; a second condition had to be met, a condition about which I could do nothing. Indeed, if the event I was expecting didn't happen soon, this very morning and here in this café, my chance was lost, and I would have to start from scratch. Furthermore, in that case the mystery of the Hardware-Store Horror would doubtless never be solved. I was so tense and preoccupied that I inadvertently allowed my croissant to dissolve in my coffee cup, a bad sign: I always dunk my croissant in my large coffee with cream, but just a little bit, so that it can be separated into moist but still firm bites. I didn't even say hello to Alexander Vladimirovich, who, contrary to his usual practice, was in the café that morning. Now, since I sense that you, the Reader, are in a state of great impatience, that you are dying to find out the meaning of my sibylline words (and since the Author won't let me make you wait any longer anyway), I'm not going to make you wait any longer. This is what I had discovered.

I had in fact discovered something—you guessed it—having to do with the mystery of the Hardware-Store Horror. But before revealing my discovery to you, I must make my position clearer: I'm a journalist, but, since I was a cub reporter at the time, the "Hardware-Store" story was in no way part of my beat, and I was only interested in it, for the first few months at any rate, in the same episodic and distracted way that everyone else was. And then, roughly a month before the moment when I went into the Gudule Bar, the moment that is the present tense for my story, I had an idea that struck me as absolutely brilliant. By applying my idea, I succeeded, after a great deal of effort, in obtaining an interview. This interview was an apparent failure. To rescue my idea and correct this failure, I had to come up with another idea (hardly independent, as will be seen, from the first). I spent many sleepless nights, but I found it. Here's how I arrived at my hypothesis. I didn't make use of any special information outside of what was available to the general public—that is to say, the information published in the press. I read everything. From that vacuous mass of documentation, I retained two things: a list of all the hardware stores struck by the criminal, and the color photos of the state of the premises after the attacks—photos taken and published through the efforts of a weekly that had run them for its readers. I took eight days off, locked myself up in my house with these documents, and pondered them for six days and six nights. I found it.

The number of victims at that time was 34. Using little flags to mark, on a map of the City, the locations of the 34 hardware stores that had been attacked, I saw with blinding clarity that the criminal had followed a spiral path; this spiral was very clear, and each time he had chosen the hardware store closest to the outline of the spiral; more exactly, he was moving in toward the spiral's center. By constructing the most accurate possible representation of this spiral, I saw that he was, without any possible doubt, working his way toward Grands-Edredons Square. I set about making a list of the hardware stores in the neighborhood nearest the spiral path. A few days later, the Hardware-Store Horror struck for the thirty-fifth time, and the hardware store hit was one of the three possibilities I had marked on my map. My hypothesis had been confirmed. A simple calculation based on geometric distance and progression showed me:

1. that there should still be one more hardware store attacked;
2. that this would be the 36th and last;
3. that the unfortunate victims would necessarily be Monsieur and Madame Lalamou-Bêlin.

Hence I found myself impaled on the horns of a dilemma: if I revealed what I knew, I ran the risk of not being believed; worse yet, I also risked destroying the result that I was hoping to produce with my discovery, which, even more than just the solution of the riddle, would offset my initial failure. I hesitated for a good ten minutes before finally doing nothing. And my prediction was borne out. But I had discovered something else (more important still in my eyes): by counting the fallen saucepans in the stricken shops—taking into account slight variations due to the quality of the negatives and the unpredictable bounces that took some of the saucepans out of the camera's range in one case—I discovered that the number was apparently always the same, *and that this number was 53,* meaning that the criminal's spiral path was leading him to 53 Rue des Citoyens, the very building in which I lived!

I finished my croissant and drank my coffee. The Saint Gudule clock tower had just struck nine. The door to the Gudule Bar opened. Two men walked in. I had won.

Maybe!

6

IN WHICH
INSPECTOR
BLOGNARD IS NOT
UPSET BY THE
OPPORTUNITY
FINALLY GIVEN HIM
TO EXPLAIN THE
NATURE OF HIS
RELATIONS WITH
THE NARRATOR

About six months before the events reported in the previous chapter, I was sitting in my office. It was a midwinter day like any other, one of those colorless days in black and white, the kind I call administrative days because you get the feeling that nothing interesting can happen in such drab surroundings, and because boredom keeps you from feeling like doing anything but digging up old files, finishing up reports that have been dragging on for a long time, and obstinately but listlessly disposing of current work. It was about ten in the morning. My report had been finished for nearly half an hour, and it had been very short. Three days earlier the Hardware-Store Horror had struck for the twenty-third time on Rue [. . .]; and as usual there was practically nothing to add to my previous reports—nothing, not a single clue. I had finished my

report, and I wasn't in a very good mood. I had just nervously
opened a new box of Callard and Bowser's and was in the process of
nervously struggling to open, with my left thumbnail, the clear
covering on one of the eight candy parallelepipeds it contained
when the inside line rang.

"Is that you, Blognard? Could you please stop by my office for a
second?"

Nothing surprising there. Every day, or just about, the chief
ended up calling me into his office at least once on unofficial
business: I had known him since childhood. He had often spent his
vacations with us in N., having been one of my father's friends. It
was so dreary that morning that his desk lamp with the yellow
shade was on. Next to it, in an armchair, was a young man who
got up to offer me his hand as we were introduced.

"Inspector Blognard, Monsieur Mornacier, a journalist . . ."

"Not a journalist, a novelist," the young man smilingly protested.

"There you have it—a professional journalist, but an aspiring
novelist. Monsieur Mornacier, who is the son of an old friend of
mine, would like to follow you around on one of your investigations—
for his novel. If that's not a problem for you, of course."

I barely glanced at the young man, who must have been about
twenty-four years old, was thin, and about whom I can at least say
that he looked as though he didn't have any doubts about anything—
and certainly not about himself. I wasn't exactly thrilled to death,
but then again I didn't really have much choice, after an introduc-
tion like that. I figured I'd stick him with the case of the jewel
thief; it was already practically solved, so I'd be rid of him in a few
days. I gave a vague grunt through the piece of candy and asked
him to follow me into my office.

"That's the ticket," he said. "That's just where I have to start,
with the office of the famous Inspector Blognard."

I smiled to myself, since it happened that at the time my office
was being redecorated. Ad interim I was occupying an old-
fashioned administrative office on the mezzanine. The office was as
dusty as they come, with black wood furniture and a coal-burning
stove like you used to see in certain train stations in the provinces
thirty years ago. It was the office where I had started out and
worked for fifteen years as an inspector, and I must admit I had a

soft spot in my heart for that big cast-iron stove; I loved to watch it turn red in winter.

"Sit down, Monsieur...?"

"Mornacier, *i-e-r*. What a marvelously anachronistic spot," he immediately added with relish; "makes you feel like you're right here in 1927–1928! I didn't dare hope for as much. But I want to let you know right away, Inspector Blognard," he said before I could even open my mouth to mention the case of the jewel thief, "there's only one thing I'm interested in: the Hardware-Store Horror!"

Enough, enough, enough already! The Narrator's role is to say "I" and tell what is happening to him as the Author has decided what happens to him ought to be told when it's happening to him (actually *after* it has happened to him). Under no circumstances should the Narrator usurp the Author's rightful position and put himself in the shoes of another character in the story and, what's more, make himself the star! How could the Reader figure out where he stood? And to top it all off, copying almost the entire scene from another novel! If that's what the Narrator imagines the novelist's duty to be, things are really looking up for French literature! So let's move on, but now the one speaking, as it should be, is the Narrator, and he's saying what he's supposed to, in his own name.

Inspector Blognard's reaction was extremely unfavorable, I saw that right away. At first he didn't say anything; he looked at me in a quiet, friendly way, all the while chewing on one of his famed candies. Then he finally spoke:

"No, Monsieur Mornacier, no! The Hardware-Store Horror—no!"

I had failed. I immediately got up to leave, but I must have had such a pitiful, downcast look on my face, after the self-confidence (purely artificial and nervous; I am modest and reserved by nature) I had shown in the chief's office, that he felt just a hint of remorse and added:

"Listen, young man, that's a hard case, without a doubt the hardest of my whole career. I don't want anyone on my tail, get that straight: I just can't have it! But I'll make a deal with you: find me a lead on the case, *a valuable lead that I haven't found,* just one, and come back to see me. If your idea holds up, then you can follow the whole investigation. Now, isn't that a square deal?"

He offered me his hand, and I left the office. He was sure I'd never set foot in it again; that was clear from his grip and his look. He had already practically forgotten me; he had felt a twinge of remorse because of my disappointment and because of the chief's recommendation, then he had felt remorse over his remorse and had added at the last moment the clause that eliminated me once and for all in his eyes: "... *that I haven't found.*" I was back on the sidewalk, no farther along than I had been an hour before; worse, I had gone backward. My brilliant professional idea had apparently just bitten the dust.

I had started a little over a year earlier at the powerful daily of a seaside provincial metropolis, and had just recently been put on the editorial staff of the City's *Paper.* Because I didn't wish to spend a long time in the uninteresting subordinate position in which I found myself, I had a double purpose: to accompany Inspector Blognard on his investigation and be there at the key moments, and at the same time (I hadn't lied to the chief) to write a novel, the first novel in a series whose hero would be the Inspector (or rather, of course, a fictitious character based largely on the real Inspector Blognard) and whose inevitable popularity would ensure my wealth and glory.

Because of the passionate interest its enigmatic nature aroused in the public, the case of the Hardware-Store Horror seemed like the chance I'd been dreaming of. Working outside normal channels, I had managed to obtain the interview on which my future would ride. But there I was, fooled by the image the papers gave of the Inspector. I had failed to realize that in fact he put his job well above fame, and that my fine idea was nothing but a pipe dream. At first I experienced a moment of intense discouragement, but I pulled myself together immediately. I still had one chance: if I could find the definitive lead the Inspector had demanded, not only would my failure be erased, but I would guarantee myself the best possible position for my project; winning Blognard's respect was the only way to reach him, to finally get him to talk, to reveal the secret of his method, the method that had made him the century's most extraordinary sleuth! I set to work with determination.

I had come up with an idea (I told you which one), but if I was sure it was valid (and that certainty, subjective at first, had just been made objective by the accuracy of my prediction concerning the thirty-sixth attack), what I was still unsure of was whether this alone would be sufficient to win Blognard's respect. His walking into the Gudule Bar showed that he had reached the same conclusion I had, but anyway I needed something more than just a valid hunch; I had to come up with something that he had missed. I couldn't be sure of that, although I had a candidate-idea that I haven't shared with you yet. And now, since the criminal, if I was not mistaken, had come to the end of his diabolical spiral and was likely to disappear, time was of the essence. Inspector Blognard and his companion had sat down in the back of the café. I got up and walked over to them.

"Inspector. . ."

He looked at me, and I could see that I hadn't been wrong about the meaning of his proposal, since he didn't recognize me at all. For Inspector Blognard had a fabulous, a phenomenal, a downright infallible memory, meaning that he forgot everything not having to do with his investigations, everything that couldn't help track down the criminal; his having forgotten me thus meant that he hadn't thought I would be able to find anything useful that he had missed.

"Inspector, you don't remember me, but I came to see you six months ago. I wanted to follow your investigation of the case of the Hardware-Store Horror, and you told me at the time to come back with a lead, a useful lead that you hadn't found. Here I am, and I think I have what you requested."

Inspector Blognard gave me a second look.

He simply said, "Sit down, I'm listening."

I sat down and told all very quickly: the spiral, the path, the center, the prediction of the thirty-sixth attack, the saucepans, their number, the address 53 Rue des Citoyens. I stopped. That was the first part of my game plan; I couldn't really hope that there was anything in all of that that the great Blognard hadn't discovered or deduced. He had listened to me without interrupting, chewing one of his ever-present candies and looking as if he were half asleep and hardly paying attention. When I stopped, he looked at me with perhaps a smidgen of respect (I wouldn't have sworn to it), but all he said was:

"I know."

"Excuse me, boss," said his companion, who was sitting across from him and hadn't opened his mouth until then, "Excuse me, boss—you *think* you know."

"Arapède, let this young man continue, for, if I am not mistaken, young man, you haven't finished. You know quite well that your having reached this point in the solving of the mystery is, according to the terms of our agreement, most useless to you—since I have already reached the same point—unless you have *something else* certain or even likely that I don't know about. You don't know if I don't know, but you hope so, isn't that it? Well, what is it?"

I couldn't postpone it any longer.

"Well, then," I said. "I spent quite a long time walking around the scenes of the crimes, all around each of the thirty-five hardware stores that have already been attacked, and I discovered the following: in each case someone used black paint on a blank wall located no more than fifty-three paces from the store to draw the silhouette of a man standing up and pissing. It's hardly a work of art, the silhouette is very crude, but there's still no mistaking it, the drawing is definitely of a man pissing. Nor, to the best of my knowledge, do any such silhouettes appear on any of the city's other walls. I haven't gone everywhere, but I have walked the streets a great, great deal, and I have never found such a 'wall painting' elsewhere. Secondly, when, following the reasoning that guided both of us, I foresaw that attack against the Lalamou-Bêlin hardware store, the one that brought you here, I inspected the area, and I discovered something I couldn't have known before, and for good reason: the 'paintings' precede the attacks, *since there was already one there the day before*. Finally, something is going to happen—something different, since the location has no hardware store—at 53 Rue des Citoyens, because since last night the wall of the building facing the church on Rue des Milleguiettes *has been adorned with a silhouette of a man pissing!*"

7

THE NARRATOR

Inspector Blognard remained silent for quite some time, and when he spoke it wasn't to congratulate me on my excellent reasoning or, and this was even more important to me, to acknowledge that the last of my deductions had escaped him; I was now practically sure of that, but I needed confirmation. He looked at me intently and said:

"How do you know it's been there *since last night*?"

"Because I live in that very building and go past that wall night and day."

"And how long have you been living in that building?"

"For a year, but..."

I was about to add "what does that have to do with anything?" when a horrible thought crossed my mind, causing me to leave my sentence unfinished: *the Inspector suspected me*! He was so sure of himself and so used to figuring everything out before everyone else that he could see only one possible reason for my success: I was the culprit! Upon my arrival in the city a year earlier, I had immediately found the small apartment in that building that I've been living in ever since, a miraculous (ha, ha—*Author's note*) stroke of luck given my modest means. That building must also have been the very one sheltering the criminal. It was, of course, a mere coincidence (ha! ha!—*Author's note*), but the Inspector's question seemed to indicate that his thoughts were oriented in that troubling direction. And, I thought, I don't even have an alibi! Inspector Blognard smiled:

"I don't suspect you, young man. I had completely forgotten your face, and believe me, that's proof enough that you aren't mixed up in this business as either a perpetrator or a victim. *I am never wrong*. Besides, you've only been here for a year, and the attacks started eighteen months ago. Arapède?"

"Yes, boss."

"I'm thirsty. Another round."

Inspector Arapède, Blognard's right-hand man, got up and went to the bar, where Madame Yvonne served him a double Shirley Temple for the Inspector and a Guinness draft. Inspector Blognard crumpled another silvery candy wrapper with diagonal black stripes and took a sip from his double Shirley Temple (the red and the black, I thought).

"Arapède, my dear boy, how you can drink that bitter tar at nine in the morning is beyond me! Why not Campari or Fernet-Branca, if that's the sort of thing you're up for?"

"How do you know, boss, that Guinness gives me a taste of tarred bitterness, as you put it? And even if it was thus previously, how can you know that this particular Guinness will have exactly the same tarred bitterness as all the other Guinness I've drunk before, whose tarred bitterness I will admit for the sake of argument? Is not honey, boss, sweet to some, bitter to others? Can it not also become bitter for me if, for example, I taste it while still having a bit of the taste of the Guinness in my mouth? The senses, boss . . ."

"Please, Arapède, no philosophizing on the job, that's not what we're paid for!"

But Arapède hadn't finished his discourse.

"Excuse me, boss, but can we really trust in what others tell us about their senses? What they say is true for them, but how can the least certainty be drawn from their statements, boss? Do not those who suffer from viral hepatitis state that objects that appear white as snow or flour to us are in fact yellow, and do not people whose eyes are bloodshot say that those same objects are red? And since some animals have yellow eyes, others have bloodshot eyes, and others still are albinos, can I not assume that they too see objects according to the color of their eyes? And what about you yourself, boss? If you hunch over a book after having looked at the sun for several minutes without a break, don't the letters look as if they were gilded and surrounded by bright shades? Does that not make you distrust all testimony, boss?"

Inspector Blognard let Arapède's tirade, which did not seem to surprise him, come to an end before going on:

"Well, young man, you have won. You have come up with two valuable leads that I'd found myself, and one that I hadn't. Consider yourself part of the investigation from now on. But everything's off the record until I give the green light, O.K.? I don't want the hoodlum to be tipped off. Let's let him think we aren't on his trail for a while. So swear: 'Cross my heart and hope to die, stick a needle in my eye.'"

I willingly recited the oath demanded by the Inspector. I was overjoyed.

The sun now lit up the upper half of Saint Gudule and, going house by house diagonally down Rue des Grands-Edredons, came to lap the green plants behind the mirror of the Gudule Bar and began to crawl lazily inside the café between the legs of the tables. I was overcome by a sweet, optimistic warmth, similar to that obtained by consuming a strawberry sundae topped with whipped cream and strawberry sauce. Alexander Vladimirovich, who seemed to have been listening attentively to our conversation from behind his princely, indifferent, half-closed eyelids, stretched and gracefully went out into the street, crossing with all due precaution before disappearing into the square through two bars in the fence. Inspector Arapède drank his Guinness in little swallows, from time to time wiping his mustache—occasionally turned brown by the dark foam of the Anglo-Irish beverage—with the back of his hand.

"But, young man," Inspector Blognard went on, "I don't want you tripping over my heels, if I dare express myself in such a way, with your pen and paper in hand. If I'm going to make you a part of this investigation, you have to contribute."

"I couldn't ask for anything more."

"Good. We'll draw up a battle plan. But first I'm going to bring you up to date: there's something else I know, which you haven't found out. You have no reason to feel ashamed; you didn't have all the necessary evidence at your disposal. It's something that you can see by looking over the hardware stores' inventories. I've had that done after each attack. Before . . . but let's not speak ill of our colleagues. All of that is routine and quite boring. The job is eighty-nine percent routine and eleven percent habit, isn't it, Arapède?"

"Yes, boss," answered Arapède, whose mind was obviously elsewhere.

"At this moment there are four people who know what I am about to tell you: there's me, there's my wife, and there's Arapède."

"And the fourth?" I said stupidly.

"The fourth is the criminal!"

And the Inspector smiled at having thus scored a point.

"So I had the most accurate inventory possible drawn up of everything that was found in the store after each attack, and where it was—its geography, or something like that (that's how I saw the number of saucepans: you're right, it's 53 in every case). I compared the result with what I could deduce about the stock beforehand. I wanted to know whether there was really nothing missing. It wasn't easy—nothing valuable anywhere, and apparently nothing missing anywhere either. Hardware-store owners have particularly bad memories; not one of them really knew what had been in his store. I thought about it again and again, and finally I found it. But I didn't say anything about all that to the papers; there's no reason to tip the guy off."

"Maybe he doesn't read the papers," said Arapède.

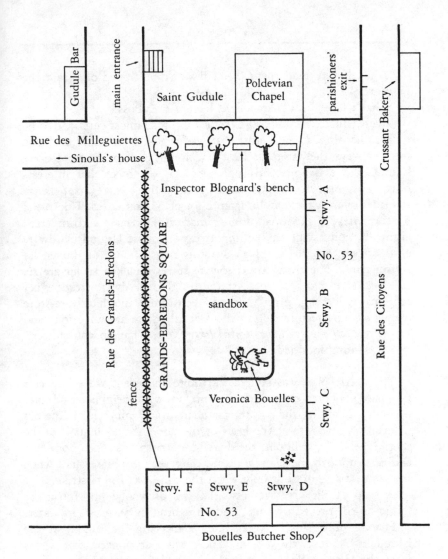

Gudule Bar

main entrance →

Saint Gudule

Poldevian Chapel

parishioners' exit →

Crussant Bakery

Rue des Milleguiettes

← Sinouls's house

Inspector Blognard's bench

Rue des Grands-Edredons

GRANDS-EDREDONS SQUARE

fence

sandbox

Veronica Bouelles

Stwy. A

No. 53

Stwy. B

Stwy. C

Rue des Citoyens

Stwy. F   Stwy. E   Stwy. D

No. 53

Bouelles Butcher Shop

Rue Vieille-des-Archives

Hortense's house

MAP OF THE AREA

"If he doesn't read them, he still won't be tipped off," said the Inspector.

"That's true," said Arapède. "Excuse me, boss."

"Well, then," resumed the Inspector, "it's almost certain that he took something: in each store that was attacked, he spirited off one item, always the same (at least one item, perhaps more, I don't know). There is apparently only one sort of object that interests him. This object, which has no retail value, is a *glazed pottery statuette,* one of the samples from a lot of 53 statuettes, I do mean 53 statuettes, of Poldevian origin, 'made in Poldevia,' and imported eighteen months ago by the import-export house United Hardware and Turpentine, to be given away as free gifts to all buyers of frying pans. The thirty-six hardware stores attacked so far are *the only ones* that received these statuettes. No hardware-store owner remembers having given one to a customer, no hardware-store owner has any recollection of them at all, there are none left, and *no one can tell me what they looked like.* Well, what do you think?"

I was dumbfounded.

The battle plan was simple and quite consistent with Inspector Blognard's unorthodox methods: mix in with neighborhood life, naturally including the square, the church, and number 53 Rue des Citoyens, which was at the heart of the case. Above all, talk to the shopkeepers, the children, the dogs, the housewives; open both eyes and ears, unearth the unusual detail, the revealing phrase, and, when the time was right, but only when the time was right, strike.

A map of the area was essential; we drew one up. It can be found on the preceding page, under the heading MAP OF THE AREA.

Having done this, we scheduled a meeting for Sunday at the Blognards'. I took the day off. There was a stationery store across from the Gudule Bar, on the other side of Rue des Milleguiettes, and I decided to buy a special notebook to write down, as a sort of battle log, all that happened during the investigation; this would be useful for the book I was going to write afterward, the first of my collaborations, from now on assured, with the great man. As I was leaving the café, I heard Inspector Arapède's voice.

"Boss, you say the *guy;* but are you really sure the perpetrator is a man?"

THE FIRST
BETWEEN-TWO-CHAPTERS
WHAT'S GOING ON HERE?
WHERE ARE WE?

Like ourselves, our Readers are, we are sure, asking themselves a fair number of questions. Now is the time to take a short break and list a few of those questions. The authors of novels, as we have learned through much experience, rarely have the courtesy, we might even say the common decency, to include, as we have, rest areas for their readers, places where they may be reassured that their queries are not being ignored and that they share their confusion with the author himself as well as with most of the characters. These free spaces in the novel are an innovation that we propose to our contemporaries, colleagues, and successors, and that we suggest be called a between-two-chapters. Everyone is invited; you can rest and reflect along the banks of a few questions before resuming your journey through the rest of the story.

52

The questions are numbered, and our Readers may practice by answering them.

1. From what novel did the Narrator steal the description of his first meeting with Inspector Blognard?
2. What is the identity of the mysterious young man glimpsed by Alexander Vladimirovich in the bedroom of the empty apartment on the right side of the fourth floor of Stairway C, 53 Rue des Citoyens?
3. Why are there 36 hardware stores in the criminal's battle plan?
4. Why is the criminal tracing a hardware-store spiral on the map of the city?
5. Why does he steal statuettes?
6. What is Poldevia's role in the case?
7. Where is Prince Gormanskoï?
8. Why does the criminal draw a black silhouette of a man pissing near the scene of each attack?
9. What is the criminal's motive?
10. Is Hortense mixed up in the case?
11. What did Alexander Vladimirovich see in the half-open suitcase?
12. Inspector Arapède's question: why is Inspector Blognard sure that the criminal is a man?
13. Will Inspector Blognard emerge triumphant?
14. Why the clatter of the saucepans?

Special Question

Why did Alexander Vladimirovich abruptly stop listening to Inspectors Blognard and Arapède's conversation with the Narrator, even though this conversation seemed to interest him tremendously? (See Chapter 6.)

An Immediate Answer to the Special Question
(by popular demand)

You're right, the reason could only be Love. Love had struck Alexander Vladimirovich in the heart and whiskers (Love enters man through the eyes, but it invades cats by the whiskers, as Galen teaches us).

Love was waiting for him at 53 Rue des Citoyens, Stairway D, third floor left. And she was red-haired.

Alexander Vladimirovich could make out a desk through the windowpane that was just being lit up by the sun. A philosopher in a mauve silk dressing gown was seated at this desk: he was thinking. On the desk in front of him, he had placed a beautiful young red-haired cat, whose soft young fur was strewn with patches of the purest white. She was purring.

She was purring professionally, not for pleasure. She was purring with determination, with perseverance. For this was the job she had been hired to do: purr; purr while the Philosopher thought; purr so that he would think; purr as long as he was thinking. Alexander Vladimirovich's heart beat faster beneath his whiskers. He gently scratched at the windowpane.

(To be continued at the end of chapters 9 and 11, the second between-two-chapters, and chapters 18, 23, and 26.)

8

HORTENSE

Utterly unaware of the five pairs of eyes differentially following her hindquarters, so clearly visible beneath her scanty clothing, Hortense walked down Rue des Citoyens and disappeared behind Saint Gudule. Her destination, indicated ahead of time on the map included in Chapter 7, was the Crussant family bakery/pastry shop/ice cream store. When Hortense entered the bakery all out of breath, the owner's wife, Madame Crussant, was happily sitting behind the counter and, in her usual slow and clumsy way, doing her best to serve her many customers. She welcomed Hortense with calm relief; she did not reproach her for being late.

"There she is," was all Madame Crussant said, as if that explained everything.

Indeed, that did explain everything, for Hortense was, if one may say as much, a gift of love from Monsieur Crussant to his wife. Madame Crussant was endowed with a well-rounded body, a creamy complexion, and a mass of intricate, chocolatey hair, making her in many ways similar to the countless high-quality eclairs, custards, and fruit tarts her husband turned out daily; she was plump like an almond croissant and slow like warm pudding. This natural slowness was exacerbated by her notorious inability to do arithmetic, as well as the stormy demands made upon her by the nine little Crussants, turned out annually by the conjugal oven with the same success and enthusiasm as their father's celebrated lemon meringue. Monsieur Crussant had finally been forced to acknowledge the insurmountable difficulties his wife encountered in handling business and had given her a gift: Hortense. Twice a day, mornings at eight and evenings at six, Hortense came to help sell bread and pastries; and on Sunday mornings, a crucial time, she was brought in for the after-Mass rush. The Crussant bread and pastry shop was located, not tritely and profanely directly facing Saint Gudule's main exit on Rue des Grands-Edredons, but rather, much more subtly and strategically, to the rear of the structure, where a drab little door allowed the good women of the church to indulge in the smooth, titillating escapade of an eclair without fear of being fixed by an infidel's all too ironic look; they only encountered others of their ilk.

Madame Crussant was extremely proud of Hortense. First of all, she was a gift and a demonstration of love (of an essentially different nature than the nine little Crussants or the countless cakes and creams she was asked to appraise, for Monsieur Crussant never put a single batch out without first obtaining her opinion); furthermore, in some vague way, she likened Hortense, whose tender flesh was obviously delicious, to a new sort of pastry that had merely been given the gift of movement, and whose inventor was therefore, in some sense, her husband. Finally (and this was a sort of bonus—like an extra little bit of whipped cream—that was particularly tasty for Madame Crussant, who had never finished high school), Hortense studied philosophy. The vastness of this fact filled Madame Crussant both with excitement (she remained motionless and calm, in spite of it all) and with something like terror. While Hortense, still not completely awake, and made nervous by being late, groped for a Vienna loaf in the bin reserved for whole wheat and bran, Madame Crussant would never fail to point out to her customers:

"She studies philosophy, you know!"

This usually impressed female customers quite a bit. It impressed male customers as well; however, it must be admitted, alas, that the latter were more likely impressed, with only rare exceptions, by qualities that had precious little to do with philosophy. Madame Crussant had indeed noticed the unusual throng that accompanied Hortense's presence in the bakery, but her innocent soul attributed it to her husband's excellent business sense, along with the powerful draw philosophy's prestige must have on the neighborhood's residents. Not only were there more customers, but certain husbands, contrary to their usual practice, were seen buying the family bread themselves, thereby relieving their wives of one of the household chores. An even stranger result of Hortense's presence was the sudden increase in sales of certain specialty cakes and breads, particularly those on very low shelves that forced Hortense to bend down or lean forward, be it facing the customer, who drew very near to make sure that she was getting out the right item, or turning her back, in which case the customer's view of the pastry was blocked by a vision no less appetizing.

On one count, however, Hortense's presence hadn't really lived up to Monsieur Crussant's expectations: Hortense, contrary to what her employers naively imagined, didn't calculate any better than Madame Crussant; she was simply more decisive. Never really distinguishing between one coin and another, unable to subtract 2.60 from 5 or 1.95 from 10, she soon gave up and made change practically at random. It made scarcely any real financial difference, since the female customers, churchgoing or not, corrected her mistakes themselves; and the male customers were much too excited about the nearness of Hortensian breasts and other accessories to pay much attention to what they had been given back, meaning that, with the help of the law of large numbers, the books balanced. Madame Crussant was in seventh heaven.

So on that morning, as on other mornings, she greeted Hortense happily and said to her customers (all gentlemen):

"There she is! She studies philosophy, you know!"

But, you will say to us, what is Hortense, a philosophy student, doing in the Crussant bakery? Could it be that, endowed with uncertain and insufficient financial resources, abandoned to her fate by her family, sacrificing herself to her passion for study and her own ambitious nature, she was dedicating the wages—generous per se, but still moderate—that Monsieur Crussant payed her (in addition to petit fours and cream puffs at cost) to the purchase of books, that she drew her only sustenance from bread and fresh city water, using up her eyes and her youth deciphering Plato or Schopenhauer published in expensive editions acquired with her last francs? Could it be, contrary to appearances, since Hortense is, as we have already mentioned, the novel's heroine, that this novel is in fact about the Starving Student in Today's World? But if this is the case, how can it be that, as we have previously mentioned, Hortense's minimal dress on that warm, beautiful September morning could have been referred to as "pricey," making it inaccessible to someone living on an assistant baker's salary? Furthermore, how could her apartment possibly be termed "huge"? We have a mystery here that must be solved at once, to avoid red herrings.

Hortense's parents were far from being in financial straits. Because they were members of the upper strata of the very closed world of the *Haute Delicatesserie,* shouldering the cost of Hortense's studies did not force any intolerable sacrifices upon them. Furthermore, they were perfectly ready to make whatever sacrifices were necessary; they adored their daughter and were no less amazed than Madame Crussant by the intensity and elevation of her intellectual activities. The only problem was that Hortense was put off by the gifts they never stopped giving her; she found their generosity tactless, their determination misplaced. And a recent event had been the straw that broke the camel's back of her exasperation: at the beginning of the summer her father, claiming the excuse of an exceptional return on a brilliant deal, had sadistically given her the apartment in which she now lived. The apartment was not uncomfortable or badly located: she had chosen it herself. But she found the principle of the thing intolerable and felt it necessary to react. So she decided to earn her own living, and she put up posters in the neighborhood saying: "Philosophy student looking for any kind of work." Monsieur Crussant called her that very day. She was paid weekly, and on the evening following her first day's work she put down the deposit on the dress she was wearing that morning, the first day of this novel.

Everything seemed to be going very well for Hortense: she was writing her thesis under the eminent direction of Professor Orsells, and she was working in the Crussant bakery. But, alas, the picture had a dark side as well: her personal life was not oriented along lines of force in harmony with her capacity, imagination, or desire. Surprised very early on by the excitement (which did not diminish with the passing years—quite the contrary, in fact) that members of the sex fundamentally different from her own demonstrated when appraising her physical appearance (which continued to surprise her, since she was quite modest), she happily entered into amorous relations, which she found, shall we say, "not unpleasant," with a minimum of hesitation, delay, or doubt, sensitive as she was to the suffering a refusal on her part might cause. But she soon ran up against insurmountable problems. The first was that of simultaneity, which inevitably generated timing difficulties and, worse, vehement reproaches from certain men whose indignation frightened her, given her inability to understand the reasons for it. Moreover, since she did not make a clear distinction between the strictly physical activities of amorous relations and other activities, primarily those that we might deem linguistic, she attempted, with an admirable persistence in the face of obvious reservation, to make the souls dwelling in the bodily envelopes that found themselves in her bed (or in whose bed she herself had ended up) share her intellectual and essentially philosophical anxieties. After numerous unhappy experiences, she had been forced to face the facts: they fell asleep, then they ran away. And on one occasion, when, as an experiment, she had attempted to reverse the order of operations by first bringing up a point of Spinozan ethics that had her perplexed, the reaction, although quite different, had not struck her as more satisfying, since the young man, a philosophy student like herself, had become so engrossed in the question that he completely forgot about the rest, and it was finally she who fell asleep, untouched and disappointed.

She recounted each experience to Yvette, who was both her confidante and her gynecologist. From time to time Yvette explained the hows and whys of some of the strange behavior she came to confront in the course of her adventures. Hortense also tried to extract advice of a less specifically anatomical nature from her, concerning the meaning of life and the best strategy to adopt in order to lead her lovers to pay more attention to her philosophical soul. Yvette responded willingly, but her succinct aphorisms were all deduced more or less explicitly from a fundamental axiom with two parts: a) all men are bastards; b) all women are bitches. Although extremely enlightening for Hortense, this axiom did not seem easy to translate into practical action. Increasing proportionately with the passing of summer that year, Hortense's dissatisfaction took on the ever-clearer countenance of an aspiration that, had she been pushed to the limit, she would have called Meeting the Man of Her Dreams. Basically, this man would embody all the positive attributes of her finest conquests while at the same time having a receptive ear for her never-ending supply of philosophical questions and commentary. But he did not appear, and Hortense began asking herself if she were cursed by fate and her horoscope, or if she had some horrible hidden physical defect. She looked at herself in the mirror and found nothing particularly repulsive about her appearance. Futhermore, male enthusiasm for her person was hardly diminishing. Oddly enough, it seemed especially lively that morning. Doubtless it was something in the air.

9

THE
YOUNG MAN
FROM
THE
T-LINE BUS

Mornings, Hortense worked until about nine, when the crowd in the bakery began to thin and all the little Crussants were at school. Hortense then gathered up her purse and her notebooks and left for the Library. Madame Crussant would kiss her on both cheeks and give her a little brown bag with a midmorning snack: a fresh, juicy, piping hot pizza wrapped in aluminum foil, and two almond croissants or a few petits fours, for example. She was afraid that the intense intellectual activity her employee was about to undertake in such a harsh place as the Library would make her lose weight, thereby reducing her chances for a good marriage. So it was quarter past nine when Hortense went out onto Rue des Citoyens. The T-line bus stop was obviously not on that street, since that street, as you have known since the very first chapter, was one-way west to east; instead, it was to be found on a parallel street a bit farther north, Rue Flaminio-de-Birague, toward which Hortense walked rapidly.

You will notice, I think, how hard it is for a novel to move forward in time; not the time of the telling, but rather the time of what is being told beyond the initial moment. This is the third time we've tried, on this morning of September 6, 19——, and still, with Inspector Blognard's conference, we haven't gotten past midmorning. There are so many things to explain dating from the before-novel era that it's a miracle if time manages to move forward even one minute. We would very much have liked to have been able to ask some of our colleagues questions on this subject, especially Alexander Dumas—to leap *Twenty Years Later* in a single bound, what a tour de force!

Four people were waiting for the bus, which appeared presently. It was tightly packed, and the driver scornfully passed the stop without even slowing. He then stopped at the traffic light thirty yards farther down; Hortense, who had seen this coming, used her usual tactic: she stood in front of the forward door of the bus and tried to attract the driver's attention by jumping up and down two or three times with her feet together. The driver, who was the same every morning, waited until she had jumped those two or three times (causing her breasts to bounce under her dress in a most convincing way) before opening the door for her, for which she rewarded him with a big smile; the T-line bus moved away, trailing the four frustrated candidate-travelers' indignant protests behind it.

Hortense worked her way to the middle of the bus, rubbed and touched by the lucky few who happened to be in her way. A woman tried to blind her with her umbrella, which she carried despite the fine weather for just such occasions. She hadn't yet succeeded with Hortense, but not for lack of trying. She was a huge, bony housewife, most often accompanied by her son, a lanky lad full of doubts and discomfort. That particular morning he was carrying a pot of geraniums; the whims of internal traffic on the bus had isolated him from his mother, who in a loud voice regularly recommended to him that he be careful with the pot of flowers for his Aunt Monique. Upon running into sweet-smelling and upsetting Hortense, he turned redder than his flowers, then thought, in a rather more intense way than usual: "I like Mom, but gee whiz, she can be annoying!" (The young man, contrary to what you think, is not the one alluded to in the chapter heading; this isn't a situation comedy.)

The T-line bus unloaded the greater part of its cargo not much later, the third stop after Citoyens-Birague being across the street from a department store; for the rest of the trip, the nine other stops until the Library, Hortense usually found a seat, opting normally for one as close to the door as possible. She sat down facing in the direction the bus was moving and arranged her packages on the empty seat across from her. On the other side of the central aisle, the seats were arranged in dissymetrical groups of four; the two seats facing her at an angle were occupied. The window seat belonged to a young mother, holding in her arms a newborn made invisible by its cocoon of blankets, the existence of which could be deduced from its pronounced wriggling (on the inside) despite its silence. The young mother, whose skin color was rather like that of skim milk, was trying to control these movements by making rocking movements of her own with her arms, but without any great conviction. An immense ecclesiastic dressed in purple was sitting next to her and reading from a little black breviary. As the bus lurched forward after the stop, he put the breviary down on his knees and, pointing to the baby package, said to Hortense with a smile: *"E pur si muove!"*

Traffic was heavy. Cops on foot blew their whistles at the intersections, carrying the world's weariness on their shoulders. The T-line bus majestically forged a path through the frenetic subcompacts; the jolly deliverymen, cyclists, and motorcycle cops darted through like skiers running a giant slalom on a foggy day. The pedestrians, those heroes of modern times, risked their lives to cross the street, be they fathers going to buy the rib steak that would feed their dear little blond cubs, schoolchildren, or malnourished senior citizens subsisting on Meow Mix and Cal-Can whom certain pranksters would try to terrify by using their horns in an amusing if illegal way. Cars both foreign and domestic flung themselves into the lane reserved for buses, taxis, and ambulances. Hortense liked this slow journey, so soothing for her because she was comfortably isolated from the vicissitudes of traffic by the consummate ease of her friend and admirer the driver; she felt utterly invulnerable; at this time she really began to wake up and think about the coming day's work in the Library.

This was the year of her master's thesis, and she was soon to have a critical meeting with her Master, Professor Orsells; she was planning to give him a first general outline and ask him several key questions. The long bus ride gave her time to gather her thoughts, check the condition of her paper, pens, pencils, notes, and quotes, and choose from among the books on her list those that she was going to attempt to draw from the stacks for reference. She felt a bit like a warrior checking his gear before going into battle, like a nose tackle getting ready to come out onto the field for the Super Bowl, like . . . (fill in those three dots as you please).

She suddenly looked up: someone was standing next to her in the central aisle, and the look on his face showed that he wanted to sit down. The purple priest and the young skim mother with the baby package had gotten off. Hortense hurriedly gathered up her things and put them on her knees, thus freeing the place across from her, which this person immediately occupied.

The person was a young man of about twenty-five, dressed in black, with a calm, dark, serious look on his face. He sat down wordlessly and placed an overnight bag, also black, next to him in the central aisle. The bus moved forward a yard, then fell back into inactivity. They went past an open-air market (Rue de la Modestie-Descendante), and the smell of cabbage and oranges climbed through the open back window. Children crowded around a man selling roasted chestnuts, holding out their coins in exchange for a bag of the steaming nuts, which they blew on to cool down; their breath turned to blue mist in the chill air (please be so kind as to excuse us and not pay any attention to the preceding sentence, which found its way in by mistake; it comes from the description of a winter street-scene having nothing to do with this novel. *Editor's note:* After an exhaustive financial inquiry, it turned out to be more cost-effective to insert this note than to eliminate the sentence, which slipped by our proofreaders). Hortense looked intently at the young man's face as it appeared in the slightly dusty window. He had a straight, slightly long nose that was somewhat exotic but noble. His hair was well groomed but looked mussable, and Hortense had a weakness for young men with hair that was well groomed and looked mussable. He was a little taller than she, making her think that his height was not impossible. Despite a certain flexibility in her criteria, it was completely out of the question for her to be interested in someone enough to go out with him if he was shorter than she; but here this was not the case. Still, she had a day of important and difficult work ahead of her at the Library, so this was certainly not the time to notice that a young man (he was a young man) was graced by a long straight nose and so on and so on, mussable hair, a stature that was not unacceptable, and elegant hands that he kept carefully folded in his lap.

At that moment, by the reflexivity principle of looking and light, Hortense realized that the young man was looking at her. He was looking at her very openly and intently and doubtless had been for quite some little while now, judging by the amount of information that his look said he had gathered; and she hadn't noticed, having been so caught up in looking at him via his reflection in the window of the bus, which was now approaching the Library stop. At that moment he spoke and said:

"You have beautiful eyes, mademoiselle, especially your right."

It was true.

Hortense hurriedly gathered up her things and got off. The bus and the young man simultaneously moved away.

Hortense headed for the Library's reading room, into which we shall naturally follow her, but which we cannot enter at the moment; there are two reasons for this:

—The first is that it's not ten o'clock yet, and the reading room doesn't open until ten. That's a fine reason.

—The second is a more novelistic, we might even say structural, reason. The next chapter, the tenth, is itself entitled "The Library," and the title of the present chapter, which hasn't ended yet, is "The Young Man from the T-Line Bus." Now, the young man in question stayed on the T-line bus, which left with him. We thus find ourselves in a sort of narrative no-man's land, and we could not, even if the time of day would allow it (that is to say, if it were suddenly to be later than ten o'clock), enter the Library's reading room. All we can do from now till the end of the chapter is accompany Hortense, who has just taken her place in the line of readers waiting for the doors to open.

It was barely quarter to ten, but there were already several people in line. The front of the line, as on every morning, was made up of the Elderly Sextet, regulars who appeared at the door by nine so as always to be the first inside and assure themselves of their rightful places. Four of them were old men; two, old women. Their reading interests were all completely different one from another, and their political, religious, literary, and cinematographic tastes were hexametrically opposed, but they found themselves united, despite all of their differences and dislikes, by a common interest in combating all the other readers, who, they were sure, were jealous of their places; that's why they met every morning in front of the door and smiled at one another, even though each was convinced that the other five were involved in idiotic research, as well as being stupid, dirty, and old; furthermore, no one of them ever dared arrive later than the others for fear that someone would take advantage of the situation to usurp his place, which was certainly the best.

The dean of the Sextet was a dashing nonagenarian. He dressed young, wearing, for example, a raspberry-colored suit with a yellow neckerchief clinging to his throat like turkey wattle. He was amassing information for a definitive work: *Advice to an Aspiring Centenarian.* To achieve this goal, he dabbled in vegetarian diets, kefirs, Oriental mysteries, and the memoirs of all his illustrious predecessors. He was the Sextet's dean and idol, and all listened to him as to an oracle.

The five others, the *young ones,* were between seventy-six and eighty. The next oldest after the aspiring centenarian was only eighty years old and was not, strictly speaking, one of the Library's readers; his card hadn't been renewed for ten years, but no one dared refuse him either admission or his place, for fear of a scandal. He had been a reader when his eyesight had allowed, after a long career in customs inspection, and had spent the large amounts of leisure time afforded him by his retirement taking copious notes for his *Universal History of Smuggling,* which he now resolved to finish as soon as his vision improved. If he came morning after morning to join the Sextet's other members and play his part in their polemical exchanges, it was for one very simple reason: to piss. As soon as the doors opened, he would show his expired card, secure his place and rush (if one may put it that way, since in fact he was able to move only slowly on his two elephantine feet, huffing and puffing all the while) to the basement bathrooms, where he would remain for a solid quarter of an hour, waiting for the inspiration that, he told the others, never failed to arrive in this place consecrated by his bladder; and he regularly added: "As the Duke of Wellington said, 'a gentleman must never allow an opportunity to piss to slip through his fingers, for he never knows when he shall have another'" (he also said that to infuriate the seventy-six-year-old baby of the group, a woman who wrote love letters to Napoleon). Then, feeling relieved and optimistic, he would return to his place and doze.

The activities of the other three old people were more mysterious; Hortense had never succeeded in arriving at any firm conclusion about them, and perhaps they themselves hadn't either. Since she was usually the first reader to appear at the door after the Sextet, they had adopted her, after a fashion—as soon as they had determined that she wasn't out to get any of their places—and gave her advice, drawn from their vast experience, on the way in which one had to proceed in order to overcome the fearsome obstacles the Library placed in the path of those who had the unfathomable audacity to aspire to consulting the countless works harbored by its august flanks.

CONTINUATION OF
THE IMMEDIATE ANSWER TO THE SPECIAL
QUESTION ASKED IN THE FIRST
BETWEEN-TWO-CHAPTERS

The young red-haired cat whom Alexander Vladimirovich was looking at through the window at the beginning of the answer to

the special question asked in the first between-two-chapters (see
First Between-Two-Chapters) was named Tjurmska (pronounced
Tyucha). She had been hired by Madame Orsells, nee Hénade
Jamblique, as a purrer for her husband, the philosopher Orsells,
who had requested her as an aid to his thinking while he
completed his latest work, which would (like all his previous
works) create a Revolution in Thought.

She carried out her task conscientiously, but the results, alas,
did not seem to satisfy her employer. In fact, her soft purring,
which electrified Alexander Vladimirovich's whiskers, had a very
different effect on Professor Orsells: the purring waves, transmitted
to his cerebral cortex by the appropriate circuits, were mistaken for
the seductive vibrations of paradoxial sleep. And that is why,
while Tyucha purred, Professor Orsells snored. Upon awakening,
he certainly had the feeling that he had thought both extensively
and intensively, but he had no idea what he had been thinking
about. He would also be in a wretched mood and hence would
cruelly punish his employee by making her read whole chapters of
his work so she would carry out duties more effectively. All the
same, Tyucha and Alexander Vladimirovich silently looked at one
another through the window. Their whiskers quivered in unison.

(Read the continuation at the end of Chapter 11.)

10

THE LIBRARY

One could only cross the threshold, protected and defended like a spaceship's entry hatch, by presenting one's card, complete with a thick, translucent, orange plastic rectangle indicating the number of the bearer's seat (his usual seat), and then leaving the whole thing (card and rectangle) at one of the Library's counters, where it kept them as hostages (in much the same way that, if one is to believe gangster movies, one's identity and personal effects are confiscated when one enters prison). After completing this task, Hortense threw her purse and notebooks down onto her table, not forgetting the snack prepared by Madame Crussant. She then rushed to the card-catalogue room to locate the call numbers of the books that she dreamed of finding the most quickly. The Library's defensive strategy—forced upon it by the laws and customs permitting readers authorized by the possession of a card (obtained, not without difficulty, after a long security check and the filling out of an insidious questionnaire that led to the weeding out of more than one aspiring borrower) to consult works belonging exclusively to it, works that are its glory, its dower, and its treasure, and that it never stops caressing, contemplating, and loving in the dim silence of its stacks—consisted of putting off for as long as possible the moment when it would have to give out the books and subject them to the defiling gaze of those ignoramuses, whom it also suspected of secretly wishing to stain, slash, scribble in, or damage them if they didn't simply steal them outright.

While handing as few books as possible over to the lusts of those barbarians, it anxiously awaited the blessed moment when the afternoon bell (an alarum for the readers, a joyous chiming for it) announced that no more works could be checked out that day. This was why a reader, as soon as he had succeeded in entering the fortress, had to act with great swiftness and deftness, and it was also the reason for the mad dash to the stairways leading to the card-catalogue room, a race in which Hortense was taking part that morning from an excellent starting position.

The first difficulty consisted in unearthing the work's call number, something that had been carefully concealed. Indeed, there was not, as one might have expected, a series of volumes alphabetized by the authors' last names that listed all the available works of each author; no; if, for example, Hortense wished to read *Pierrot mon ami* by Raymond Queneau, she had to know when the book had been acquired, not when it was published (that would have been too easy); for each section of the alphabet there was a volume located in a perfectly random part of the room and good only for certain years. One had to find the appropriate volume, look up the author, look up the work, write down the call number, and then discover in which other volume the real call number could be found, since the first call number was an old call number that had been shelved in favor of another, more modern one at the time of a particular shift of power inside the librarian empire. It goes without saying that only a great deal of practice, the inheritance of secret traditions, or a librarian's friendship could allow one to find his way. More than once Hortense had been obliged to console some poor American college girl, fresh from the reassuring shores of the Library of Congress, as she sobbed into a dozen tissues at the foot of some dark bookcase.

But that wasn't all! Let's assume that by some miracle you had managed to find the call number of the book you were looking for, or that, having simply given up on finding it, out of desperation you had noted down the first number you came across; that you had—let us even say correctly—filled out the request cards for the book and deposited them in the box reserved for that purpose. You still would not have come to the end of your troubles, and the Library, although it had lost the first skirmish, would not have been defeated so easily. For then there began a long wait, during which, you may naively have thought, people were rushing to find your works, having ceased all other activity so as to be able to bring them to you. You wait. A half hour goes by, an hour, nothing. You have finished your letters, lifted your eyes several times toward the immense glassed-in cupola through which, despite its dustiness, a bit of daylight slips in, and there at last is one of the book boys, who appears before the row in which you are sitting. And he even throws a book onto your table! Feverishly, you pick it up: but, alas, it is not Queneau's *Pierrot mon ami* (whose call number you had discovered, thanks to a hot tip, in a special subcatalogue devoted to works on the circus) you have before you, but rather *Einführung in der Theorie der Elektrizität und der Magnetismus* by Max Planck, Heidelberg, 1903. You rush to the complaints desk, where you wait for ten minutes: a Finnish girl doesn't understand why *The Critical Review of French Discus-Throwing* for the year 1910 is not to be found in that room, while the issue for the year 1909 is; in something resembling German, the librarian patiently explains that the head librarian decided, for reasons of security, to transfer all sports magazines dating from precisely 1910 into another room, which has just closed for the day. At last it's your turn. The comparison of your request card with the call number on Planck's book clearly indicates that you are right: the Z is not a W, and the 8 is not a 4; there can be no doubt, but what to do? Wait another hour? The book that will reach you, if it is not *Pierrot mon ami,* may be even less interesting. Resigned to your fate, you return to your place and begin studying quantum theory.

Thus the Library's first strategy was that of *error*, with the variant of sending the right work to a *different* reader. Hence in the reading room's central aisle one often saw feverish hunters seeking to trade, often triangularly, a work on pygmy cooking habits for the original edition of Father Risolnus's *Prolegomena Rythmorum*. But there was a higher rung on the ladder of *dissuasion:* the use of a particularly formidable weapon, that of the host of delaying answers the stacks could send to the reader by means of his own request card. These answers could prolong the struggle for several days; if this was the strategy chosen, the order of events would be as follows: the book boy would appear in your row with his cart; there would be nothing for you; another half hour would go by. You would then receive your request card, usually worn-looking, with the following notation: "Not on the shelves." The next day you would request the book again; this time the answer would be: "Incorrect call number." The third day it was "Being rebound," and finally, on the fourth day, a stroke of delicious cruelty whose refinement you can only admire: "Issued to you yourself on . . ." and there would be written the date of your first request. That was the highest level of the Library's escalation, since you would now find yourself in the uncomfortable position of trying to explain that the book had never been issued to you, all the while having the miserable feeling that you were being taken for an absent-minded idiot or a thief. The librarians would try to console you, and you would be able to read in their pitying look a judgment leaving no room for appeal: the poor wretch, *it* has struck again!

It goes without saying that you would learn—if you hadn't grown discouraged for good and taken the next flight to London to drown your sorrows in the British Museum—that you would learn, with practice, to elude some of these traps. The counterattack corresponding to the delaying tactic, for example, consisted of immediately giving up in favor of another work and several days later recommencing your probe for the work you had initially desired, forcing the enemy to perform considerable mnemonic feats that it would, before long, find overtaxing. Furthermore, for readers even the slightest bit battle-tested, the current dissuasive measures, of which we have just given a sampling, were not sufficiently effective. That was why the Library was constantly inventing new strategies: fire alarms, or setting back the clock in the entryway, allowing for the gain of a full half hour (during the day the clock was reset to the correct time, or even ahead, allowing for gains at closing time as well). The latest strategy, which had unsettled even Hortense and sent a member of the Institute to the hospital with a nervous breakdown, consisted of suddenly shutting down an entire wing without warning for an indefinite period of time. Thus, on Monday, no poetry was issued; on Tuesday, no mathematics; on Wednesday, no books on the history of navigation, nor any at all published after 1863. This newest offensive, only recently begun, was proving to be a smashing success; some of the Library's most tenacious readers were seized by despair. There was even the sad spectacle of a famous specialist in Renaissance rhetoric calling a press conference and, surrounded by his wife and four children, all in tears, announcing that he was abandoning his research and going into real estate. Many naive readers believed that the course of events could be changed through direct appeals to the powers that be; they formed a readers' committee, launched a petition drive, called upon their representatives to the national legislature, and lobbied the alumni associations of famous universities. The Library smiled behind its beard: a users' assembly was selected through a two-stage election process conducted with a list ballot, the winners to be chosen semiproportionally, and split-ticket voting allowed; a complaints box for the readers' use was put up in the entryway, the heat was fixed in the sporting-manuscripts department, a few political careers took off, and that was all.

During her year of frequenting the Library, Hortense had become a wily veteran as far as eluding its traps, and her success rate in obtaining the works she sought was the envy of quite a few readers, since it approached twenty-five percent on certain days! (She had even been nominated for the readers' prize, which, as a result of sordid political maneuvering, she had not received.) But, like the other readers, she had a second serious problem to solve, that of neighbors.

There were neighbors who fell asleep and snored; there were some who chatted and snickered; there were frightening ones who came up and tried to pick her up. Hortense had, of course, put into practice strategies adapted to each of these—let us say, normal—situations, but that still left two particularly formidable cases:

The first was that of the Ancient Stinker. The Ancient Stinker did not, alas, belong to the Elderly Sextet of the entryway, meaning that one never knew when he would turn up or where he would sit. The Ancient Stinker had once been a prolific reader; following an amorous misadventure, he had stopped varying his reading, limiting himself to Epictetus' *Manual,* which he would put down on the table next to another work (this one belonging to him) by Louis Veuillot. He would take this book out of his satchel, where it had been sitting next to a cheese that, according to the majority of experts surveyed, must have been a Reblochon dating from earliest antiquity. It was not really the smell of the Reblochon, however, that made being near the Ancient Stinker so formidable— one might grow accustomed to that—but rather the fact that, upon ceasing to vary his readings as a result, as we were saying, of his amorous misadventure, he had also ceased to wash. The most direct effect was on the nearest seats; it then spread, if one may say as much, in concentric waves out to a radius of approximately three rows. Evacuating the room had never been considered, for, being too unhappy to stay in the same place for very long, he would depart after half an hour for another library. Hortense obviously feared his visits, which forced her, when she was disfavorably placed, to flee for at least an hour so as to escape the effects of love's sorrows.

The other formidable neighbor was Lady Mortadella-Face. Lovers of this particular cold cut—once quite popular but now a bit passé, I fear—will recognize, without it having to be spelled out, the physical peculiarity that had earned this reader her title. Certainly her appearance was not especially pleasant, but this detail was not what made being near her something that had to be avoided absolutely (the redundant "had to" and "absolutely" here being used to underline the imperative nature of the recommendation). Lady Mortadella-Face was in the habit of sitting down at her table and cluttering it with a considerable number of books (most often very voluminous dictionaries) that she arranged into a sort of three-sided fortress protecting the territory she stubbornly defended.

In these walls, however, she left cracks similar to the machicolations in a medieval castle, through which she poured onto those next to or across from her the molten lead and boiling oil of looks so nasty that few were able to withstand them; and if her opponents didn't flee quickly, she would bombard them with carefully penned notes attacking their physical appearance, family origins, manners, and fate in such crudely obscene language that the author of a dictionary of slang subjected to this treatment had been seen to blush like a Victorian schoolgirl.

On this particular day, however, Hortense was lucky enough to be free of those disturbing neighbors. While waiting for the hypothetical arrival of the works she had requested and that appeared, another miracle, bearly an hour later, she had gone into the Library's garden to eat the culinary treasures prepared for her by Madame Crussant; it was very hot, but a wonderful gentle breeze made the leaves, which weren't very sure of themselves in the first place, quiver on the linden trees. The fountain in the pond with 53 red fish spat a river out of each of its four mouths—the Seine, the Rhone, the Loire, and the Garonne—and the little bit of wind created a most refreshing spray. Moreover, it was the conjunction of this soft moisture and the breeze that, along with certain especially insistent looks, revealed to Hortense the fact, of which she had been unaware until then, that she wasn't wearing any underwear. Since she had little faith in the opacity of her dress, and even less given the rather determined sunlight, she felt embarrassed and swore to be more careful from then on. Having wiped off her fingers, which now smelled of oily, pizziatic tomato sauce along with custard and flour and sugar, on a tissue, she went back into the room and sat down. In front of her were several books and articles on the works of the great Philosopher Philibert Orsells, the subject of her thesis; she was ready for a productive working day. At that exact moment, a foot touched hers. Lifting her eyes, she saw before her, and looking straight at her, *the young man from the T-line bus*!

11

DINNER AT THE SINOULSES'

(PART ONE: GETTING READY)

On the evening of that very same day, Yvette ate dinner at the Sinoulses'. By five o'clock, she had finished with her last patient, fed the Sinoulses' number into her answering machine in case of emergency or essential gossip, locked her office door, gone down the two flights on 53's F Stairway—the one nearest Rue des Grands-Edredons—crossed the square, and taken Rue des Milleguiettes (away from Saint Gudule); she covered some thirty-five feet on that street, then pressed the button marked with the Sinouls' code, PL 317: there was a muted buzz; she pushed hard on the old-fashioned door and walked in. Having crossed the vestibule and passed by the staircases that beckoned (had she taken one, she would have found herself in a novel completely different from the one you are currently reading), she came out into a courtyard that, surprisingly enough, was rather large and might better be termed a garden. It was clearly separated from the sides of the apartment building by a grate through which could be seen another garden some hundred feet long, which was closed off in back by a high wall, and, inside it, a little rococo house, countless examples of which are to be seen in the southern suburbs of Paris, but whose presence a stone's throw from Rue des Citoyens could not help but be surprising (albeit not for Yvette, who had had the time to grow accustomed to it). We can see from here the smile of disbelief playing about the Reader's lips, but we shall take this opportunity to insist that this fact is rigorously accurate, and we resolutely await any refutation.

The house was one story with a basement and a laundry room, and raspberry bushes and a cherry tree in the garden. The usual thundering sound of Old Man Sinouls's stereo blaster (at that moment playing a Frescobaldi organ toccata at full volume) reached Yvette's ears through the living room window. Fine light from the already setting sun came from the west and filtered through the open window.

"Hey there, old lady!" Sinouls said.

Balbastre barked enthusiastically.

"Down, you son of a bitch!" Sinouls said, most appropriately.

"Women!" Yvette said as she collapsed into an armchair.

Sinouls went over to turn down the volume on the blaster and gave her an understanding look. For various reasons—Yvette's stemming from her profession, Sinouls's from theoretical conviction— they were both misogynists. It was not the least of their affinities: they were also about the same age and both beer lovers, which is why Sinouls now hurried to pull two tall cold ones out of the refrigerator. We want to make it clear right away (we know our Readers) that their relations were perfectly proper; a certain number of shared points of view drew them together. Furthermore, Madame Sinouls was a book dealer and art lover, both things for which Yvette and Sinouls had little appreciation; she also differed with them over religion and beer. But because she was a discreet, careful soul, she didn't show it too much. Yvette gave Old Man Sinouls an accurate, detailed summary of her latest cases. Then, beer in hand, they went back to the kitchen, where Sinouls began preparing the evening meal.

He loved to cook, composing his menus like programs for organ concerts, using spices like stops in a way he planned to explain in a treatise he had been in the process of composing for a good ten years now, entitled *Cooking Thought Of As Organ Music*. Every dinner was a chance to experiment. That night he hoped to create a *coq au vin* worthy of a Clerambault. This dinner, which is going to hold our attention for the rest of the present chapter and continue into the next, unfortunately will not, because of the need to save on both effort and paper, be what it should have been: a huge dinner uniting all the story's key characters; the hero and heroine to be placed by the narration (and under the Narrator's perceptive gaze) at two initially opposite ends (we're speaking here about the position of the hero and heroine, not that of the opposite ends themselves, which would remain stationary) of the vast hall— cluttered with tables and chandeliers, gleaming with white table-cloths and dazzling light respectively—only to then come together little by little in a labyrinthine fugue of great symbolic significance that would gradually reveal, through narrative asides, the plot's central conflicts and the characters' convoluted psyches (in a way that the critics, upon beoming aware of our novel, would not fail to notice. They would then sing our praises, punctuated with flattering comparisons to Monsieur P., for example). We will try that another time. No, this is just a family dinner, necessary for the narration because it will be interrupted for a moment by a phone call for Yvette.

The only ones present at the dinner were Yvette, Balbastre, who was a dog usually called Babou, and the members of the Sinouls family, with the exception of Marc, the son. Sinouls opened another bottle of beer in the already strongly scented kitchen. At that moment the front door was flung open and Armance, the elder of the two Sinouls girls, made her entrance. She kissed Yvette on each cheek (three in all, left right left: we are speaking here of three kisses, and not of three cheeks—*Author's note*). Then she called over to her father:

"Hi there, Daddy-o, don't forget the money you owe me."

Sinouls staggered under the blow. The wine vapors, the beer, and Yvette's friendly, understanding presence had put him in a state of slightly confused euphoria. Without immediately comprehending what he was being asked, he happily nodded his head, realizing too late that he had just lost a key point in the battle he was constantly waging against his daughter.

"But . . . ," he began, not soon enough, alas.

"Oh no, you said yes; Yvette's my witness," Armance shot back. "He won't buy me the panties from Chantal Thomass he promised me," Armance added for Yvette's benefit. "I don't have anything left to wear."

Sinouls had pulled himself back together. Sensing that the situation was hopeless, and having nothing left to lose, he gave vent to his indignation:

"First of all, they're too expensive, and I don't have any money. And besides, don't think I don't know what they're for!"

Old Man Sinouls had a hard time accepting the idea that his daughters, after having been nubile, something that had struck him as improbable to begin with, had now reached the age at which they were taking on lovers, as he put it; this idea struck him as mind-boggling, and he put a great deal of effort into an utterly ineffective rear-guard (so to speak) action. The kitchen door opened again. This time it was the younger, blond twin, Julie.

"By the way," she said, "Nicole is staying for dinner."

Nicole was standing in the doorway behind her friend. They had both just stepped out of the bath and were completely naked.

"See what it's like?" said Sinouls as he took a long pull on his beer for fortification. "That's the way it is all the time! There's always one or two of them prancing around naked as a jaybird. I know perfectly well that I'm an impotent old alcoholic, but still! All those little breasts and bottoms and brand-new tufts of hair, all tender, all different colors, jiggling around every which way—it keeps me from concentrating; I'm always hitting wrong notes."

"That," Yvette said in just the same way Madame Eusèbe would have said it, "is today's youth for you! It used to be that you only let your lover see you naked when you were married, if then. But you shouldn't complain. At least your girls don't have bad bottoms."

That was true.

"That's true," Sinouls said with a sudden rush of paternal pride. "Actually, they're delectable."

He didn't add, as he certainly would have if his wife or someone else had been there, "Too bad incest is illegal nowadays, even within the family!" since he knew it was perfectly hopeless to try and shock Yvette; she had seen everything.

"After all that," he said, "I don't know what I did with the bay leaf. Christ almighty, where'd they put the bay leaf? God bless, I can't even get them to keep things halfway organized in this damn dump!"

"Sinouls," Yvette said patiently, "the bay leaf is right there in front of you."

And indeed it was.

Returning to the living room, they sank back into the armchairs, leaving the various culinary ingredients to steep, marinate, mix, or cook, as the case might be. Dusk was deepening, the slanting beams of the setting sun were gilding the tops of the trees planted perpendicular to the ground. Sinouls, who couldn't live without a musical background (music and radio, he would say, are what thicken the sauce of existence), turned on the radio. A solemn voice announced:

"When questioned today at the bishopric, Monsignor Fustiger revealed that the dedication of Rue de l'Abbé-Migne will take place in the very near future, and that he will attend the ceremony personally in the company of the Poldevian ambassador. Poldevia, which has signed a treaty of petroleum friendship with our country, is particularly interested in this event because of the presence on that site of the chapel, once located on Avenue de Chaillot, dedicated to the memory of that unfortunate Poldevian, Luigi Voudzoï, who died in a horseback-riding accident. You will recall . . ."

"Would you believe it?" Sinouls said to Yvette. "I see that bastard Fustiger this morning, and he goes and asks me to play at the dedication!"

Old Man Sinouls's daughters were then seventeen times two (that is, they were each seventeen). Armance was the elder (by very little). Armance was a redhead just beginning her redhead career, which is to say that she was in the process of becoming a menace to any peace and quiet. She was pouty, whiny, and enchanting, one at a time or all at once, depending on the day and the hygrometry of the air; she bitched about her father, her mother, her brother, her sister, her dog, her parents' friends, and her own playmates, both boys and girls; to Old Man Sinouls's great consternation, she was starting to stay out for the better part of the night. He was both terribly proud of having unleashed a redhead on the world, along with the havoc she could not help but wreak in the hearts of men (bastards all, as Yvette would have said), and terribly jealous. Being a redhead, and in order to meet the obligations following therefrom for a girl aware of her duty, Armance had discovered England, the English colors of autumn leaves that she carried over to her clothing, and Jane Austen novels. For her upcoming eighteenth birthday, Old Man Sinouls had promised her a trip by boat to Portsmouth and a short stay in Lyme Regis, the town in which some of the most famous scenes in Jane Austen's novel *Persuasion* are set (we can recommend both trip and novel to our Readers). Old Man Sinouls promised himself that he would take advantage of the opportunity to make a series of extended comparative visits to pubs, those temples of beer and Britishness (even if not of the same kind, at first glance, as that of Jane Austen). Armance suffered from a fairly constant lack of affection and money. She balanced her budget on both counts by baby-sitting with all her might for the most productive breeders among her parents' friends and for the nicest of the mothers among Yvette's patients; this gave her some most enlightening insights into numerous interiors (often the same ones her father visited because of the blasters therein housed), of which several were located precisely in 53 Rue des Citoyens, which is not without significance for our story's development.

If Armance was redheaded and as unpredictable as the California sun or the Bléonne (which, as everyone knows, is the river that runs into the Durance from Digne and whose spectacular mood swings have led the residents to name the road bordering the river Ready to Go) (from the inception of the genre, has not one of the novelist's roles been to elevate the general cultural level of his readers?—*Author's note justifying the preceding parenthetical remark*), her younger sister, Julie, was blond and calm-looking like her mother; she grew angry rarely and, in those days (but unfortunately for Old Man Sinouls, that was the last year of this), more or less exclusively with her sister, brother, mother, dog, or other people, and even then only if they visibly, invisibly, or supposedly attacked her father. Her studies went along smoothly (Armance was volcanic in this respect as well), particularly in science, which requires careful thought; but, for some strange and inexplicable reason, she was completely undone by any sort of test if it was called as much or gave rise to a grade. This oddity, which disturbed her parents and caused her teachers more than a moment's perplexity, had developed suddenly one morning long before, just as she was getting ready to go to school. Still a little blond child, and not a blond girl as she was at the time of the story we are telling (one must never forget to put the reader in a position such that he can distinguish the relative position in time of various narrative threads) (all communication between us and the Author had broken down at the time this chapter was being written, following our refusal to give him an advance against the sale of thirty thousand copies, as he was demanding. We don't know whether this parenthetical remark is an exhortation by the Author to himself, entered into the typescript by accident, or whether it is really part of the text; not knowing for certain, we have kept it as is, not without some trepidation—*Editor's note*); she (Julie, that is) suddenly burst into tears at the kitchen table (not yet the beautiful "culinary worktable" that Old Man Sinouls later built) and, in the presence of her breakfast (hot chocolate and bread and butter with apricot jam) and her surprised parents, said: "Don't you see, there's a test today; and they're going to ask me, and I'll have to say that 22 times 14 makes 308, *and I won't know!*"

Having devoted two paragraphs, presented in order with respect to primogeniture, to Armance and Julie, we must say a few words about their brother, absent at the time of the novel. He was in the process of crossing New Zealand with his girlfriend and his viola da gamba, playing concerti by Monsieur de Sainte-Colombe (from which our musical readers will be able to infer that his girlfriend played the gamba as well, since the Sainte-Colombe concerti are for two viols!) before amazed audiences of sheep and shepherds.

CONTINUATION OF THE END
OF CHAPTER 9

We will now continue with our account of the loves of Alexander Vladimirovich and young Tyucha. We could easily have worked this account into the human and canine narration that makes up the body of our work's chapters, but we denied ourselves that facile solution, for two reasons:

a) Under no circumstances should Alexander Vladimirovich's loves be confused with those of other characters, because:

(i) they are noble (I don't mean to say that there are no other noble loves in the body of the story; rather, Alexander Vladimirovich's noble loves are doubly so, which is not the case with any other amorous intrigue we allude to).

(ii) they are feline.

b) Cats are loners, and the paths they take in prose belong to them alone.

Reasons a) (i) and (ii) and b) thus force us to avoid any overlap.

(To be continued in the second between-two-chapters.)

12

DINNER AT THE SINOULSES'

(CONTINUATION AND END: THE DINNER PROPER AND THE PHONE CALL)

Old Man Sinouls sent his daughter to buy bread and reinforcements for the beer supply, which he was afraid would run out. It was now really dark. The pungent smell of the linden trees wafted in, as did a few mosquitoes. The lights were turned on; five plates were taken out of the cupboard, along with knives, forks, spoons, and glasses; Yvette was given a clean napkin; Old Man Sinouls agreed to turn off the radio. They ate buttered radishes with salt, creamed cucumbers, and a few marinated mushrooms. Old Man Sinouls remained standing with his beer mug—an immense German stein he had brought back from Dusseldorf, where he had once gone to play a concert—in hand. He didn't like to sit down until the end of the meal, for, rather than be obliged to get up continually to check on one or another of his dishes, he preferred to spare himself a few such efforts, which were made unpleasant by his girth. After the appetizers, they ate the *coq au vin*, which was compared to other *coqs au vin* in family history as well as to those prepared by friends and competitors; it was deemed excellent. Occasionally someone would step on Balbastre's tail or one of his paws, since he was always in somebody's way; he was bawled out each time.

Yvette and Old Man Sinouls carried on simultaneous but independent monologues each aimed in the other's direction. Armance bitched. Julie was beginning to be troubled by Desargues's theorem (or perhaps by Pappus's; our information is incomplete on this subject). Madame Sinouls maintained a pleasant silence. The cheese was brought out, and everyone admired the smoothness of the Brebis and the way the Brousse was still runny. The dirty dishes piled up and disappeared. The pastry was brought out; there were six nice creamy sweets from Madame Crussant's: a cream puff, a coffee eclair, and a chocolate eclair, another cream puff (this one was chocolate, the other being coffee), a double-crusted strawberry tart smothered in whipped cream, and a multicolored creation whose undetermined contents were split into diamond-shaped sections, which Armance immediately grabbed. Old Man Sinouls turned down the pastry. He offered Yvette raspberries from the garden, which were precociously beginning to darken the bushes and scent the air. Everyone took some, then added heavy cream and dusted the combination with sugar; a mixture of raspberry juice, the slightly ocher-colored cream, and sugar streamed pinkly down the plates. Old Man Sinouls went to make real coffee for himself and Yvette, then poured out two small glasses of pear liqueur as well as a finger of herbal tea for Madame Sinouls. Armance stood up, kissed Yvette on all three cheeks, and said, "Ciao"; on this note, she left. Since her destination has no direct bearing on what follows, we are not going to reveal it. Old Man Sinouls's face was contorted with jealousy.

The table was now empty; all the food and drink had disappeared, having been gobbled up and gulped down. A sense of the ephemeral and transitory inexorably combined with digestive contentedness; the sounds of the night arrived: the noise made by insect mandi-

bles in the garden, the faint, distant rumble of traffic, all punctuated by Gudule's clocks. The time for reminiscence was at hand,
whether it preceded or accompanied drowsiness. Piles of crumbs
were randomly strewn about the various diners' places. It was hot.
A few moments' worth of languorous digestion in the garden was
proposed, before they parted for the night. In the garden were
gleaming white metal seats called "garden chairs," folding chairs
whose stability was uncertain, and a cane chair (we don't know
what cane is, but such scenes in novels always have a cane chair).
Before going outside, Sinouls turned on the blaster.

The blaster was Old Man Sinouls's pride and joy. Having neither
the financial (because of beer and family) nor geographic (his house
wasn't large enough) means to treat himself to an organ, he had
built the next best thing (at least in terms of acoustic power, as the
neighbors had learned, to their chagrin): his blaster. As the years
went by, the blaster gradually improved, benefiting, through
successive accretions, trials, and approximations (it approached
perfection, the existence of which was assured by an upper-bound
theorem), from all the latest technical developments in materials
for sound and hi-fi systems. Old Man Sinouls installed everything
himself. He changed the connections, did the soldering, and
rigged the wiring (which ensured a not insignificant number of
imcomprehensible breakdowns, since he was always losing the
circuit diagrams he had drawn up), which was in a general tangle
and had leads of every color shooting out in every direction,
creating a most appealing effect.
    To this end, Old Man Sinouls had put a highly refined system
into practice. All his friends had blasters, which he himself
installed. He would go to their houses, look over the premises,
question them about their musical and aesthetic needs, inquire as
to their financial possibilities (to be ready for these visits, they all
had to keep a stock of beer on hand, providing Sinouls with a
support system when he went around town scouting out stores of
material for blasters), accepted their intimate confidences, and
pronounced his verdict: the least experienced saw their blasters
constructed from parts handed down from a blaster belonging to
another member of Sinouls's network who was more financially and

musically advanced. Finally, after a long series of such trades, moves, and reinstallations (accompanied each time by beer and confidences), Sinouls himself could at last acquire the indispensable new part he needed for his own blaster, for next to nothing and with complete assurance that none of his friends' blasters were in any way superior to his. Yvette often came to the Sinoulses' to listen to music, forcing him to keep Verdi operas in his record collection. But on that particular evening he put on a record of C. P. E. Bach clavichord music, the only possible choice for that time and place. Balbastre had fallen asleep and was sighing as his paws twitched convulsively.

"I'm sure he's dreaming of Voltige," said Sinouls.

Voltige had been Balbastre's one great love, a white curly-haired dog who had lived, a long time ago even then, in the house across the garden from the Sinoulses'. At that time a fiery young dog, Balbastre had run frantically up and down the length of the fence while she played coquettishly in the grass on the other side, shielded from his attentions by an iron barrier and the snobbery of her masters, who had refused to allow any association between their noble Voltige and an unpedigreed commoner, even in the face of the pleas of Armance and Julie, who had been moved by their dog's suffering. Then they had left, and Voltige had disappeared, but her memory remained intact in Balbastre's heart.

Old Man Sinouls, with his organlike voice, shouted, "Voltige!" and Balbastre immediately awoke with a start, rushed frantically to the back of the garden, and ran the length of the fence several times, barking in a register closer to that of Gounod's *Ave Maria* than to his usual range, which was firmly based in the tradition of late-eighteenth-century French organ music and which had thus earned him his name. Sinouls and Yvette doubled over with laughter.

"Stop torturing the poor animal," Madame Sinouls said softly.

Balbastre lost heart, threw a reproachful look at his master, lay down again, and fell asleep. Silence settled over the quartet of characters seated in the garden.

Yvette and Madame Sinouls were planning to see an exhibit that Sunday; they were hesitating between Getzler and Guyomard; or perhaps a bit of Victorian painting; good things were being said about the exhibit of ancient Poldevian sculpture. Julie got up to do the dishes before going to bed. Old Man Sinouls felt vaguely out of sorts; maybe he'd had one too many, he thought. He couldn't manage to concentrate on the ever more pressing problem of the program for the dedication. He felt, and feared, oncoming insomnia. He suffered more and more from insomnia brought on by beer and by the worries caused by his financial situation and his children's untimely and accelerated maturation, particularly that of his daughters.

"I drink to forget," he would sometimes say to Yvette.

"To forget what?"

"To forget that I drink."

The family hedgehog had begun to root around in the big oleander next to the raspberry bushes. Old Man Sinouls had, in turn, fallen asleep; he and Balbastre snored side by side. At that moment, the telephone rang.

"Yvette, it's for you! Phone!" (Julie's voice.)

"Who is it?"

". . ." (For the moment we are taking Yvette's point of view; we are indicating that she didn't hear the answer.)

"What?"

"It's Hortense! On the phone!"

"Coming! Coming!"

Time passed.

Old Man Sinouls, awakened by the ringing and the subsequent conversation, was now impatiently awaiting Yvette's return, since he loved to hear all his friends' and acquaintances' latest little stories, and Yvette, by virtue of her profession, her frankness, and her capacity for alcohol, was an inexhaustible source of such news, allowing Sinouls to improve the quality of his judgments on the state of "our fine society" (we quote). A neosociophysiognomist, descended from Lavater and Souriau, Old Man Sinouls had a most interesting theory classifying all human types, which we would not fail to share with our Readers if, of course, we had the narrative time.

More time passed, as the earlier blank space and now this phrase indicate.

After this time had elapsed, Yvette came back. Her face was gleaming with a secret burning to be passed on.

"Well," said Old Man Sinouls.

"That was Hortense," Yvette said, which everyone already knew, even Balbastre, who always eavesdropped on phone conversations.

"So?"

"She's in love!"

Old Man Sinouls's interest fell a notch. Hortense's being in love was a piece of news whose frequency diminished its novelty; it was certainly always charming for the girl in question, but it lost quite a bit of its intensity by the time it was received secondhand. A variation was: she isn't in love anymore, she split up, she has a broken heart, he left, the bastard, oh, the bastard; you know what he asked her? Yet another variation was: she's in love. "You already said that," Sinouls would say. His memory, normally so faulty, was absolutely infallible when it came to such matters. "You already said so, last Tuesday." "Yes, but last Tuesday it was X, and now it's Y." "But you never said she didn't love X anymore." "I didn't say that because it isn't true; now she's in love with X *and* Y." This variation was the most interesting of all the possible amorous permutations, but it was certainly not the case this time, Sinouls told himself, since Hortense had recently gone through a phase that had amounted to an oasis of philosophy in the midst of an emotional desert.

"Ah," Sinouls said with a hint of indifference, "and who is it this time, or rather, to start from the beginning, since when?"

"Since this afternoon," said Yvette.

Sinouls's interest suddenly perked up again. Here was something really new. This was the first time he had found himself in the front row, so to speak, since Hortense usually waited a little while before confiding in Yvette and revealing the current state of her soul's tribulations (as they said in the eighteenth century), this admission being accompanied on occasion, as the need arose, by an on-site inspection (if you catch our drift); and furthermore, Yvette herself did not immediately rush off to her friend Sinouls's house to catch him up. The event's being announced by telephone, along with Yvette's actual presence, gave it an unusually provocative flavor, like that given by paprika to goulash or by saffron to fish chowder.

"Let's have it," said Sinouls, now fully awake.

"So this is what happened," said Yvette.

13

THE SEDUCTION OF
HORTENSE

At the end of the last chapter, we left our Readers hanging, like Old Man Sinouls, on Yvette's lips, waiting to find out from her what had led her, following the phoned-in confidences, to pronounce the verdict "She's in love!" in the Hortense case. Our intent in subjecting you to the trauma caused by such a wait was not, as was said at another time in essays about Hitchcock's films, to create mere "suspense"; we find such facile methods repugnant, but, basically, we did it because we felt like it, and what could be more appropriate for the occasion than a chapter numbered 13 (our marketing director, I mean our publisher's marketing director, who graduated from an American "business school" where he concentrated in hotel management—making him specially qualified to work with books—pointed out to the readers' committee, which passed along his observation to us, that, just as the great New York hotels, the ones that do a brisk business, have no thirteenth floor so as not to frighten the 63.12% of their customers who are superstitious, it would be a good idea to suggest to the author that he not have a thirteenth chapter {readers of novels, who of course make up only 46.29% of all hotel customers, are nonetheless superstitious 79.11% of the time} and instead go directly from Chapter 12 to Chapter 14. But we were adamant: given the way the novel turns out, something that we alone know {neither the marketing director nor the readers' committee being any more likely than the critics to read that far} before our numerous readers, it is important that the key event told here be the subject of precisely a Chapter 13, and we are perfectly well aware of all the ritual and existential implications attached to this figure {which is, by the by, a prime but not a Queneau number}. So we have politely but firmly dismissed the marketing director's suggestion, pointing out, with a certain discreet irony, that under such reasoning [his], a character in a novel would no longer be able to walk underneath a ladder, which would certainly undermine the already shaky quality of the prose. We won the point in question, and that is why there is a Chapter 13, which we shall now hurry to resume before the presentation of this clarification, necessary for ethical reasons, takes up so much space that it ironically relegates to Chapter 14 that which we have taken such pains to prove can only be related here). (End of the parenthetical remark.)

Which, then, could be more appropriate than this thirteenth chapter for the firsthand telling of the series of words and gestures that led Hortense, if we are to believe Yvette, to express herself over the phone in such a way that she (Yvette) could feel justified in summarizing the conversation for Balbastre and the Sinoulses (it was certainly hard on Balbastre, given his hopeless love for the long-lost Voltige) in these terms:

"She's in love!"

So here we are, back at the end of the morning on which Hortense, lifting her eyes from her books because of the leg that has just rubbed up against hers under the table in the Library, found herself nose to nose (albeit with a proper distance separating the noses) with the young man from the T-line bus.

He smiled at her.

She smiled at him, not knowing exactly what to do. He was in the process of reading a newspaper, which he immediately dove into again. It was the *Times* (of London). A bit disconcerted by the apparently random nature of this coincidence, Hortense returned to her reading. Then she got up to check a call number. When she came back, she found on her table one of those slips of white paper much dreaded by the Library's readers, the kind of slip that informs the reader sitting there that he must appear in the reading-room office to hear someone tell him harshly that the book he has requested is unavailable for one of the forty-four reasons invented by the Library.

But this particular slip bore the following inscription, written very legibly in red ink: "The reader seated in place number 53 would be very pleased if you would agree to have a drink with him."

Hortense took a quick look around the table. It was he.

Never before having been approached in such a manner, she hesitated for a moment. But the young man's first words on the bus (where had she heard or read them before? She didn't know. And you, dear Reader, what do you think?), his sudden appearance, his reading the *Times,* the nice, hot, sunny weather, which was, all the same, not *too* hot—it all inclined her to be agreeable. She looked at him, and her look said yes. He stood up, and they both left the Library.

Tête-à-têtes like the one for which Hortense and the young man from the T-line bus were readying themselves took place in the Wrong Number café, located across the garden from the geographic fountain, so attractive to the readers on these pleasantly seasonable days. Meetings often took place there for work-related reasons as well—the exchanging of bibliographies or secret tips for the tracking down and procuring of books. As she crossed the garden, Hortense became more and more aware of her clothing's extreme lightness and resultant insufficiency, but she wasn't exactly sure how to shield herself from her companion's gaze without drawing even greater attention to the chinks in her armor. The young man, however, did not seem to be particularly interested in such matters, which Hortense found reassuring yet disappointing. Idly commenting on the wonderful weather, which surely would not last, they crossed the garden and entered the café.

The waiter, a big fan of Hortense's, gave her a broad wink that she did her best not to notice; at that time of day he was usually in a fairly advanced state of jolly drunkenness that nonetheless left him functional, which is to say that one could still be reasonably confident he wouldn't spill the drinks he served. Hortense and the young man ordered tonic water and coffee respectively. Gastounet, the waiter, made his usual remark to Hortense:

"They're awfully lucky to have you over there, that must pull them out of their dusty old books."

His invariably wine-colored face had as yet only attained the hue of a Beaujolais (toward the end of the afternoon it would reach the deepness of certain Bordeaux, and sometimes that of the darkest Burgundies). Hortense had long wondered how he reached this state of inebriation while being watched by his boss, a woman with an extremely severe manner who certainly didn't allow him to drink at the counter. She had finally discovered his strategy: the tables in the Wrong Number were separated from the counter by an aquarium that was full of red fish and topped by green plants practically as high as a man's head. Gastounet, the waiter, would carry his tray of glasses and dirty dishes to the counter, where he would empty it and fill it up again with the new orders: a tonic water, a coffee, two beers, a bottle of Vichy water, and a glass of Beaujolais, for example. He would then deftly take the bottle of Beaujolais or Côte-du-Rhone out from under the counter and add a glass of wine for a phantom order, which he would carry on his tray with the others; finally, after he had served the customers and as he was returning to the counter to fill a new order, he would, while hidden from the boss's view by the tallest of the green plants, empty the still-full glass in one lightning-quick gulp that took no more than a tenth of a second, carrying it back innocently with a small glimmer of satisfaction shining in his wineshot eyes and a most noticeable new darkening in the color of his cheeks. Hortense, perhaps alone among the regulars at the Wrong Number, had caught on to his little game, and Gastounet, who was very proud of his tactic, considered her a member of the family from then on. He looked over the company she kept, using an extremely wide range of grimaces and faces to indicate his opinion of the assorted lovers, past, present, and future, who joined her on occasion in the café. His reaction when Hortense had her only and therefore memorable meeting with her master, Orsells, was extremely unfavorable, and Hortense had of course been in no position to explain to him that her relations with Orsells were of an entirely different nature. On this particular day, he contented himself with giving the young man an amused look that showed nothing. Hortense felt very grateful to him, without knowing exactly why.

14

MORE OF THE
SEDUCTION
OF HORTENSE
(CONCLUSION)

"The left one isn't bad either," said the young man, picking up the topic of conversation started on the bus and then dropped.

Unfortunately, we cannot refer to him as anything but "the young man" since Hortense, our heroine, whose point of view we have been adopting since the previous chapter, still doesn't know his name. Nor, because of an unfortunate narrative imperative, can we describe him, outside of saying: he was dressed in black, with a little overnight bag that he kept close by, under his chair in the café. His overall manner gave the impression of a slight lack of distinctness about his features, almost as if he were, in some odd way, his own brother. After his introductory remark, he began questioning Hortense about her presence in the Library, what she did there, and whether she came there often. He offered no explanation for why he had been there himself. Hortense, who had at first been sure that she was the reason, came to wonder whether their meeting was a mere coincidence. She happily spoke of her work, which thrilled her, and launched into a lengthy explanation of Professor Orsells's philosophical system. The young man seemed to be paying close attention: he sat very still, his elbows resting on the table, listening, looking, occasionally asking a question to indicate his unflagging interest. Hortense continued to talk. Suddenly she became aware of two things.

First, that the young man's gaze had clearly moved from her lips to a point located a half a foot or so lower down, and second, that the parts of her subjected to this gaze and protected precious little by her dress (for Hortense, if she had unintentionally neglected to wear panties, nevertheless almost always limited her undergarments to that) had, without a shadow of a doubt, reacted in an unmistakable way that, furthermore, was utterly impossible not to notice. She nearly lost her breath. Some sort of warm feeling was rushing through her, and she said to herself: this is it. Hortense had just experienced what Madame Eusèbe in her old-fashioned way would have called *love at first sight* (she, Madame Eusèbe, had never experienced that with any Eusèbe—neither the father nor the son, her husband, for whom she had a longstanding if somewhat contemptuous affection—or even with Alexander Vladimirovich, whom she loved passionately all the same. That doesn't mean that she only knew of this sensation from books, or rather illustrated novels, shall we say; Madame Eusèbe had fallen in love at first sight once. All that is part of her guilty secret, which we have partially revealed, but which must now be covered up again). As she went on talking without knowing exactly what she was saying, moving without realizing it from the Orsellian system to an involuntary memory of an oral presentation she had given on Hume in her last year of high school, at the time of her first lovers, Hortense wondered what was going to happen now, since the young man didn't seem to suspect a thing, even though the fixed direction of his gaze, which couldn't have been more blatant, made that hypothesis incredibly unlikely.

Several minutes went by. Hortense's agitated state was overtaking her nether regions, fortunately protected by the table; her speech was, she realized, growing more and more incoherent. She had the (false) impression that she was blushing. Her dress weighed on her, which was paradoxical if nothing else and would certainly have upset whoever had conceived and designed it. Finally, after what seemed to be an eternity (in fact no more than six minutes), the young man took a black wallet from his pocket and, after inspecting the scrawl added by Gastounet to the cash register's invisible imprint as carefully as if it were a twelfth-century manuscript, pulled out a fistful of coins whose values he appraised as if he didn't recognize them, picked out a few, looked again at the region of Hortense's body that had held his attention before, and said:

"There are really too many people here. We must go elsewhere, for I am no longer following your presentation very well."

"Since it turned out this way," said the young man (they were once again on the T-line bus), "what is your name?"

"I'll give you three guesses," Hortense answered, feeling that she was plummeting back into adolescence.

"Agathe?"

"No."

"Clémence?"

"No," Hortense managed to get out with great difficulty, for *Clémence was her middle name.*

"Well, how about Hortense?" he said.

Hortense's apartment, a gift from her sadistic father, purchased with profits from the *Haute Delicatesserie,* was located in a renovated seventeenth-century building on the other side of the corner of Citoyens and Vieille-des-Archives, catty-cornered to 53 Rue des Citoyens. She lived on the top floor, aloof, in an expanse of four large split-level rooms opening onto a terrace that looked back over the gardens of the Amandine convent; this meant that street noise barely reached her. Upon returning home, Hortense immediately ran to pee and put on a pair of panties. This may have been a bit absurd, given the fact that, in all likelihood, she wouldn't be keeping them on for very long, but the convolutions of the female mind, we know, are infinite, and even a novelist who has dedicated, as we have, numerous hours of his life to studying those convolutions (since that, it would seem, is the standard training for novelists) still cannot pretend to be capable of elucidating all the motivations thereof.

The operation was quickly accomplished, but Hortense took advantage of the opportunity to sneak one last peek at herself in the mirror to check that everything was in place and acceptable. She knew (men's looks, words, and deeds, and not men's alone, could not have been more explicit on this subject) that she was not at all bad-looking, that she could pass for pretty and sometimes even beautiful, that in any event she was stimulating, but she was highly modest and very unsure of herself. She believed that there had been a sort of general fatal oversight that would not fail to be cleared up one day, at which time she would be left among the fundamentally plain. She only acknowledged one definite good point when it came to her body: her buttocks, and particularly the way they turned into thighs in an utterly seamless, indiscernible manner, describing a curve that, upon turning around, she could view and appreciate as elegant. She put her dress back on and returned to the living room. The room was very big, with soft white carpeting (a nightmare for her cleaning woman), and was cut in half by a two-step difference in floor level. It was bordered by a large bay window that gave onto a terrace where, on sunny days, she could—to the great enthusiasm of the retired Colonel Bigondaze, who, armed with his binoculars, didn't miss a minute—ensure that her whole body was a uniform light-caramel color, essential because of the anatomical peculiarity we have already pointed out, which would have been spoiled if a white tan-line caused by a bikini bottom or pair of panties had artificially reestablished the transition from buttock to thigh that nature had wanted so perfect.

The young man was immersed in his examination of the little trinkets, gifts from her grandmother, that Hortense had arranged on the mantelpiece. She asked whether he was thirsty. He said he would love a bit of mineral water. She went over to her huge white refrigerator, which was stocked with a few bottles, the only food being a dozen eggs next to a package of Panzani spaghetti. She took out two glasses, put them on a low table near the sofa, and filled them with Badoit sparkling water; the glasses immediately misted over. She sat on the edge of the sofa while he sat in an armchair on the opposite side of the low table; he didn't look at her directly, but the phenomenon from the café repeated itself, leaving no doubt about the overwhelming reality of her feelings.

They drank.

There was something like silence.

"Where were we?" the young man asked.

Hortense would have been hard pressed to answer that question: if he was asking about her oral presentation on Orsellian theory, begun at his request in the café, she no longer had any idea where she was, and, more importantly, she didn't care. If he was asking about something else, she thought she knew more or less where they were but was anxiously awaiting the continuation. While maintaining his unwavering gaze, as if afraid that failing to do so would make the effect it seemed to produce on Hortense's breasts disappear, the young man smiled. Hortense swallowed a big gulp of cold Badoit and put her glass back down on the table. The young man put his down as well and took her hand. Then he stepped over the low table and sat on the sofa, on her left. Hortense felt relieved, for she had been afraid that he would sit on her right (as happened with twenty-eight percent of the men who wished to seduce her, and which she didn't like at all). Everything was still going perfectly.

As soon as he was seated on her left, the young man took Hortense's face in both hands and kissed her gently on the lips, but without lingering. He then kissed her temples, cheeks, and chin, finishing with the left cheek, the left temple, and the forehead, thereby completing one complete revolution counterclockwise, which is, as everyone knows, the trigonometric direction dear to non-Poldevian mathematicians (Poldevians reckon in the opposite direction). He then lifted her chin, kissed her on the neck, and went around her neck to the nape, where he allowed himself a sharp little nip in that downy, sunny, sweet-smelling place. It ran the length of her spine, an effect that Madame Eusèbe's illustrated novels would have called a great shiver but that was in fact merely an extremely pleasant transfer of nervous influx. The young man's left hand, now liberated by the more serious kiss he was giving her (his right hand was holding the nape of her neck), was bearing down decisively on Hortense's leg. It passed slowly and carefully over her left knee, then went under her dress and up the length of her thigh, checking along the way for firmness and shape. The result must have proved very favorable, at least if one could attribute his tongue's insistence and ardor to such a judgment. Upon reaching the top of her thigh, his hand stopped short when it ran into the edge of her panties. The pair of panties was for special occasions. They were well tested, pink and soft and scanty. Hortense didn't hesitate for a moment in choosing them, proving the intensity of her condition. But the young man's hand was obviously not anticipating this encounter, his previous glances in the Library's garden and on the bus having certainly given him the impression that he wouldn't run into any obstacle at all, not even such an enticing one.

After a perceptible moment of hesitation, the hand resumed its journey; meanwhile, the kiss broke off, and the right hand moved down onto Hortense's right hip (completing a rear-enveloping maneuver on the heroine, if you are following us), which it began assessing insistently (it must be said that the hip's round fullness merited such treatment). The left hand resumed its forward march, but far from attempting to slip between the minute bit of material and the flesh underneath to reach the most critical areas, it moved onto the panties, in a caress that gave its palm an exact measure of the volume of what we will allow ourselves to call Hortense's intimate coiffure, for the lack of a better term and because we are not sure where we stand in relation to current obscenity law.

This act brought Hortense to the limit of her patience, neither resisting nor initiating, which struck her as yet another sign of the event's importance, since it took away all her power of movement. But at that moment she could not keep from gasping. The young man, with brisk decisiveness (and helped by Hortense's spontaneously lifting her buttocks at the right moment), took off her dress. Hortense was again naked, with the exception of her panties, of course, which turned out to be a caramel color almost the same as that of her skin. The young man did not try to take them off, and Hortense sensed that this was meant as a very gentle reprimand, a punishment for the surprise they had caused him. She was not the slightest bit worried or disappointed; quite the contrary. Her breasts had not ceased to be in the hopeful state they had already experienced in the Wrong Number, and the young man set about lightly biting first one and then the other while lifting them to his face. He remained in that position for some time before finally standing up, still dressed impeccably in black, and taking Hortense by the hand; she led him to her bedroom.

It was a large room, spacious and comfortable, with a very large, low bed and several pillows. On the mantelpiece . . . (but we will halt the description of Hortense's room there. Although it is fascinating and necessary, it is probably not what our readers are looking for right now). Hortense stretched out on her back. At that point the young man opened his ever-present overnight bag and pulled out a shaving kit from which he extracted a green toothbrush, a tube of Sensodyne toothpaste, a Gillette razor with the blade already in place, and a can of Williams shaving cream. He went unswervingly to the second door—the one to the bathroom— opened it, made a small space in the medicine cabinet for his belongings, put them in it, came back into the bedroom, closed up his (black) overnight bag, and put it at the foot of a chair over which he began to carefully drape his clothes as he took them off. He took off his shirt after his jacket, then his pants after his (black) shoes and (dark blue) socks, and finally his (red) briefs. He was naked. He turned his back to Hortense, waiting on the bed, and she could admire what there was to admire, for he was a handsome young man. When he turned toward her, she could ascertain, even from a few inches off the ground, that he was not indifferent to her. He said:

"You have a perfectly perfect pair of buttocks. Perfectly perfect buttocks are those that change without transition into thighs, without it being possible to state precisely where the buttocks end and where the thighs begin. Your buttocks are the second such pair it has been my privilege to see. Thank you."

Hortense knew then that she was in love. And jealous.

The young man drew closer to the bed and, bending over but still standing, took off her panties. At last she was completely naked. This is thus the time to complete the portrait of Hortense, our heroine, promised in Chapter 2.

We apologize for the portrait's not being presented under ideal conditions, in which the reader would be alone with Hortense and able to gaze upon her at leisure. The young man is there, with very clear intentions that are entirely his own, necessitated by his lascivious desires and the development of the plot, and the Reader will not be able to hold things up for long, since the climax appears to be at hand. We further apologize for making a voyeur of the Reader. There is nothing to be done about it in any event; if it were not the young man in question, it would doubtless be another, perhaps not even young at all, perhaps it would be the Author alone, and in any event we would be in the process of looking together at a pretty young woman reclining nude on her bed, her right leg slightly raised, her thighs slightly spread, and her breasts in a state of agitation for which we don't have a word (let us specify, before we forget in the coming rush of events, that Hortense had adopted this waiting position not to be coquettish or provocative, but rather in hopes that the reward for the view she had created by slightly spreading her thighs, as a result of raising her right leg, would be a diversion of attention from her knees, of which she was inordinately ashamed). In any event, it is to be feared that the Reader cannot help but be a voyeur, and the more copies of the book bought and read by more people, the more voyeurism engendered; from which it follows, if one holds voyeur-ism to be morally repugnant, that there are precious few ways out of this dilemma: either the Reader must be denied the chance to contemplate Hortense nude, which would be unfortunate, or the book must be handled in such a way that it will have very few readers, thereby minimizing the damage. This ethical paradox has been masterfully explored by Professor Orsells. But let us return to our heroine.

We will follow the usual order of operations when it comes to describing the heroine—that is to say, from top to bottom: her hair, we shall say, shone more brilliantly than threads of spun gold; more precisely, we will say that she was practically blond, possessing light-brown hair that was quite soft and arranged in a wedge of medium length; beneath each arm was a tuft made of similar material (she didn't shave, thank God!) that was lighter still and scented (rather differently under each arm) with a strong, slightly peppery smell, which seemed to have an aphrodisiac effect (at least that's what Hortense had often heard said, and the young man reconfirmed that for her a bit later in the afternoon) and which, unfortunately, we cannot describe more precisely for the pitiful lack of a linear scale for smells similar to the one for colors, or even the one for earthquakes (ah, a smell that was 7.9 on the Richter scale), or storms (8 Beaufort, for example); her forehead surpassed the water lily, her eyebrows were arched like little rainbows, and a milky little path separated them from the bridge of her nose so equally that no more or less was necessary; her eyes were brighter than emeralds, shining underneath her forehead like two stars, her face was beautiful like a summer mourn, for it mixed ruby red and fairest white in such a way that neither color was displeasingly dominant; her mouth was small and her lips full. Her neck was long, her hands slight.

Her breasts (average in size, tending toward small) had very sensitive tips and were slightly rounded on the bottom but firm, both dense and full; her hips each comfortably filled one hand, her navel was small and circular, her stomach slightly rounded and endowed with an all but colorless down, arranged symmetrically around a median line equivalent to the one running from the small of her back to the cleft between her buttocks (one quarter of whose praises we have not yet sung, but time is of the essence), and this down was like that on the willow that sprouts in the spring in the Sierra de Cuenca, whose beautiful mountain maidens Gongora immortalized in song; beneath her belly, she was almost blond, being even lighter there than under her arms, her hair being planted in a clear, decisive, abundant manner that was neither desert nor steppe nor brush but ran above the mound of Venus. Her sensitive spot, easily found with a tongue or finger, was very evident. She had naive knees, and her shoe size ran 7½–8. She didn't paint her nails.

The young man, who had been standing in front of her during this entire description, looked at her for a long time from the front, then from the back, and then again from the front. His interest remained indisputable, visible and intense. Hortense held out her arms. He leaned down to her, and the chapter drew to a close.

THE SECOND BETWEEN-TWO-CHAPTERS

IN WHICH, AFTER THE INTERRUPTION FOR A FLASHBACK,
THE STORY OF THE SEDUCTION OF HORTENSE,
TOLD OVER
THE PHONE TO YVETTE AND PASSED ON
FROM HERE TO
OLD MAN SINOULS, COMES TO AN END,
AND CHRONOLOGICAL ORDER IS REESTABLISHED

"So she's in love?" Sinouls asked.

"He's the man of her dreams."

"He was there when she called you?"

"He'd left."

"Already?"

"Because of his work, dummy."

"And what's so special about him?"

"He's a wonderful lover, and he told her that her buttocks were perfectly perfect, because there was no discontinuity between her buttocks and thighs."

Old Man Sinouls pondered this problem for a moment.

"Is that really true? I didn't know that Hortense..."

"Oh yes, Hortense has that quality, among others."

"So what does this phoenix do?"

"Well, he guessed her name, practically straight off."

"You don't say," said Sinouls.

"Yes indeed. And the reason he works nights is because he's a roving night antique dealer."

Old Man Sinouls raised one eyebrow.

"Come again?"

Yvette repeated the phrase.

Old Man Sinouls kept the one eyebrow raised. He looked at Yvette, who raised an eyebrow.

Let us all raise an eyebrow.

CONTINUATION OF THE END OF CHAPTER 11, IN WHICH WAS TAKEN UP THE ANSWER TO THE SPECIAL QUESTION FROM THE FIRST BETWEEN-TWO-CHAPTERS

While Yvette, Sinouls, the Author, and the Reader raise an eyebrow (which one?), let us go back to that time of the afternoon when the chapter devoted to the seduction of Hortense was slowly drawing to a close.

It was hot, and Tyucha was purring Tyuchishly. She was purring not only because it was her duty, but also so that the purring waves, entering Alexander Vladimirovich through his whiskers and stirring his heart, would reach all the way to his claws and the ends of his paws, which would then sink into the wood of Professor Orsells's office windowsill, where Alexander Vladimirovich was perched.

Professor Orsells was thinking as he snored.

But it had been so hot that, before commencing to think under the influence of purring, he had opened the window. Alexander Vladimirovich jumped into the room. Tyucha redoubled the sweetness and seductiveness of her purring.

Alexander Vladimirovich jumped onto the desk. His muzzle brushed against the tender young muzzle of Tyucha. Their whiskers intertwined.

15
INSPECTOR
BLOGNARD

"The real trouble, Louise," Inspector Blognard said to his wife, "isn't when you don't have a suspect, it's when you don't have a motive!"

"You're right, Anselme," she answered. "But why?"

It was Sunday, and it was hot. It hadn't stopped being hot since the beginning of summer. The Inspector was sitting in his living room in shirtsleeves while his wife Louise, just back from Mass, vacuumed with a new vacuum cleaner she had bought on time at the recommendation of a most convincing traveling salesman, Monsieur Sauconay Vacuman, who lived in the very building her husband was staking out. That couldn't be a mere coincidence, she thought. She put the tarts bought from Madame Crussant on the kitchen table. They lived on Boulevard Marivaux, not very far from Saint Gudule, where Madame Blognard went to Mass. The kitchen table had an oilcloth cover with an old-fashioned pattern imitating the second Mondrian from the left on the back wall as you go in the right entrance to the museum in the Hague. Madame Blognard was vacuuming. The Inspector, who was not in his office because it was Sunday, took advantage of the opportunity to think out loud in front of her and sum up the current state of his investigation; his wife heard him over the noise of the vacuum cleaner and answered him from time to time as one would answer Socrates, because it helped the thinking process.

"Why?" Blognard said. "Because knowing the motive is halfway to having a suspect. And having a suspect is half of solving the case. And solving the case is half of making an arrest. And making an arrest is half of a conviction. Which means that the motive is one sixteenth of the conviction and no more than one sixteenth, but it is still an essential sixteenth and more important than all the other sixteenths. And why is that?"

"Why is that indeed, I wonder?" said Madame Blognard, turning off the vacuum cleaner for a moment.

"You will grant that an investigation is like a house," her husband said.

"You're right, Anselme, now that you've told me, I can see clearly that a police investigation may be compared to a house; the simile is bold but well founded."

"Well founded, that's what it is! To build a house, you need a foundation, and the foundation for building a case is the motive! Some people think it's the suspect, but to my mind that means starting in thin air on the second floor—there's no surer way to bust up your face. And that's why a matter like the Case of the Hardware-Store Horror is so difficult. Now, you take your garden-variety murder, on the other hand..."

Louise took it.

"What do you do? You find out who knew the victim, because in our country we only kill people we know, it's not like Chicago or Nevyork. You make the rounds, and bingo, you have a motive."

"You usually have more than one, in fact, if I am not mistaken," said Madame Blognard, making a momentary but daring departure from her role as echo.

"Without a doubt," her husband said indulgently, "but that doesn't change a thing. Suppose you have several motives, but at the same time you already have the suspect needed to go with those motives. In that case you've built the foundation and the ground floor in one fell swoop."

"The second floor, Anselme, you said suspects were the second floor."

Inspector Blognard furrowed his brow, for he did not wish to lose his train of thought.

"And if I understand you correctly, Anselme," said Madame Blognard as she moved in for the kill on a dust-mouse under the television chair, "you don't have a motive in the Case of the Hardware-Store Horror?"

The question was purely rhetorical, or rather secondarily rhetorical (for rhythm and breathing), since Madame Blognard knew full well that her husband hadn't made much progress yet. He even dreamed of it at night, not a good sign.

"Not the slightest hint of one! We have a thug nobody has seen, who goes through this whole song and dance each time just to steal some worthless Poldevian statuette and then fades back into the woodwork, who paints black silhouettes on walls of a man pissing—excuse me for using that kind of language, Louise. Not half bad, the way little Mornacier came up with that clue. He'll go far. But why, why? What does he want? What's he going to do now? It's infuriating!"

"Don't get all worked up, Anselme, you'll solve the case. You always do!"

Blognard looked lovingly at his wife; he unwrapped a candy and tossed the packaging into the vacuum cleaner, which swallowed it up with a muted rustling sound.

"Why do you have such confidence in me?" he asked, moved.

Louise could honestly have answered her husband, as she often did: "Because I love you, silly!" or "Because I know you're the best," but the real reason for her confidence was both deeper and darker, dating back to before she had met him. Of course, she had never let any of this come out. Perhaps she was afraid of seeming ridiculous, or maybe she just didn't want to embarrass her husband. (We don't know, either, but are in a better position than Blognard to shed some light on certain motives, because of our relation to the novel.) The daughter of a police officer—a high-ranking officer, no less: her father, Commissioner Leonart, had been director of the Saint-Frère police academy in Montdargent until his recent retirement—Louise, from the time she was sixteen, a prim, pretty girl in braids, bobby socks, and Little-Boat panties (one of the great charms of old-fashioned eroticism), had known that she would marry someone in her father's field, for she adored him. In coming to this decision, which was in any case more an inner conviction than an act of will, she asked herself the question *who*. It was true that she had ample choice, for all the men whom the country's police department considered to be their future finest passed before her eyes. She served them tea on certain Sundays when her father invited them (and she was the lady of the house, since the Commissioner was a widower); they all looked her over, timidly or brazenly, sincerely and ambitiously. She was in no hurry to decide.

She decided to marry the best, the most perfect, the ideal one. At that moment she came to wonder whether such a thing was really possible; in other words, could she be sure that such a being existed, and that he would be the one to be her husband? A simple bit of reasoning proved to her that she had nothing to worry about on that score, since the very idea she had within herself of such a perfect ideal could not have come to her unless the idea corresponded to a real and potentially extant being; otherwise how could she have thought of it? "A shoemaker," she said to herself as she dreamily poured boiling-hot tea onto the fingers of a stoic young cadet-inspector who, out of deference, blushed but remained silent, "a shoemaker cannot imagine a shoe for which he does not already have a model in his mind's eye, whether a whole shoe or one assembled from various pieces. And he can only make a shoe thanks to the image, which his memory puts before him, of shoes he has already seen. Thus," her thought continued, "when the one I am seeking appears, I shall recognize him as such," and she smiled at the blushing young man who was not the one. By thinking about it often, she had, sometime before her seventeenth birthday, on which her father was to invite his best students to tea, worked out a fairly satisfactory proof of her future husband's existence: "I believe he is someone such that I cannot think of anyone greater, or more perfect, or better (for me, I mean).

"I say this, and even if I doubt the veracity of what I am saying, I understand what I am saying, and that being exists in my mind. But if that being exists in my mind and in reality as well, he is greater, more perfect, and better in reality than if he only existed in my mind. Thus, since he about whom I am thinking must be such that no one could surpass him, he cannot exist in my mind alone. It then follows that he must exist both in my thoughts and in reality. Therefore, he really exists."

On her birthday, she was in the company of those with the best hopes for promotion, most especially a young man by the name of Joubert, who was first in his class. This Joubert, who was both brilliant and ambitious, had set his heart on Louise, whom he courted as ardently as his strenuous studies and her strict father would allow. On that particular day he was accompanied by his best friend, Anselme Blognard, whose class rank was only seventy-three. He was also in love with Louise—which of those young men wasn't?—but knew that he had no chance with his friend Joubert around, and had refrained from coming to the girl's teas until then. Louise took one look at him and knew he was the one. They were married six months later.

She hadn't regretted her marriage for one minute. The matter dubbed the Case of the Hardware-Store Horror had her worried, however, not only because Anselme was losing sleep over it and was even irritable from time to time, but also because this impending failure was like a stain on the slipcover cover of her love for him. Let us explain this simile.

The Blognards were not rich; the apartment on Boulevard Marivaux was in their name and all paid off, but it was of a modest size and modestly furnished, with the exception of a set of four very beautiful armchairs given them as a wedding present by an old aunt of Louise's. Louise was an extremely careful homemaker, with a passion for cleanliness. In the course of a meal, which she would most often spend standing, she would run a crumb-catcher around each diner's plate at regular intervals (and she acted no differently when she and Anselme were alone) to keep the crumbs from marring the splendor of her waxed red parquet floor. She had embroidered four slipcovers to protect the armchairs, which she covered when there weren't any guests in the living room. But after a time the slipcovers struck her as being so beautiful that she grew fearful of seeing them dirtied; accordingly, she added four slightly less beautiful slipcover covers. A stain on the slipcover covers made her unhappy, but certainly much less so than a stain on the slipcovers themselves would have, to say nothing of one of the splendid armchairs. And it was the same way with her love: a failure in this investigation would be a stain on Anselme's perfection, but the stain would only be on the slipcover covering the slipcover protecting the armchair of her unsurpassable love. That is why she was upset, but not, however, *too* upset.

She had suggested the get-together for that Sunday, the one for which the tarts had been purchased from Madame Crussant and which was to include the consumption of a hearty stew. (There's nothing like it in hot weather for making you think, strange as that may seem.) Inspector Arapède, a bachelor, was to come for lunch, and Madame Blognard had insisted on having young Mornacier, the Narrator, share in the meal and subsequent strategy-planning session as well. She was more than a little curious to meet the man who had succeeded in uncovering a clue that had eluded her Anselme, not to mention other clues that only Anselme had found.

Time was marching on (the guests had been invited for quarter of twelve, since Madame Blognard maintained her provincial customs, meaning that meals were at noon and seven o'clock sharp except, of course, when Anselme's work kept him in the office long past those deadlines). Louise sent her husband off to shave and brush his teeth—after all those candies, they had turned black—and then moved into the kitchen to put the finishing touches on her stew. It was a dish over which she took great pains, since it had touched off the first and only fight of her married life.

The Blognards had been newlyweds living in their first apartment in the provincial city where he started his career, and the young wife (she was not yet eighteen) was cooking for her husband for the first time; the tiny apartment was on the sixth floor of a modest building on a run-down but quiet street; it was a hot September day, and Louise had made a stew: she had simmered the meat in wine and bay leaf all night over a gentle flame; in the morning, before refrigerating it, she had carefully drained off the fat; she reheated, gently, then redrained; shortly before Anselme was due home, she had cooked the carrots; finally, she had leaned out the window from time to time to watch for the silhouette of her massive and beloved Anselme, so as to be able to throw the grated Gruyère onto the boiling and aromatic dish at the last moment. And then he arrived. She heard him open the door with his key. He walked in, and suddenly—without saying a word, without kissing her—he scrunched up his (then dark) eyebrows in a terrifying way, snatched the aromatic, cheese-covered tureen from the table, and threw it out the open window! He couldn't stand cheese!

16

THE SPIDER'S
STRATAGEM

"Here's how we're going to proceed," said Inspector Blognard.
Inspector Arapède and myself, stuffed with stew and tarts,
listened to him carefully.

"The nerve center of the whole case, its Gordian Knot, as it
were, is, I am now, like you [that was said to me], convinced, to
be found at 53 Rue des Citoyens. I can feel it in my bones," he
added, unaware that he was translating a favorite expression of his
friend and colleague Inspector Lovatt of Scotland Yard (who had
made him join the society he headed, Friends of the English
Badger—Inspector Lovatt had a passion for that animal. See
Blognard in London, to be published in the same series, subject to
the commercial success of this book, if you see what we are driving
at with this parenthetical remark). "Somewhere in that building,

on stairway A, B, C, D, E, or F, our villain is hiding. He flits about hither and thither like a crafty but careless fly. We are the patient spider; we must spin our web and lure the fly—that is to say, the Hardware-Store Horror. Now then, where do we anchor our web? In the square facing the building are three benches with their backs to Saint Gudule. I will spend my days on the middle bench, disguised as a beggar. That will allow me to ask questions off the record in local stores—especially Madame Eusèbe's grocery—and in the café, without attracting attention. Inspector Arapède, who, no matter where he went or how he was dressed could never pass for anything but what he is, a police inspector, will ask the official questions. You, young man, will pump your friends in the neighborhood for information. There's no need to be subtle about it. Just the opposite; the criminal must know that we are on his trail and be frightened, causing him to make a mistake. And the mistake he makes, that he can't help but make, will be the equivalent of the careless tack that lands the fly in the waiting spider web, in the middle of which will be I, Blognard."

"O.K., boss," Arapède said unenthusiastically.

There was nothing he hated more than those days spent copying down witnesses' stupid answers to the stupid questions he felt obliged to ask them; then he had to type everything out in triplicate and explain the contents to Blognard, who didn't even have the time to read them and preferred to be briefed orally.

"Where do I start?"

"The grocery store."

When I left the Blognards' (Inspector Arapède had stayed behind to discuss a few procedural matters), I went down Rue Saut-de-la-Chèvre, passing by the store where I had bought the bottle of sparkling wine I had presented to Madame Blognard (a charming and very refined woman, even if she *is* a bit of a housewife), and slipped into the garden at Place des Ardennes to sit down and daydream for a moment. I thought about the case, about its likely looming solution, and then I thought about Hortense, whom I hadn't seen since the morning of the novel's beginning. She no longer walked by the Eusèbe grocery at eight each morning; maybe she was sick. I promised myself that I would question Yvette, who seemed to be her friend, about that, but I was already less interested in her—the critical moment had passed.

Two children, apparently a brother and sister, were playing Frisbee on the grass near me under the watchful eye of a charming girl with whom I did not hesitate to strike up a conversation: she was a young Poldevian au pair by the name of Margrska (pronounced "Magroorska") who had come to the City for the summer (the reason for this narrative scene is to assure the Reader that the Narrator, who, for reasons of veracity, had to be denied any chance with Hortense in spite of his wishes, is alive and well. We can reveal that Margrska, the Poldevian girl, was neither reserved with nor cruel to him). I left her an hour later to go draft a summary of my encounter with Blognard, and we made a date for her day off. Grands-Edredons Square was empty.

As I now reread the blue notebook in which I recorded my thoughts as they came to me at that time (I am writing this two years later), I see, much more clearly than in the heat of the moment, immediately following the case's conclusion, when I wrote the book (a best-seller) that allowed me to dedicate myself to my calling as a writer (the book in question is *Blognard and the Hardware-Store Horror,* the first in the Blognard series of sensationalist popular novels, which is not to be confused with our own work— *Author's note*), that the turning point in the investigation was that lunch and Blognard's clear-sighted, efficient decision, reached before his wife, Arapède, and myself as we were finishing Crussant's tarts, to anchor his web on the bench in Grands-Edredons Square. No doubt the storm on the night of the equinox gave fate that last little push that provided the proof that might otherwise have been lacking, but I am convinced that without the almost constant presence on the bench, day and night, of a Blognard who, even in disguise, radiated good will, intelligence, and determination, the criminal probably would not have committed the careless fatal mistake that the wind, that instrument of fate, made catastrophic for him.

From Monday morning on, Blognard appeared dressed in a big old moth-eaten and grimy bathrobe from the Pyrenees and a beret he had doused with the murky liquid from Madame Blognard's French-fry bowl; his face was smeared with candy, and his feet were shod in sneakers, which he later replaced with sewerman's boots. I am all but certain that the criminal felt his presence, his aura, his lawman's determination, almost instantaneously, and that he began losing his grip.

The first lead emerged from the mass of testimony and details gathered by Arapède, who came to the square every morning at ten to give his report as inconspicuously as possible (I would be sitting on the next bench over, blue notebook in hand, taking down everything that seemed likely to be of use for my future book). The lead was given to us by the concierge, Madame Croche: according to her (and this had to be extracted from the torrent of venomous curses upon and accusations against the building's residents that she showered on poor Arapède), no one had moved into the building recently, not for two years at any rate; there were two or three empty apartments whose owners were away either in the south or abroad, but they were not being secretly sublet; she told Arapède as much, and we believed her. From this, Blognard concluded with striking dispatch that the criminal was someone from the building, someone who looked respectable but was doubtless hiding the Hyde side of their nature behind a Jekyllian facade that fooled even his nearest and dearest. That was the first step.

The next one was taken thanks to young Veronica Bouelles, in exchange for a few candies that Blognard was smart enough to hand over to her so as to win her confidence and gain a chance to snare the pearl of knowledge borne on the stream of her babble. No doubt in hopes of receiving another gift from the generous man, she casually mentioned on several different occasions that the black painting was most interesting, that little girls her age, contrary to her mother's claims, were perfectly capable of using black paint without soiling their tunics, fingers, or hair, and that it was not true (and all this was said in installments spread over intervals of several days, meaning that without Blognard's phe-nomenal deductive memory the link would likely have been missed), again contrary to what her mother said, that they were no longer selling black paint in stores, for one night she had seen a man out her window (which was on the ground floor on Stairway C, opening onto the square; she climbed up there with the help of a chair to let Alexander Vladimirovich in when he visited her) playing with a can of paint. How Blognard got her to show him the spot where the man in question had been without promising to buy her a can of black paint is still a mystery to me, despite my best efforts to clear it up, but that is not the key point. Veronica's testimony suddenly narrowed the possible list of suspects considerably, since the man in question (it was impossible to get a description out of her, but you can't have everything) *had left by Stairway D.*

The implications of this revelation were enormous, and a quiver of excitement shot through me when I heard the news. Blognard himself, normally so impassive, seemed worked up; had he been a real beggar, I would have sworn he was drunk. Only Arapède remained indifferent. He went so far as to shrug his shoulders, but there was nothing unusual in his doing that. All at once, the number of possible suspects had been reduced to nine, nine being the number of occupied apartments on Stairway D (likewise Stairway C [this remark is idiotic; there is no fathomable reason why the number of occupied apartments on Stairway C of 53 Rue des Citoyens should interest us—*Author's note*]); the building was five stories high, with an apartment on either side of the stairway on each floor, making ten apartments in all; but one of the apartments was one of the two that were unoccupied, according to Madame Croche—leaving nine.

Arapède then took a plan of the D stairway out of the large black ledger he always carried under one arm, in which were to be found all the documents relating to the investigation. Together we looked at the list of tenants. It read as follows:

Left Side

Ground Floor: Monsieur Anderthal, antique dealer.
Second Floor: Sauconay Vacuman, traveling salesman (vacuum cleaners and frying pans).
Third Floor: the Orsells family.
Fourth Floor: Monsieur and Madame Yvonne.
Fifth Floor: Mademoiselle Muche.

Right Side

Ground Floor: Monsieur Joseph, Saint Gudule's beadle.
Second Floor: Madame Anylline, dry-cleaner.
Third Floor: the Crussant family.
Fourth Floor: vacant.
Fifth Floor: Sir Whiffle, porcine writer, retired.

Blognard pensively looked the list over for quite some time. Then said, "We can certainly eliminate Mademoiselle Muche. This is a man's crime."

"But . . . ," Arapède began.

"No buts about it," Blognard said curtly. "And besides, if my memory serves [it did], and if your report is correct [it was], Mademoiselle Muche turned seventy-three on November fourteenth of last year, and I have a hard time imagining her going out at night with a can of black paint to paint walls with silhouettes of men pissing, much less forcibly entering hardware stores. Prince Gormanskoï is away, and his apartment is unoccupied, which makes two. That leaves seven."

I didn't see the baker Monsieur Crussant or the beadle in the role of criminal, and Blognard acknowledged that it was hardly likely, but he said the unlikely was not a firm category when it came to crime, and he therefore refused to strike them from the list. Nonetheless, he acknowledged, he would soon be able to eliminate them.

"I'd even be happy to give you a list of the suspects in order of likelihood as I see it," he said.

Here is the list, as I copied it down at that very moment. It can be seen to what an extent Blognard was already closing in on the truth.

List of the Suspects in Order of Likelihood,
According to Inspector Blognard

1st (tie): Sauconay Vacuman and Monsieur Yvonne

3rd: *Orsells*
4th: *Anderthal*
5th: *Sir Whiffle*
6th: *Crussant*
7th: *Joseph*

"Well, my children," the Inspector said as he rubbed his candy-covered hands, "things are starting to take shape!"

17

ORSELLS

Hortense's joy knew no bounds. She was as happy as a lark, if utterly exhausted by the repeated amorous exertions she gave herself over to in the company of her new lover. His imagination and inventiveness were vast; sometimes they overwhelmed her. His enthusiasm did not diminish. It was all certainly delightful but a bit tiring, and after two straight days of arriving half an hour late at the Crussant bakery, she was reduced to pleading a sudden development in her work as an excuse for skipping the morning rush, which the Crussants were happy to let her do with no decrease in her wages, at least for a while. But the work that she had used as an excuse was also suffering, for—outside of the quite natural fatigue resulting from her amorous excesses—she was unable to concentrate on the hardest aspects of her thesis, instead spending her best time—when He wasn't with her, on top of her, around her, or behind her—either dreaming of him or giving Yvette a detailed account of what he had said or done.

Yvette, who immediately gave a faithful retransmission to Sinouls (and they both raised eyebrows more and more often), thus learned that the young man from the T-line bus was named Morgan (and that is what we shall call him from now on; it isn't his real name, but we can't give his real name yet; if that one was good enough for Hortense, it will be good enough for us); he was called, Hortense told Yvette, Morgan; his mother was English, his father unknown. Every night around nine, after wolfing down a few eggs, a can of sardines, or some spaghetti that she fixed for him with a hand still trembling from unspeakable activities, he would take his little overnight bag and go prospecting, part of his job as a roving night antiques dealer, leaving Hortense panting on the bed. Despite Yvette's insistence, Hortense was not in a position to say anything more about his occupation, and to tell the truth, it apparently didn't interest her much.

The problem of her thesis was becoming urgent, however, since she had promised her master, Professor Orsells, that she would have a detailed outline for him by the end of the summer; that end was drawing near, and the outline still wasn't finished. Nor, given her current activities, was it likely to be done on time. After hemming and hawing for several days, she decided to go see Professor Orsells and ask him for an extension. To ready herself for this ordeal, and as was her custom anytime a problem was worrying her, she went shopping the day before the morning she was to meet with him, and bought herself a dress and two pairs of shoes.

She had a huge closet in which she heaped dresses and shoes bought under such circumstances. She never wore them, since their value was purely tranquilizing; the dresses and shoes she did wear were those given her by her father each time he invited her to lunch and, in an attack of paternal sadism, gave her money, salmon, or an apartment. She did not choose clothes of the same fabrics, colors, or price ranges; they were two entirely different collections, and she obviously never put them in the same place. Hence, on that day, she bought two pairs of blue shoes and a red dress, which she stuck in the closet as soon as she got back. She had had the vague impression that the closet was almost full from the last time she had been obliged to make such purchases—on the occasion of her last breakup—and that she had told herself she would soon have to have another closet built. She must have been mistaken, however, for there was in fact still a great deal of space left in this one.

At that time, Philibert Orsells was without a doubt the City's most visible intellectual, and therefore the country's (that does not mean there were no intellectuals elsewhere, but simply that they could not hope to be seen in the City if they did not live there). His thirty-five published works had all been excerpted in the papers, and they were issued in editions of as many as five thousand copies; he gave his opinions on the key questions and events of the day in books most often titled according to the formula *Modern Philosophy and X*—*Modern Philosophy and the Revolution in Machine Tools,* for example. He was continually calling on his countrymen to open their philosophical eyes and finally realize the consequences of the fact that there was: a new mass media; AIDS; science fiction; unemployment; the sexual, antisexual, or parasexual revolution; Islam; Buddhism; etc. He always did things decisively, and the papers put his words in their rightful place by giving them roughly one or two percent of the importance they gave to statements made by cyclists, singers, or the leaders of the party then in fashion. His was an indisputable success. He was still in vogue among young student intellectuals because of his feeling, which was essentially that of most of his fans, of being on the cutting edge, a spirit outside of all categories, censured on every side by the powers that be (and God knows there are enough!), overshadowed, repressed, stifled under the yoke of silence on the part of "people in high places"—the paper pushers, the conservatives, and this, that, and the other thing. He had based his entire personal hodgepodge on that image, which he also genuinely believed in (making it that much more effective).

His private life was simple and modest. When he was not on a lecture tour in the U.S., Japan, or Germany, he lived with his wife and twin nine-year-old daughters, Adèle and Idèle, in their modest apartment at 53 Rue des Citoyens. His wife was a former student, eighteen years younger than he, who was calm, kind, blond, and pale; she hadn't said a word for a good ten years. Her maiden name had been Hénade Jamblique.

Orsells welcomed Hortense heartily and invited her into his study. He excused himself for a moment; he was going over the proofs of his soon-to-be-published, thirty-sixth book and asked that she allow him to finish the page he was in the process of editing. Hortense took advantage of the opportunity to examine the room carefully (which could have been our chance for an insightful, all-encompassing description making the essential traits of two characters apparent by means of the judicious choice of the objects catalogued, but we will not allow ourselves to take this easy out, which our nineteenth-century predecessors used and abused, turning bourgeois homes into so many "moralized land-scapes"). On the left corner of Orsells's desk, opened to the page beginning the chapter entitled "Fine Arts," was a guide to Poldevia.

Abandoning the usual scanty dress demanded of her by Morgan (in memory, he said, of their first meeting), the primary character-istic of which was the absence of panties and a certain transparency, she had worn somber clothes for this meeting. Their unaccustomed weight (it was still hot) caused her a bit of discomfort, as did, no doubt, the guilt she felt over her behavior and the disappointment it would certainly cause the great man, who had been so supportive of her scholarly pursuits.

"Well," said Orsells, "what's up? How far have you gotten?"

Hortense had already made up her mind not to answer that question honestly. She chose a middle road, describing her genuine symptoms of fatigue without elaborating on their cause, which she left unclear, hinting only that it had something to do with her work in the Crussant bakery. She concluded by asking for advice, which struck her as the best way to proceed. Orsells was an incorrigible giver of advice.

She was not disappointed. Not that she was really looking for advice in a situation that she did not feel necessitated it and that, furthermore, she had only described very partially (how do you explain to your thesis adviser that your need for an extension is essentially due to excessive fornication?). Besides, Orsells's advice (whether given to different segments of the left, center, or right, to weight lifters or coin collectors), although plentiful, was so general and abstract in its absoluteness that she was risking nothing. By starting him down his favorite path, however, she had a good chance of obtaining the desired extension.

"My dear child," Orsells began in a voice sugary with theory, "in every case, and particularly in yours, one must go back to the beginning—that is to say, to the foundations, which are both metaphysical and moral, stemming from both Ethics and Ontology or, as I prefer to call it (you know my little pet word), *Ontethics.*"

"Addressed in Book One, Chapter One, subheading one, line one," Hortense mumbled mechanically.

"Everything, as you know, rests on the moral connotation of the word *should.* The proposition 'One should do A' necessarily stipulates that one desire that A be carried out in all possible worlds where the problem may arise, which furthermore is, as you know from having taken my fall-semester course of 19[. .–. .], the *possbeing. Should* also involves the universal in the sense that if I say 'One should do A,' I am implicitly asserting that whoever (that is to say, myself or another, in all possible worlds) *should do* A under identical circumstances (that is to say, the same circumstances, independent of the position in space-time of the individuals in question). It follows that 'One should do A' may be paraphrased as 'I, by this, strongly prescribe, as expressing my sincere desire, that anyone do A in any situation having the same abstract properties!'

"I derive from these premises, which no philosopher in his right mind should doubt [and here his face clouded for a moment at the thought of such of his brethren who, incredibly, had doubted], what I call The Golden Rule of Ontethics, which is particularly 'relevant,' as our friends in Cambridge would say, in your case:

"'One must treat another in a certain way if and only if one is prepared to: (one) do the same thing in all possible worlds; (two) accept that the same thing be done if one is ONESELF the object of the contemplated operation.'"

"In all possible worlds?" asked Hortense.

"Naturally, in all possible worlds. That is a trivial consequence of the Rule in the condensed form I have given you. You must surely see, dear child, how this applies to the present case of your thesis, for which I am, in this world, the 'object' of your extension operation," he said with a smile.

"Yes," said Hortense, "but perhaps another less personal example . . ."

"Well, let us suppose that I pose the following question: *Should I push my neighbor so as to be the first to board the bus?* There you have a crucial and concrete problem that comes up very frequently in our day-to-day life. The bus arrives, we see at a glance that it is packed and that if we do not act we will be not the last to board but rather the first *not* to board. To push or not to push, that is the question. One must apply The Golden Rule of Ontethics with lightning speed. That is why one must be in complete command of all its nuances. What does the Rule tell us in this case? That I should push if and only if, *in the final analysis,* I would prefer pushing *and* being pushed to neither of the two of us—my neighbor in front of me in the line waiting to board the bus and I—being pushed. It is this way because the situation's abstract properties imply that *pushing and being pushed* are essentially the same thing, which, you will grant, is an extremely profound result. Only the people change. But the beauty of the thing becomes even more apparent [Orsells had, in his excitement, latched onto Hortense's right knee] if one considers that the moral theorem I have just stated is the one reached if the person 8 question, the one in front of you, has exactly the same desire you do. But if it so happens that this person is a mild-mannered gentleman or a timid old lady who has no desire to push and no great objection to being pushed, then one *must* push. Push, push, it is the only morally justified course of action! Furthermore, one may extend the problem to three people, which has allowed me, Orsells, to obtain a definitive solution to the so-called three-body problem of planetary motion, which the physicists and astronomers had so little inkling of how to approach."

Hortense freed her knee, thanked Orsells for his enlightening advice, and said that she indeed needed to contemplate Ontethics intensively to see how the Golden Rule applied to the case of her thesis. She would come back in two months with a definitive answer to the question, she was sure of it (two months was the length of the extension she had requested for turning in her thesis outline; it would be November, and perhaps by then Morgan's flaming desire, along with her own, would have cooled sufficiently to leave her a little bit of time to concentrate).

And she left.

18

THE GREAT STORM
ON THE EQUINOX

There was a build-up. Several days before the fall equinox, as if by heavenly decree, the heat intensified, growing heavier and heavier. Children began to whine, scratch, and generally drive their parents up the wall; parents screamed over a yes or no; soft-drink salesmen prospered, as long as they didn't run out of stock; dogs panted; the trees, houses, and sky were covered with a film of sweaty sweat; refrigerators panted; on café terraces, the customers looked like whales beached at Hendaye. Old Man Sinouls never sobered up, without even doing it on purpose: each beer he sweated out made him even thirstier. Even Inspector Blognard had tripled his consumption of double Shirley Temples. The great storm on the equinox was drawing near. The weather forecasters, their satellite weather maps at the ready, predicted it six days running, but in vain. Big, heavy, black clouds like swollen sacks of cement or flour would gather above Saint Gudule; they would shake their heads, hesitate, then go off to unburden themselves over Poland or Trieste.

Finally the moment arrived. Dusk came at three in the afternoon; the sky was the color of pewter, a gray-green, a storm-gray... whatever. Monsieur Anderthal, the antique dealer, having hurried back to the ground floor of 53's D stairway to close the windows, which he had left open to let in the slightest breath of fresh air, thought the sky looked like an Anglo-Saxon pewter mug that had just been sold to him dirt-cheap and on which he hoped to make a handsome profit. The lowest clouds began to come together into a threatening ceiling.

First a few drops fell around six, two hours before the time of the actual sunset, given daylight-saving time, the immortal invention Senator Honorat of the Lower Alps (today Upper Provence) gave the world at the beginning of the twenties. It was a false alarm. Nonetheless, the birds disappeared, and the streets emptied out. The heavens had planned their opening salvo for eight o'clock. Monsieur and Madame Bouelles were in the butcher shop chatting with their last customers; Monsieur Bouelles was hunting the flies that had taken refuge inside and were too frightened to go after the roast beef. Little Veronica Bouelles was all alone in her alcove in the back room; she could see the sky out the window, and she didn't like it at all. She was very scared and was getting ready to cry and scream to bring her mother running—something her pride usually kept her from doing—when Alexander Vladimirovich crept up next to her and rubbed the remarkably cool end of his muzzle against her nose; her mind was set completely at ease.

"Alex!" she said lovingly.

Alexander Vladimirovich gave her a few short, raspy licks, then climbed up her chest as if it were an eiderdown; Veronica soon fell asleep, and Alexander Vladimirovich himself took a catnap while being pleasantly rocked by the regular movement of her little chest as it rose and fell beneath him.

The wind grew fiercer; the sand flew around the sandbox; to show what it could do, the wind knocked over several trash cans, then stopped and waited; the streets emptied out again. On the radio they were continuing to forecast nice sunny weather for the next day. The wind started to really let loose. Three tiles and a piece of a cornice came tumbling down a little farther up Rue Vieille-des-Archives. And that was the stormily raging storm on the equinox. All the half-closed windows banged in the wind, and the damage began in earnest (cf. Victor Hugo and Conrad for more details). Alexander Vladimirovich woke up and stole out quietly without awakening the little one.

Monsieur Bouelles had closed up his shop, and Madame Bouelles was in the kitchen, where she was heating up the evening meal. It was the time of day when Alexander Vladimirovich made his ritual visit, the time for his ongoing conspiracy with Monsieur Bouelles, for they had a common lust that even the storm couldn't keep them from sating. And the ceremony necessarily took place at that time, far from Madame Bouelles's disapproving gaze and in the absence of any customers: at the end of the day, Monsieur Bouelles would prepare the meat for the meat locker, placing it on the butcher-shop stall beneath the nineteenth-century painting of which he was so proud (cf. Chap. 2), and as he was scraping the surface clean he would find all sorts of scraps of raw meat composed of some amount of fat mixed with mutton, pork, veal, or beef. Whatever the scraps were, *he would eat them;* more precisely, he would share them with Alexander Vladimirovich, who had the same passion he did. Madame Bouelles had caught him doing this alone one day and had been horrified by this vile lust of his, so Monsieur Bouelles was happy to share with Alexander Vladimirovich, who served as an alibi in the event of a surprise visit by his wife. Alexander Vladimirovich also preferred sating his lust discreetly, safe in knowledge that Monsieur Bouelles would never betray him to Madame Eusèbe, and with good reason.

Having stilled his appetite, Alexander Vladimirovich left quickly through the square and went out into the storm, moving along carefully from tree to tree to resume his nightly stakeout. For he was shadowing the young man from the T-line bus, when Hortense, whose lover he was, knew by the name Morgan, and about whom we may now reveal (as the Reader certainly guessed right away; the Reader is certainly more perceptive than our publisher's editorial board, which requested this utterly and idiotically unnecessary clarification, but what can you do?) that he was precisely the same young man Alexander Vladimirovich had seen in the apartment on Stairway C in Chapter 3, and whose presence, as we have known since Arapède's investigation, was utterly unknown to Madame Croche, the concierge, therefore making him, in all likelihood, a squatter (careful, we didn't say it was true!).

Alexander Vladimirovich followed him everywhere; thus he had trailed him to Hortense's apartment, was aware of all of our heroine's charms (about which, we may tell you, he couldn't have cared less), and had on several occasions, for purely documentary purposes, witnessed their amorous contortions, which were infinitely less dignified, in his eyes, than the delicious dance done by Orsells's little red-haired cat, to whom he dedicated all the free time left him by his surveillance. Following the young man was essential, for, if he understood correctly, he was still missing one key link in the chain. In spite of the storm, or perhaps even because of it, he knew that the young man would go out that night, and Alexander Vladimirovich felt that he was working up to a revelation of the greatest importance for his own future.

The storm now let loose on the City; cars carried off by the wind zigzagged in their efforts not to end up wrapped around one another; a T-line bus wound up broadside in the middle of an intersection, and a little old lady in a little old car that barely came up to the ankle of the bus began cursing it in language that caused the passengers to quiver in amazement, at least at as much of it as they could make out between the tremendous gusts of wind that stuffed air down your throat and didn't even allow you to digest it and exhale before filling you up again. The two lovers, unaware of all this commotion, were in the process of enthusiastically giving themselves over to a variation on a certain method you could find mentioned (under the name Corkscrew Movement) in one of the volumes of *My Life and Lovers* by Frank Harris, a work that had been one of Hortense's favorites at fourteen. She had stolen it by forcing the lock on the drawer in the "special" section of her parents' library, choosing it over Krafft-Ebing and Havelock Ellis. And Freud.

Alexander Vladimirovich sighed, settled his paws under his fur in a waiting position, and thought about other things.

The storm raged all night. Between two assault-waves of wind, it rained. Torrents of rain poured onto the City and carried all sorts of debris into the overworked sewers, thereby doing a good bit of the streetcleaner's work by eliminating many of the countless canine deposits that make our streets the luckiest in the Western World.

The young Pr—(we mean the young man; please excuse this regrettable misprint), as Alexander Vladimirovich had foreseen, was outside for a very long time on that particular night. He was well prepared for the storm, wearing an oilskin raincoat and rain hat. But Alexander Vladimirovich, despite his litheness and knowledge of the streets, could not help getting his paws wet; it was his fervent hope that the case would soon draw to a close. The young man returned home (if it may be called that) at around three in the morning, his arms full of the usual suitcases and packages; he did not stay there for long, soon leaving to rejoin Hortense and enjoy a rest (we won't call it *well deserved*).

The storm had all but exhausted its bag of tricks. The clouds, or what was left of them, reformed into cohorts, files, and divisions as they went off to the east. The sky cleared little by little to make ready for a tender dawn over the rather seriously devastated city: branches and chimneys were lying on the ground; burst water mains were adding their chlorinated contents to the pure streams of celestial water; there would be quite a bit for the city's firemen and streetcleaners, not to mention the army, to do when the floods, which would not be long in coming, arrived.

For the moment, however, everything was calm and peaceful in the gathering dawn. The residents, relieved by the perceptible change in barometric pressure and the level of air hygrometry, had at last found their long-awaited rest, and everyone slept late in expectation of a general moving back of the city's activity. The birds returned to the trees, drank from the puddles, and chirped à la Messiaen as they perched on the branches between the damp leaves. The sun (which had hidden its head under the covers, it had been so afraid) now began planning a modest comeback. Much sand and dirt had rejoined the gutter of Rue des Grands-Edredons.

As the streams of rainwater receded, they left designs made up of dunes and banks, which could easily have been confused with the Loire at low tide. Researchers from the university's hydrographics laboratory, affected by budgetary restrictions decided on by the minister at breakfast, came during the day to study the streets since they couldn't afford to build expensive life-size mockups complete with bellows, soils, and water flows.

Alexander Vladimirovich checked to see that the young man was indeed asleep in the arms of Hortense, who slept naked and most innocently, without budging, through all the commotion, as if she had come upon the remorseless sleep of Veronica Bouelles. Then he recrossed the intersection with Rue des Citoyens and returned to the square, where an unexpected sight caused him to stop short on his front paws. At the foot of Stairway C, more precisely under the second window from the right, which was part of the young man's apartment, lay some bits of a clay pot; no, they were the remains of the statuette that Alexander Vladimirovich had spotted on the windowsill next to the milk bottle in Chapter 3. A particularly strong gust of wind had sent it tumbling into the void and, with the help of its mass and an acceleration extremely close to g (we have naturally taken air resistance into account), it had shattered into x pieces (he didn't have the time to count them) upon striking the ground. Alexander Vladimirovich saw the danger threatening his plans in a flash; again in a flash, he saw what he had to do and acted immediately (the whole business had taken little more than a second; cats have extremely quick reflexes). Looking around to make sure no one would see him (it was six o'clock in the morning, a glimmer was barely beginning to make itself seen in the east, but Grands-Edredons Square was still completely empty), he used his paw to move the pieces of the statuette, one by one, just the right amount.

Then he smiled behind his whiskers and went back to the grocery.

COMPLEMENT TO CHAPTER 18
WHICH IS AT THE SAME TIME A CONTINUATION OF
THE ANSWER TO THE SPECIAL QUESTION FROM THE FIRST
BETWEEN-TWO-CHAPTERS
WHICH WAS THEN ELABORATED IN CHAPTERS 9, 11
AND THE SECOND BETWEEN-TWO-CHAPTERS

Cats have extremely quick reflexes, and moving the remains of the statuette thrown from its source of support by the great storm on the equinox had taken but a moment. Still, we must ask ourselves a bit more insistently than does the chapter *why* Alexander Vladimirovich committed this deed with its not insignificant consequences. Chapter 18 (to which the present note is an addendum, which does not prevent it from also being a continuation of the account of the loves of Alexander Vladimirovich) attributed to Alexander Vladimirovich one motive and one alone, which it left shrouded in mystery to boot. And doubtless Chapter 18 has its reasons (we know it, we're the ones who wrote it). Furthermore, it must not be overlooked that the actions of cats, unlike those of humans, never have one specific cause, or even a principal one. When, by chance, several causes fight over a human mind, there is always one that reigns preeminent in that mind (this ties in with the inadequacy of speech, which is incapable of expressing everything in a single harmonious sound like meowing, and must instead layer thought upon thought in sentences. Not to mention the ridiculous differences in languages, obviously imperfect because several).

Alexander Vladimirovich had *at least one other reason,* no less pressing, for moving the remains of the statuette. It will be revealed in two installments (which are logically and chronologically dependent), in chapters 23 and 26 respectively (at the end).

19

ARAPÈDE'S DREAM

Inspector Arapède was dreaming. He was dreaming that he was in a very large, clean, modern police station in which he had his own office and his own interrogation room. The dream he was dreaming was the same one he had dreamed the night before and every other night since the first night of the novel. He was perfectly conscious during this dream and therefore made a great effort to pay close attention, so as to be able to decipher its meaning, which, he sensed, was continuing to escape him. There were three people in his dream office: himself, represented by the gaze that saw and knew that it saw because, at the same time, he was watching himself dream (or rather, he knew he was there as one of the dream's characters even as he was dreaming); Inspector Blognard, who was holding a Shirley Temple that was at least a quadruple and a huge Callard and Bowser's that was like a chocolate bar; and last, the suspect, Monsieur X, who was seated on an unupholstered yellow plastic chair bought in a Dijon discount store during an investigation (it was Inspector Arapède's own kitchen chair, he recognized it clearly). He would have liked to have seen who the suspect was. Each day he felt he was coming closer to making out his face, but it was like one of those names you know perfectly well, but which suddenly escape you, or the translation into a foreign language of a word that you also know perfectly well, but which, for some reason, conceals itself from view (Arapède was rapidly discovering that words in a foreign language are like proper nouns in your own language, and he was very proud of this discovery of a fundamental principle of the philosophy of linguistics). This suspect was in the yellow chair, trying, still successfully, to hide his face, which was, in fact, as Arapède knew, the culprit's, but he *dreamed "suspect"* because that corresponded to the interrogation setting.

He and Blognard were putting the suspect through the third degree in a manner worth of Humphrey Bogart, James Cagney, or Edward G. Robinson. Arapède had always dreamed of conducting a third degree with the proper supplies at his disposal—bright lights and hamburgers, for example. The third degree in the dream was of a kind that would have left a California D.A., and doubtless Perry Mason himself, perplexed; it consisted of a dialogue between himself and Blognard on the theoretical problem of proof, and the suspect was dying to step in, that was obvious from the way he was squirming about in his chair, but he wasn't allowed, and it could be felt that, at some point in the interrogation, he wouldn't be able to hold out any longer, and Arapède would see his face and recognize the culprit (his name was almost there, on another page of the book), who would then confess. Only, that hadn't happened yet. The conversation/interrogation went something like this:

BLOGNARD: I am happy to learn that you have abandoned the extravagant positions I was told you held.

ARAPÈDE: And which are those?

BLOGNARD: It has come to my attention (and unfortunately nothing about last night's interrogation would permit me to believe that these were not your opinions) that you are someone who asserts that most indefensible thesis ever held by a police officer—that *material proof* of guilt in any crime cannot exist.

ARAPÈDE: I am now deeply convinced of the nonexistence of what police officers, examining magistrates, judges, and journalists call *material proof,* but I see nothing absurd about this opinion.

BLOGNARD: What! Can there be anything more incredible, more contrary, and more repugnant to common sense, anything more clearly the product of a skeptical disorder, than believing that proof *does not exist!*

ARAPÈDE: Easy now, my dear Blognard. And what if I prove to you that you yourself, by virtue of your asserting the material existence of things such as proofs, are a much more devilish skeptic than I, and consequently fall into a considerable number of paradoxes and contradictions?

BLOGNARD: But are you not an avowed skeptic?

ARAPÈDE: What, in your opinion, is a skeptic?

BLOGNARD: Well, a skeptic, as everybody knows, is someone who doubts the minister of justice, the police commissioner, and the procedures for establishing judicial proof, to make a long story short, someone who doubts everything.

ARAPÈDE: Therefore he who only doubts one thing concerning one *particular point* cannot be considered a skeptic?

At that moment in the dream, Arapède felt a feeling of warm certainty come over him; he felt that he was about to corner Blognard; but the suspect felt it also and began squirming frantically in his yellow chair, so much so that the bridge of dreams, fragile as a Japanese paper bridge, collapsed, and Arapède found himself back in his bed. He turned on the lights and went down to make his morning coffee.

Arapède came from a modest background. After very intensive studies, the metaphysical ambition came upon him later in life, and he entered the police force, where he became the famed Inspector Blognard's right-hand man. Arapède greatly admired Blognard and would very much have liked to convert him to Pyrrhonism, the philosophical system that, after great hesitation, he had finally espoused. He was single, slow-moving, stout, and of average height, and he wore a black suit; he lived with his widowed mother in a little apartment on Avenue Sextus Empiricus, in the same part of town as the consulates.

Arapède was an extremely conscientious police officer. He carried out the duties Blognard demanded of him—interrogations, and investigations of the most minute details—with a tenacious perfection that won him admiration, envy, and a bit of jealousy on the part of his colleagues. Blognard would often say that without Arapède he would never, so to speak, have succeeded in conducting a thorough investigation—that is to say, in carrying it through to that final stage where the culprit's conviction is certain no matter how much effort and skill the defense puts in during the trial. This was not untrue, and this perfect tenacity of Arapède's was—contrary to what Blognard had said in exasperation during several of their countless philosophical debates—the result of his Pyrrhonism, and not in irreconcilable conflict with it. He hunted down certainty into the smallest nooks and crannies, but he always eventually found some fly in the ointment of proof, the fatal flaw that he alone saw (while all the others contented themselves with second-rate certainty) and that brought to the corner of his mouth the little smile that Blognard didn't like at all (for sometimes Arapedian doubt gave rise to first-rate difficulties).

Arapède, because of both his system of thought and the seriousness with which he took his professional duties (he tried never to miss a detail around Blognard), led a full, methodical life that left him precious little time for recreation; he never went out except when invited to the Blognards', and saw movies once a week with his mother, who loved musical comedies and was a Busby Berkley fan (several times she had dragged him to see that [in Arapède's opinion] inept and unrealistic movie in which Carmen Miranda goes down, or rather is lowered down, with the help of a pulley, the length of a steamboat with an immense platter of fruit and vegetables balanced on her head like a hat—the tutti frutti hat); once a month he would go the movies alone to see American detective films that contributed to his internal filmography of interrogation scenes, which he was trying to make as complete as possible because, as at that time, these scenes fed his dreams.

The key skill he had to practice was patience. He had discovered an ideal exercise for that long ago; he did this exercise regularly. It was egg peeling. So that the Reader will have a proper appreciation for the nature and difficulty of the exercise, we will specify that the eggs in question were *raw.* He dedicated an hour to it every morning, working at a little table specially and exclusively reserved for this activity. He would set the egg down in front of him on the table, in a coconut shell sawed in such a way that ninety-one one-hundredths of the egg were left showing and the base was firmly supported. He would tap the upper part sharply, which allowed him to remove the first bit of shell without tearing the egg membrane, and would next proceed slowly, with extreme caution, until the egg was naked; then, and only then, would he nimbly toss it into the little frying pan in which his mother would cook it with bacon. The entire operation required about a week. He had never failed. On certain Sundays when he was on a particularly difficult case, he would peel an egg in one sitting, working almost ten hours straight. He kept a likeness (by means of color photography) of each egg peeled in this way on his bedroom wall, in rows of twenty-three. There were already twenty-six complete rows, and he was about to start a new one.

Having carefully washed his hands with a special soap from Marseille after his morning sitting with the beginning of a new egg peeling (he was peeling a particularly difficult egg, a duck's egg with a very fine skin, and he needed all his concentration not to botch the most difficult passages, those involving the crossing of the equator, if you see what we mean), Inspector Arapède pulled out his notebook and looked over his schedule for the day: it was the day after the day after the great storm on the equinox, and he was supposed to go to the Eusèbe grocery and take down the testimony of the couple who owned the place, Monsieur and Madame Eusèbe. He sighed. He did not, in fact, like this end of things: the testimony of the people he questioned—whether they were suspects or not, whether they answered in good faith or not—was always exasperatingly imprecise and inexact. He would have preferred some nice juicy lies, since then at least you knew where you stood; he feared the worst with the Eusèbes.

He had almost finished his assignment, having already interviewed not only the Crussants, the Orsellses, the Madame Yvonnes, in fact all the residents on Stairway D, but also, if a bit more summarily, the residents on the other stairways as well. He had completely filled one notebook with his neat handwriting, formed lovingly with an old-fashioned Sergeant-Major pen (the likes of which he had a hard time finding after exhausting the reserve left to him by his father, Police Captain Arapède, in his will. He had them made to order according to the traditional design by a craftsman on Rue des Chaufourniers). He wrote in purple ink and used a green blotter on his slightly inclined desk; each day he would photocopy the previous day's report and hand it over (the photocopy, of course) to Inspector Blognard. He would also bring Blognard his notebook, however, because Blognard preferred to read the report in the original, as he called it, saying that some of the power of the writing was lost in the photocopying.

He was careful about the editing he did each night after dinner (chicken broth, cottage pie, and flan, for example); while his mother knitted, he would check his spelling in an old Littré dictionary, the coherence of his syntax in his Grévisse grammar. He began all his sentences with a capital letter, his paragraphs with a larger capital. He would also vary the style of his presentations, sometimes contenting himself with indirect discourse, often inserting dialogues to which he liked to add his name in capital letters and stage directions like those in the plays in his mother's *Illustrated* collection; for example: September [. . .], 5:40 P.M. at the Bouelleses' home; the stage set is a butcher shop; on the floor in the sawdust are two chicken feet; young Veronica is next to her father, who is holding her hand and encouraging her to answer the nice police inspector's questions:

Arapède: Now then, was this man with the cans of paint tall?

Veronica: Yes.

Arapède: This tall? No? This tall? Taller than your father?

Veronica: No, not taller than my dad, my dad is the tallest, my dad has a big knife and he chops up meat with it. When I grow up, I'm going to be a butcher and I'm going to chop things up with my knife.

It was not just for stylistic, and more generally aesthetic, reasons that Arapède composed his reports as if they were the manuscripts of some great author. On the one hand, it helped him to concentrate and not forget potentially important details; on the other, he took advantage of the opportunity to slip into his accounts, in the guise of resting points, arguments about the general order of things, which were a part of his never-ending debate with Blognard; he would highlight certain answers' impreciseness, referring back to other passages in his notebook to bring out the contradiction between some people's statements and others', ending with some aphorism from Montaigne or Chillingworth. Finally, he knew that by acting in this way he would stimulate Blognard's interest, and thus his intellectual faculties as well, and that from this stimulation the needed flash of insight would be sparked.

20

EUSÈBE

Madame Eusèbe answered Inspector Arapède's questions eagerly and enthusiastically, frequently citing Alexander Vladimirovich as her witness; she told him everything she knew, which added nothing to Arapède's knowledge, and everything she didn't know, which was quite a lot and which also, of course, added nothing. Her eagerness and enthusiasm did not at all surprise the Inspector, who was used to this type of reaction from people of the Eusèbes' age and social status, but he sensed a very slight excess, which led him to think that Madame Eusèbe had something to hide (that was the case, and even more so than we might know) but that what she was hiding, although shameful, was probably not the sort of thing that would interest the police, and, in any event, it was certainly not something having anything to do with the case; so he contented himself with appearing evasive and raising an eyebrow two or three times. He could see the effect it had on her each time, for Madame Eusèbe would shiver, look at Alexander Vladimirovich, and become even more eager and enthusiastic.

In an indirect but clear way, she provided Eusèbe with an alibi, at least for the last few attacks, and Arapède, taking a quick look through the door at the old grocer standing at his post on the sidewalk, was not very surprised by that: Eusèbe did not strike him as a prime suspect.

He was distinctly more interested in the cat. He obviously knew something, and what was more, that something seemed to concern him, for he was trying (in vain, given the Inspector's trained eye) to hide his interest in and fascination with their conversation. The Inspector had recently read a short story translated from English in which the main character was a cat, by the name of Tobermory, who had been initiated into the charms of producing articulate human sounds by a German scholar invited to a country house for the weekend. The Tobermory in question had taken the opportunity to reveal a whole slew of discrediting or embarrassing little secrets about the hosts and their guests, making for an extremely lively weekend. And Arapède thought that he would very much have liked to subject Alexander Vladimirovich to that same treatment and then take him to the police station in his dream to put him on the yellow chair and give him the third degree; he was clearly a cat who would never be able to resist a good discussion on the value of material proof. But, sighing, he resigned himself to closing up his notebook and thanking Madame Eusèbe, who appeared greatly relieved.

As he was going out, someone entered the grocery. From the photograph (he was very careful, before each series of interrogations, to obtain photographs of the witnesses/suspects, so as to be able to get some idea of their characters and thus their likely reactions; that permitted him to choose the proper dialectical tactic in advance: you don't put the same questions in the same way to a coal peddler, a church sexton, and a civil servant), he recognized that someone as Old Man Sinouls, Saint Gudule's organist. He immediately seized the opportunity to introduce himself and solicit a brief interview. Old Man Sinouls was very glad for this diversion, since he had forgotten just exactly what it was that his wife had sent him to get (he had some trouble with his short-term memory, meaning that he would often tell Yvette something she had told him just the day before, or something he had just read in the very *Paper* she had under her arm). Old Man Sinouls explained the ins and outs of the case to Arapède, along with its sociocultural significance and its probable development. The Inspector was enlightened in general but left mostly in the dark in particular. Since Old Man Sinouls was not very high on his list of priorities, however, he was not greatly affected by this turn of events. He made his way over to Eusèbe.

Eusèbe was unenthusiastic and even irritated about seeing him come over. He sensed that he was about to be bothered for nothing. Since the storm on the equinox, the weather had been nice once again but considerably cooler than before, and the days, by God, were getting shorter, as they will at that time of year. That shortening was starting to be noticeable; soon it would be back to standard time, which put more darkness in the evening hours, and tourists would become increasingly scarce: they were still fairly numerous, but they went out later, come back earlier, and, above all, had started covering themselves up a little bit everywhere. That, of course, was a clear drawback for Eusèbe: going from a period of extreme abundance during which he didn't know where to direct his gaze and saliva, as much because of the quantity and quality as because of the surface and the transparency, to another that, although certainly not one of blight (the month of February was the worst in that respect), nonetheless required sustained attention if one did not want to allow opportunities to slip away—all that was trying. But, in fact, the advantages were almost as important, for he could put to use all the knowledge he had acquired during spring and summer, testing the accuracy of his reactions, deducing from comparison with his memory what now stood before him, partially hidden from direct sight. That had its charm; the air was crisp, some small, careless English girl went by in a transparent blouse, her pointy little breasts and pink little buttocks (a very likely assumption) all aquiver in the refreshing breeze of this last week of September, and Eusèbe's spirits were revived.

And now here was this big oaf coming along to bother him with his questions. Eusèbe let a certain amount of time pass before becoming aware that the Inspector was asking him if he hadn't noticed any suspicious people doing suspicious things on Rue des Citoyens.

"As Madame your wife told me that you are most often to be found right here on this sidewalk, and no one can pass by without being seen by you."

At first Eusèbe understood nothing of what Arapède wanted. He thought he was doing a statistical study for the city government on the number of female tourists who moved in one or the other direction according to the time of day, the day of the week, and the month of the year; he had some very precise ideas on that subject and was ready to pass them along. He would take advantage of the opportunity to ask this fatso if he knew why more tourists went from east to west than from west to east; he hoped it wasn't because they were kidnaped upon reaching the center of town by a gang involved in the tourist trade. Hence there was a moment of confusion in their dialogue. When Eusèbe gave some figures, Arapède wrote them down, then began thinking that that certainly did make an awful lot of suspects for one single street. Changing his tack, he asked Eusèbe if he could describe one of these suspects: Eusèbe wasted no time in doing so, giving comparisons of dress colors with panty colors drawn from the vast attic of his memory before finally settling on one particularly shining example:

"You can't imagine," he said, "how disappointing an ass can be when you contemplate it and compare what you're shown with what's really there [as determined deductively]; there are some...some who cheat! Incredible!"

Arapède's mind was beginning to waver. Pulling himself back together, he asked Eusèbe if, without going into more intimate anatomical details, he could describe one suspect for him, a *man*. Eusèbe suddenly looked at him with a surprise that rapidly gave way to indignation.

"What? What? A man? Are you sick, or what? Men aren't interesting, I don't know a damn thing about the men who walk by, what do you think I'd do with men, a guy like me? Do men have breasts? They have...," and he went into a whole series of indecent specifics that caused Arapède to beat a hasty retreat.

That night, as he was going to bed, Eusèbe was seized by something like doubt. He had finished his bowl of soup, making bubbles in it with his lips, as usual, when all of a sudden he remembered the Inspector's words: a good citizen should look around so as to be able to inform the authorities about suspects' activities. That is the only way our City's security can be ensured. And suddenly Eusèbe wondered whether he was a good citizen. At first, that didn't seem too important.

"Maybe I'm not a good citizen. Why should I give a damn whether I'm a good citizen or not? Men aren't interesting to look at, how hard can it be to understand that?"

And he finished his yogurt with canned peaches in a state of righteous indignation that he immediately shared with Madame Eusèbe. Still ecstatic about having escaped the Inspector's inquisitive and dangerously perceptive gaze, but worried all the same about the future, she did not agree with him: you have to tell those people what they want to know, that way you don't get into trouble.

"I have no business saying this, Eusèbe, but I think you were wrong to answer that polite, well-behaved Inspector so rudely; if it comes to anything, there are others who won't be so nice as he was!"

Eusèbe brushed off her moaning with the back of his hand; it was a matter of principle, they wanted to make him say that men were interesting to look at as well, and that was just too much, he didn't want to. What did they take him for, a faggot maybe? He left the table in a storm of moral outrage.

But when he found himself alone at bedtime (Madame Eusèbe had gone downstairs to speak with Alexander Vladimirovich), his elation deflated and he began to feel unsure of himself. He felt no remorse at the way he had answered the Inspector—he didn't regret his refusal—but rather a vaster, more penetrating, more radical doubt: he had been studying for years now, and just what exactly did he know? Asking himself that, he began trying to come up with a way to express in one sentence the quintessence, the sum of what he had learned from his thousands of acute, precise, systematic observations. He couldn't; all he could bring to mind was a confused jumble of female lips, panties, shoulders, breasts, and thighs of all nationalities and dressed in all sorts of clothes. They began to dance before his eyes, making him feel dizzy.

"I don't know anything," he said to himself, "I don't know anything at all. It all adds up to nothing, what's the use."

He rose to his feet cautiously, for everything around him had started spinning and the infernal parade of increasingly disrobed and muddled female bodies continued inside his head.

Then, as he always did when he ran up against a difficult problem in his life, he decided to take a piss. For several years it had been somewhat hard to piss—not that pissing caused him pain, no; it simply took him more and more time. He now needed five or ten minutes in front of the toilet thinking about all sort of things before inspiration would come and he could finally piss—slowly, very slowly, but surely. At first this had irritated him, but he had soon turned his weakness into a strength, for he had observed that standing there like that thinking about pissing and then pissing while thinking made all life's little problems vanish, and all those apparently insoluble problems found solutions; since he had discovered this fact, he had secretly called it The Eusèbe Pissing Method. It went like this: he would stand there thinking for a few minutes, as usual, thinking about everything and nothing in a way that put his bladder in the proper moral condition—*that* was important; and then, when some feeling inside him said it was coming, he would pick up a big glass of soda pop he had put down in front of him on the windowsill to the right of the toilet tank, and he would take a big swig that he gulped down all at once. Then, miraculously, through an effect whose physics escaped him but which he sensed was certainly a discovery as important as Nooton's concerning apple cultivation or Ineshtyne's about the relativity of things in this world, that would be that, he would be pissing, and with each mouthful he then swallowed in little gulps, a violent emptying-out of his bladder would result, from which he drew an intense satisfaction, feeling thus transformed into a cosmic cistern. Finally, when he had finished the glass of soda pop and thus finished pissing, the problem that had been bothering him would be solved!

But alas, on that particular night, it was not to be. The evil dance, the imagistic whirlwind of nude femininity, and the doubt engendered in him by Inspector Arapède's odious questions all continued; all the sights he had accumulated over the years gushed out of his head in great spurts, leaving nothing. Setting his glass back down before leaving the bathroom, he noticed his face in the mirror as he leaned over the toilet tank. He saw his old face and cried.

21
YVETTE GOES TO HORTENSE'S HOUSE

On the first Sunday of standard time, Hortense called up Yvette: she wanted to see her.

"Come over for lunch," Yvette said. She yawned; it was eleven o'clock, but she was hung-over, for she had had too much to drink at the Sinoulses' after watching the sixth round of the France-Wales rugby matches at her father's house.

"I can't," Hortense said, "you have to come over to my place, I have something to show you."

"What about Morgan?" Yvette asked, knowing that Morgan couldn't stand to be seen by Hortense's friends and acquaintances.

"He went to be with his mother for the weekend because of daylight-saving time."

"Because of daylight-saving time?"

"Yes, he has to go comfort her because of daylight-saving time. She can't get used to it, I mean she can't get used to the change in time. She's English, you know," Hortense added, as if that explained everything.

They agreed to have lunch at one; Yvette was to bring the bread and the dessert.

Hortense didn't want to say anything before lunch. She seemed nervous and tense and bore no resemblance to the happy lark with the shining complexion and glittering eyes, seemingly always just getting out of bed, that she had been for the last month (the image is doubtless a bit fuzzy, but it does say what it means). The spaghetti was overdone and stuck together; the bacon bits were slightly burnt. Hortense kept rolling and unrolling bread balls.

After lunch, Hortense led Yvette into her bedroom. She had put a big black leather trunk on the bed and now said to Yvette:

"Here's the story. I'm sure he's cheating on me. Everything must be right there, inside, but I'd rather have you be the one to open it, I don't want to go pawing through his things."

Yvette smiled and opened the trunk: it contained various tools, a long steel rod with a forked end, a large bunch of keys, screwdrivers, razor blades, several pairs of gloves . . . There was a little bundle of letters, tied in a packet with a blue ribbon. With a little cry of rage, Hortense threw herself on the letters.

"You sure you shouldn't put on gloves?"

"Why?"

"Fingerprints!"

But Hortense didn't seem to hear her. She took the top letter out of the bundle and began reading. Her face showed fairly considerable confusion.

"I don't understand a thing; what do you think?"

The letter said:

> Abbé-Faria Prison Hospital, September [. . .]
> I'm writing to you from the slammer, my poor Gogor, I don't know what got into me this time, it's one of those diseases ya can't see when ya got it, so I'm in the Abbé-Faria prison hospital.

There followed news about various girlfriends and fellow inmates and outmates. It was signed, "Marguerite, your moldy little crouton."

"If that's his madly devoted mistress," Yvette said, "you don't have anything to worry about right now."

Hortense skimmed several other letters from the bundle; they didn't seem to enlighten her any further. She sighed and sat down on the bed.

"But what's all that?" she asked, pointing to the trunk's contents, which were now spread out over the bedspread.

"That, dearie," said Yvette, rushing along, "is, if I am not mistaken, a burglar's kit. That big iron thing there is called a jimmy; there are at least three different sizes here. And that, I do believe, is a diamond for cutting windows nice and cleanly so you can slip in quietly. And what you see there is a rope ladder."

At first Hortense stood there gaping. She looked at Yvette and suddenly seemed fifteen years younger, leaving her precariously close to not existing at all. And then the corners of her mouth spread open, her lips began to quiver, and suddenly she burst out laughing.

"Oh, that's just too much! How wonderful! How fantastic!" Hortense shouted, clapping her hands and stamping her feet in excitement as she hugged Yvette's knees, choked with laughter, held her sides while looking at the jimmy, then broke up with laughter again.

"It's wonderful, just wonderful, my lover isn't cheating on me, my lover is a burglar!"

"Fine, if you want to look at it that way," Yvette said.

She waited for things to calm down a little.

"Would you care to explain to me why you thought he was cheating on you?" asked Yvette.

"Well," said Hortense as she kissed the jimmy on the lips, "it happened like this: you know how he told me he was a roving night antique dealer?"

"Yes, I know," Yvette said, "didn't that seem a little strange to you?"

"No," said Hortense, "what's strange about that?"

"Oh, did I say strange?" said Yvette.

"Only, I wanted him to spend the night with me, and he wouldn't. He goes out every night after ten and rarely comes back before seven in the morning; I don't know exactly when because I'm asleep—we make love so much I don't even have the strength to go to work. Not to mention my thesis!"

"And Morgan?" asked Yvette.

"Oh, he never runs down, he claims it's because of his ancestry. He's half English, half Poldevian, you know."

"Poldevian . . . I didn't know that," Yvette said.

"Yes, evidently his father—he's a prince—left when he was young. And that's what put the bee in my bonnet; I wondered if maybe I couldn't satisfy him, even though I do my best. He says I'm gifted, you know," Hortense said, as if he were her first lover and Yvette wasn't up to date on her personal life. "And then I told myself maybe I wasn't enough for him and he had someone else on the side. Not at night, of course, he works then, but I didn't see why he had to go out again during the afternoon after sleeping all morning. He never wants to go to the movies, they're showing all the Hitchcocks, you know, and I had thought . . ."

"I know," said Yvette. "Well?"

"Well," said Hortense, who seemed slightly ashamed. "Well, the other day I followed him. As usual, he left with a big, full suitcase. He kept walking for quite a while; I had a hard time keeping up with him. He walked over to Boulevard Cornichon-Moulinet; there's a huge apartment building there, very impressive. He rang, and a woman came down to let him in. He stayed for about fifteen minutes (I told myself she couldn't be it), and when he left again the suitcase looked less heavy. How silly I am, he was just going around peddling his merchandise!"

"And none too soon," said Yvette. "And then?"

"Well, then he kept on going. He walked into another neighborhood, and each time he would stay for a little while. I told myself it had to be one of those women but that he was just stopping by to make a date (he never makes phone calls when he's here), I don't know, I was sick with jealousy. When he got home, the suitcase looked empty. Then I came back. I said I had been at the Library (he didn't pay attention to what I was saying, he's never jealous!), and I asked him really casually where he had gone. And he said: 'No place in particular, I just walked around.' That made me absolutely sure, and that's why I said to myself that I absolutely had to know, and I called you, and there you go. Now everything's fine."

Yvette did not think everything was as fine as all that, but she didn't want to rain on Hortense's restarted parade.

"I should have suspected something anyway," Hortense said after a moment's thought.

They were having coffee in the kitchen. The trunk had been closed up again and returned to its place.

"The other day he came back with these Japanese typewriters and asked me if I knew anyone who would be interested in buying one. He had more like them. I didn't quite see how that was a line of merchandise that would interest antique dealers! He just showers me with presents—little trinkets, a dozen old-fashioned embroidered napkins, a mink coat (really not in very good shape) —he's very generous."

It was left at that.

"Still," said Sinouls, "you could have made her see that subtraction and addition are symmetric operations, and that he could very well be . . ."

"I know," Yvette said, "but she looked so relieved to find out that he definitely wasn't cheating on her (just between us, I don't see where he would find the time, he's certainly a busy young man!) that I didn't dare rain on her parade. Nothing very serious can happen to her anyway—he doesn't seem like a bad boy, even if he *is* a burglar. I could have preached morals at her . . ."

"Oh, morals," Sinouls said. "Ever since I fell off that horse . . ."

". . . you haven't had your sense of morality, we know," said his daughters, Armance and Julie, cutting him off in midsentence.

They had been hearing that quip for almost eighteen years.

"What a sucker that Hortense is," Armance said to Julie when they were alone; "what a sucker!"

"By the way," Yvette said, "how's the concert for the dedication going?"

"Fine," said Sinouls. "I've been officially chosen to do the concert. Fustiger's the one who got it for me."

"So what are you going to play?"

"Well, I conducted a little musicological investigation at the Library, since I had to find something appropriate to the occasion—something involving Poldevia. And I found it: it's a Telemann chaconne written after one of his many stays in the inns of Poldevia. He had been invited by one of the Princes and brought back twelve cantatas and eleven quartets, not to mention these wonderful little unknown organ pieces: it's a chaconne in thirty-six variations, but instead of simply varying the melody, as usual (it's an old Poldevian folk song rather like that piece from Berry—you know, the one that starts out: 'Berrichon, chon chon...'), he has six practically independent melodic lines that he then twists around each other in a manner that is quite complicated but very pleasant all the same and uses all the stops. But the best part is the way it ends at the very moment when, if it went on, it would come back to the opening theme. I don't know if the Poldevian Princes will appreciate it, but it's good fun to play in any event. Listen to a little bit of it."

And Sinouls went over to his blaster, on which his cassette player was balanced. When he was working up a piece of organ music, he would record himself. This allowed him to listen to himself later, at his leisure, and check for weaknesses in his interpretation of the music while lying on his couch with a beer in front of him. The Telemanno-Poldevian music rose up both virile and tender, with that mix of musical flowers, as popular as they are luxurious and scholarly, for which the Hamburg master, a lover of tulips as well as passacaglias, had the secret. "Berrichon, chon chon"'s melancholy melody, made slightly Oriental, spicy, and exotic by its stay in the heights of the Poldevian mountains, filled the Sinoulses' autumnal living room. It mixed with the smell of the autumn tea roses that Madame Sinouls had arranged into an *ikebana* on the table, at the foot of which Balbastre was snoring as he dreamed of his long-lost love, that little bitch Voltige.

"It's funny," said Yvette, "the way Poldevia keeps turning up wherever you look nowadays. You know, the inspector handling the case of the Hardware-Store Horror..."

"He came to see you too?" Sinouls asked.

"Yes, and he asked me if I had seen a Poldevian statuette in the neighborhood; I wonder. . ."

"What?" said Sinouls, for the chaconne was then going through a particularly athletic passage.

"I wonder," said Yvette, "if something like that wasn't in Hortense's boyfriend's little trunk."

"Like what?" asked Sinouls, who hadn't heard a thing, for he had just realized that he was playing a bit too fast between the eighteenth and twenty-third variations.

"Nothing," said Yvette, "I must be wrong."

THE THIRD AND FINAL BETWEEN-TWO-CHAPTERS
THE POLDEVIAN VENUS

But of course Yvette, as you, dear perceptive Reader, have guessed, was not mistaken: Prince Gormanskoï—for it was indeed he, the missing heir to the throne of the Principality of Poldevia, currently a burglar by trade and madly in love with the beautiful Hortense—had in his trunk one of the six original casts of the famed Poldevian Venus or Venus with Snail, the work of that brilliant Poldevian Renaissance genius, the goldsmith Malvenido Escargotdzoï.

In any event, the statuette in question was a tasteful, mannerist-style jade piece depicting a beautiful goddess holding a snail in her arms. And you must also suspect, dear Reader, that the statuettes sought by Inspector Arapède and Inspector Blognard in the context of their investigation were mediocre clay replicas of this Poldevian cultural treasure.

The snail was of a respectable size; he had put out his horns and was examining the goddess's very evident charms with unabashed admiration.

22

ARMANCE AND JULIE
GO BOATING

The first Sunday in October dawned beautifully. The sun, not as young as it would have liked to be, needed more time to get warmed up; the wee hours of the morning were already nippy, and coats were getting ready to come out. But from Friday noon on, you would have sworn it was summer; everybody rushed out of the City.

The Sinoulses and Yvette put the chaise longues back out in the garden. Armance and Julie had gotten a phone call from Madame Orsells, who needed their help taking care of the twins (hers); she had at first requested just Armance but had then reflected and realized that two was not too many. The Orsells twins, Adèle and Idèle, were real little brats, but Armance and Julie—there's nothing for twins like twins, as they say—were completely capable of handling them. Madame Orsells had unexpectedly been called on to spend the entire day typing an important typescript under the dictation of her husband, who was to turn it in to the printer on Monday. The Sinouls twins accepted the job most happily, for the pocket money, of course, but also because they really liked Madame Orsells, nee Hénade Jamblique, and her calm, sad, blond look.

53's D stairway reeked of bleach and silence, for all its residents had rushed out onto the roads after hearing the first Saturday weather report. The sound of Madame Orsells's electronic typewriter—a Smith-Corona 2000 with fabric ribbons (35.50 francs for about thirty typed pages, with automatic correction for the last ten characters, character by character otherwise)—was not yet to be heard, but only her deep yet tender voice singing a ballad in the kitchen while the twins drank their Ovaltine (bought for them by their father in New York during the last International Applied Philosophy Congress) and devoured large plates of pancakes with maple syrup (brought back this time from Montreal and the meeting of Philosophonic Philosophers of North America and Europe), six for each. Madame Orsells was singing: "You say you shall hang from the nearest tree, but Lysander, what fright to the birds that will be!" The melody dipped melancholically on the last verse, and Madame Orsells repeated "to the birds that will be!" She was standing in front of the stove, flipping pancakes one after the other before putting them on her daughters' plates: one for Adèle, one for Idèle, each dripping with maple syrup the color of honey and sap and topped with a pat of butter melting in its hot dough-prison; the Sinouls twins were already drooling. The Orsells twins, however, were content to eat without lifting a finger to help their mother, all the while criticizing her with application.

"That's the stupidest song I've ever heard," Adèle said, looking straight ahead out the window.

"You're right," said Idèle. "Birds could not be afraid of Lysander's corpse, their intellect is much too limited to draw a distinction between living and dead, at least for humans."

Madame Orsells said nothing; to Armance and Julie's great internal indignation, no smack reddened either young Orsells's cheek; their mother continued the song to its forseeable conclusion while tending to the making of her pancakes, delicious as usual. She was wearing a long black dress and one shoe (the other foot was bare), and had a long blond braid that ran down the length of her back to the cleft in her buttocks; she had a long, thick, round neck and fat shoulders on which her head lolled with a strange grace.

The quartet of young ladies departed. Madame Orsells kissed them in succession lightly on each cheek, making eight kisses in all:

"Goodbye, Madame," said Armance. "We'll bring them back at six, after their afternoon snack, O.K.?"

"Call me Hénade," said Madame Orsells. "And that will be just fine."

Going down the stairs, you could hear her voice, singing out a bit more brightly now: "With her I lived three good years, Till one day she finally told me, You look like mother and father, those dears, Brother-lover, it was my destiny! And that is why...," but at that moment Monsieur Orsells cut her off, and the rest of the couplet was lost.

Armance and Julie had put together a program designed to ensure their strategic superiority at all times. To begin with, they would go rowing on the lake; next they would go back home for lunch: there Yvette on the one hand and Sinouls on the other would each be able to answer in his or her own way any dialectic offensive the young ladies initiated; and finally, for the afternoon, the heart of their effort: they would see whether, after *Night of the Living Dead*, the little Orsellsès still had such entrenched beliefs about the difference between living and dead.

The lake was located in a slightly remote part of the City that could be reached by a bus line whose terminus was right next to the boathouse. If you arrived fairly early in the morning, you could easily rent a boat and, given the water's great expanse, find a quiet spot somewhere around the island to read, daydream, sunbathe, or kiss, if that was your purpose; Armance knew this spot well from having used it copiously all summer with different boys, to Old Man Sinouls's great jealousy. Upon reaching an intensely tranquil little nook she had spotted, Armance took the Jane Austen novel she was reading from her purse and the T-shirt she was wearing from her back, thus explosing her little round breasts to the still misty, yet warm golden air that was mild enough for her delicate skin. Julie did the same, but in a blond way, and plunged into a passionate reading of a book on the thermodynamics of flame, her latest discovery. The twins looked at each other (we mean the Orsells twins, of course; we know it's a little confusing having two pairs of twins, but there's nothing to be done about it, that's the way it happened!).

"Papa says," reported Adèle, "that girls become complete idiots once something starts to grow there."

"Yes," Idèle echoed, "he says it's either 'tits' [she pointed to her chest] or 'that' [she pointed to her head] [the twins went to a progressive bilingual school and very often spoke to one another in English]."

Armance did not react, instead continuing to read her chapter of Jane Austen; the twins realized they would have to shift into a higher gear:

"Papa says," reported Idèle, "that mama is remarkably stupid."

"She believes," said Adèle, picking up this thread as if to explain, "that everything starts from one, a philosophical opinion that was refuted centuries ago."

Without saying a word, Julie stood up and tilted the boat at a most threatening angle. The message was clear, and the girls sensed they could not go too far. They began reading their favorite comic books: *Plato's Banquet; Lucky Locke Versus Spinoza; The Moral Derby;* they would interrupt one another from time to time to make an acerbic comment about one of their classmates or, indirectly, about their mother, or to invoke one of their father's opinions, but always staying within the limits of the armed truce imposed by the grown-ups. Time passed.

The ducks came up to the boat; they were most dignified ducks, having been imported from England—Cambridge, to be exact—as part of the recently enacted cultural exchange policy; accustomed to rubbing elbows with Nobel Prize–winning physicists, watching apples fall on the lawns of Isaac Newton's colleges, or punting on the Cam between the weeping willows while discussing the virtues of the theory of definite description with Lord Bertrand Russell, they felt somewhat intellectually malnourished, but they liked Armance and Julie, in whom they detected something like a scent of their native country. Adèle and Idèle showered them with Socratic commentary and brioche, and in general a fine morning was had by one and all.

They rowed back to the boathouse. Armance and Julie sang as they rowed:

"Berrichon chon chon, your big buns buns buns, bring all the young boys on the run!"

They circled the island in this manner:

"Berrichon chon chon, your big buns buns buns, look like throw-pillows my mom's done!"

There are fourteen couplets like that (not all ending in *un* sounds, either; you move imperceptibly and artistically to variants like *in*—"Berrichon chon chon, your big buns buns buns, they first move out and then move in"—or even *an*—"are envied by my shriveled old nan"); Armance and Julie had learned this beautiful, melancholy ballad native to lower Berry from a record given them by Yvette, in which the lament is performed by that great singer Maiety Chimelel* with tympany accompaniment. The Orsells girls blushed with shame at this grotesque manifestation of bad taste.

During lunch (mostly leg of lamb and sherbet), Adèle gave a brief summary of Saint Thomas's *Theological Survey,* and Idèle, a devastating critique of Wittgenstein's *Philosophical Investigations.* Between two mouthfuls of sherbet, she remarked that, according to her father, Inspector Blognard would never solve the case of the Hardware-Store Horror, for "his approach is too Cartesian" (that was how Sinouls understood the sentence while listening absent-mindedly, for she had in fact said "Carthusian," an Anglicism, and not "Cartesian"). At another point, Idèle indicated that Poldevian philosophy was going to amaze us all, her father had predicted it. It happened that those two sentences, juxtaposed in Sinouls's forgetful mind and memory, came out the next day during his

---

* On the flip side is her famed "Dictionary Song," in which she sings selected words in alphabetical order while humming Ligeti's *Continuum,* no small feat.

great conversation with Madame Yvonne, and strangely enough Sinouls did not attribute the opinions to himself, but credited Orsells with the thesis that Inspector Blognard would not solve the case because he was seeking a Cartesian interpretation, whereas the solution was obviously of a Poldevian nature. That was the last link in the long chain of deductions that finally in fact led to the case's conclusion.

Armance and Julie brought the Orsells girls back home to their parents as planned and then had to listen to the text typed by Madame Orsells in its entirety. They would much rather have skipped this ordeal, but they hadn't been paid yet.

In this text, one of the jewels of the Orsellian method, a preamble first indicated that the text in question represented a Revolution in Thought (if one wants a text accepted by the papers and scholarly journals, it is essential that it begin by announcing a Revolution in Thought; the author should also explain that he is an outcast ignored by all established schools of thought, an intellectual dissident, a maverick whose apprehension of the truest Truth will overturn the established dogmas of his contemporaries) and that this Revolution was based on the Golden Rule of Ontethics, which we presented in Chapter 17 in the same terms used by its inventor. The Golden Rule was explained, stated, and illustrated by numerous examples. Having thus blazed the trail, Orsells entered into the heart of the matter: to wit, after years of searching like a navigator on the ocean of thought; having no other guide than the compass of the Rule, or like an explorer of the instellar abysses of morality, the Rule being his telescope, he had seen (and the reference to Galileo was made explicit here, in an allusion to the preamble) what no one else had dared perceive: The Deep Unity of Human Knowledge built around the secret central kernel that he alone was able to put in the hands of the public, since he had already begun to do so, albeit partially, in works including . . . (there followed a list of all his books currently in print); this very secret, very ancient, central knowledge was not to be described just yet, that would be the subject of a later book, but he could already give it a name, and that name was *Ology;* at the heart of human knowledge, there was and would always be, forever after, Ology; it would be necessary to grow accustomed to thinking *ologistically,* to

break out of our petty habits, to overthrow the privileged capital-
ists of knowledge in a philosophic October Revolution and tune in
to Ology (this was the text's lyric and prophetic part; storm clouds
would gather if we weren't sufficiently quick about completing this
essential transformation). All disciplines, scientific and otherwise,
the hard sciences as well as the soft, would obviously have to be
rearticulated with respect to the central kernel. Many of them
would have to change, beginning with their names; for some that
wouldn't be too difficult, as the ground had already been broken,
so to speak: psychology would become *psyco-ology,* the discipline's
ologistic basis being thereby made apparent, liberated from its
ancient shell; bacteriology would be *bacteri-ology,* geology would be
ge-ology, that all went without saying, but others would be subjected
to more sweeping changes. Mathematics could not remain in its
present state, nor chemistry, nor physics. This last, for example,
would be *physis-ology* (so as not to be confused with *physi-ology,*
which is something else entirely) from then on. In this way, things
would be made clear: for every science there would be on the one
hand its *ology,* and on the other, apart from the union, on the left
side, its analogic or nonologic residue, which would have to be
restructured in such a way that it could be put at Ology's service:
"In all things," Orsells said, in one of thse striking aphorisms for
which he had the knack, "Ology should be put at the controls."

The Master dictated this impressive work to his wife on that
October Sunday when Armance and Julie went boating.

23

SINOULS, MADAME
YVONNE,
AND THE INFINITE

Madame Yvonne was some fifty years old; she carried her age with open, graceful aplomb. She had not always been Madame Yvonne, and the Gudule Bar had not always been the Gudule Bar, yet even if these two entities were only some ten years old, they had existed under another name for a solid thirty. It happened like this: Madame Yvonne went "into service" at the same time as her fellow villager Madame Eusèbe (and Madame Yvonne knew the latter's real first name perfectly well, but she didn't see it as any sort of guilty secret and never would have mentioned it), working for Arsène in the Saint Gudule Wine and Coal Shop, We Deliver. You could still see the old sign at the entrance to the new establishment, but let's not get ahead of ourselves.

Just as the faithful, upon leaving Mass, hurried to indulge in the sin of gluttony by wolfing down cream puffs at the Crussant bakery (run by Old Man Crussant, Crussant's father, during the early postwar period we are talking about), symmetrically and simultaneously the Saint Gudule Wine and Coal Shop filled up with men who came to drink down some of the red stuff and eat sausage, head cheese, rillette, or lardon. There was a counter for Arsène, the owner, a back room with a few tables, and between the two a sort of long, taut rope where the drunkest were hung up to dry out. There were in fact two ropes that they were leaned up against; they would snore, their arms dangling at their sides; then mothers, wives, daughters, maids, or mistresses (who often filled several of these roles at once) would come fetch them and drag them back home. Yvonne waitressed against the ropes and in the back room for twenty years. Brave and strong, she was Arsène's mistress and had the drunks' respect. Serving the wine and lugging the coal gave Arsène a powerful thirst; he drank. He drank so much and so often that one day the pink elephants came to see him in the bar and wouldn't leave, until finally Yvonne decided to pack him off to the hospital.

He stayed there for a year (he was on the verge of cirrhosis); when he returned, a gaunt, aproned figure who no longer drank, he found changes. Yvonne, whom he had married not long before, had turned everything inside out: the Saint Gudule Wine and Coal Shop had become the Gudule Bar. To give Arsène, who was no longer able to serve wine because the red color would kill him, something to do, she decided to switch over to beer (he didn't like beer, there was no danger). The wine cellar was converted into a beer garden in which Arsène was the head gardener. They carried three hundred sixty-six different brands: Belgian beer, English beer, Andorran beer, Japanese beer, American beer in cans, Yugoslavian beer, cherry beer, near beer, Joseph Conrad beer (with the facsimile of a letter of endorsement from the novelist to the owner of the establishment), and Samuel Johnson beer, with the famous quote "No other institution in the world has brought man so much happiness as the pub," for that was Arsène's ambition: to turn his subterranean kingdom into a pub. He traded in his black apron for a tweed jacket and even began smoking a brier pipe. But along with the birth of the Gudule Bar came that of Madame Yvonne;

she had been Yvonne and then, for a little while during the hospital months, Madame Arsène; becoming the boss had now changed her name once and for all. Arsène became Monsieur Yvonne. He got a good laugh out of that. The Gudule Bar also began selling tobacco and newspapers. Sinouls came in frequently to resupply himself with beer and pick up the latest local and international gossip, the former from conversation with Madame Yvonne, the latter by buying the *Paper.* He had become official taster to Arsène, a.k.a. Monsieur Yvonne (who affectionately called him Consul for some reason even he didn't know), and one of Madame Yvonne's favorite customers, for reasons that will soon be made clear.

Although a longtime resident of the neighborhood, Sinouls had never patronized the Wine and Coal Shop, and it was only the remodeling done by Madame Yvonne that led him to cross the establishment's threshold. Still just starting out and with an uncertain future (the remodeling had set her back a pretty penny), Madame Yvonne always dropped everything for Sinouls, whom she thought an important customer since he was Saint Gudule's organist, a position that gave him a great deal of social standing in her eyes. That day Sinouls was accompanied by one of his colleagues, an amateur organist who was an astronomer by trade. After having a drink, they decided to buy the *Paper.* Sinouls went up to the counter (the newspapers being to the left of the cash register), picked up two copies of the *Paper,* pulled out his change purse, and said to Madame Yvonne as he was paying:

"Two *Papers,* one for him, one for me. But are you sure they're really the same? You understand, Madame, that we don't want to be reading different news."

Madame Yvonne hurriedly set him straight.

"My dear sir, all the copies of the *Paper* I sell contain exactly the same news—not one line is different, I assure you." She let her tone of righteous indignation convey that she would have immediately sent packing the wretch who dared send her copies of the *Paper* that were not completely and utterly identical, as requested by her two customers.

Sinouls bowed to her very formally and walked off without

laughing, very proud of his little joke. And Madame Yvonne, who thought that maybe he was a little cracked or a little slow, developed a certain affection for him. She protected him, served him before everyone else, and always said with a smile as she gave him his *Paper:*

"It's definitely the genuine article, I guarantee it."

Not long afterward, the American astronauts landed on the moon. Monsieur and Madame Yvonne were glued to their television (the set was in back in the large room; it was used for the big soccer matches) just like everybody else, and in the morning (because of the time difference, you had to stay up most of the night) everyone leaned on the counter with his large or small coffee, black or light, or his brandy, and was a little overwrought from the lack of sleep and the importance of the event (oh yes, at that time people thought it was an extremely important event! How the world changes, eh?). The quality of the picture and the enormity of the thing were discussed; then a debate broke out among the customers over how great a distance it really was. It certainly seemed like a long way, all right, but *how* long? Some said that it was certainly farther than Baluchistan, and others, that it was certainly as far as Bécon-les-Bruyères. Madame Yvonne turned to Old Man Sinouls because he was a man of numbers and learning—he had to be, to make music with Saint Gudule's great pipes. Monsieur Sinouls tossed out a few numbers, spoke of the sun and the planets, of antipodes and parsecs and meridians, drew diagrams with his ballpoint on paper napkins; that was all well and good, but in the course of his lecture he began talking about how the distance in question was no big deal compared to that between the stars, and before Madame Yvonne's at first skeptical eyes he worked up an impressive chart of the journey traveled by light-emitting photons in the immense spaces between the stars, spaces outside the range even of NASA's most powerful rockets. He spoke of light-years; he spoke of Proxima Centauri, of the Andromeda nebula, and for modesty's sake he threw a veil over time paradoxes. It was a veritable space opera there in the Gudule Bar.

When Madame Yvonne went to bed that same night, she began thinking about light-years. She tried to visualize them, and she thought about all those stars receding into the distance, with nothing much in between for a foothold, and about how there were even more even farther away, with poor little rays of light getting all out of breath making the trip (who knows why) and how those rays, despite their great speed, didn't seem to be making much better time than a Mercedes caught in rush-hour traffic on the highway. Madame Yvonne couldn't sleep. All those distances and unfathomably faraway stars had given her a headache, and she shook Monsieur Yvonne, who had been snoring peacefully at her side:

"Arsène," she said to him, "the thought of those infinite spaces frightens me."

This episode, which she had not forgotten, had redoubled Old Man Sinouls's prestige in her eyes, and during the numerous breaks from his parching task that he spent in the Gudule Bar, she frequently consulted him on the great problems of the day, for her own entertainment and edification as well as for that of her clientele, for such is the duty of any self-respecting bar owner, and Madame Yvonne was, above all, a conscientious bar owner.

And that is why, on the day following the Sunday on which the Sinouls girls had taken care of the Orsells girls, Madame Yvonne asked Old Man Sinouls what he thought of the case.

"Now that Inspector Blognard is on the job," she said as she had been saying every Monday for months now, "the criminal really has to watch his p's and q's."

It was at this moment that Sinouls's memory, through one of the short circuits it was famous for, simultaneously called up two thoughts that it did not first recognize as being indirect in origin, having been transmitted from Orsells by way of Adèle and Idèle and then Armance and Julie. They instead struck him as being his own, emerging fully armed from his brain. And since it is preferable, if one is even slightly in his right mind, to make of two simultaneous ideas one unified thought instead of two simultaneous or successive but independent statements, Old Man Sinouls said:

"Blognard will never solve the case."

Madame Yvonne was a bit taken aback, for Old Man Sinouls,

although he was always making ironic comments about the police in general, had never before given evidence of a particularly marked skepticism regarding the great Blognard, to whom (as he had once confided to Yvette) he even "tipped his hat." She therefore pressed him for an explanation, which he wanted to give anyway since the double-idea-made-one that had just come to him was burning to be let out:

"It's quite simple," he said. "Blognard is using a Cartesian approach; that's all he knows. But this case clearly reeks of Poldevia. He must look on the Poldevian side, otherwise he'll never get anywhere."

And since Madame Yvonne, sensing a great "topic of conversation" for the day, pressed him for a further explanation, he added (to his great surprise, for he didn't know where the remark came from):

"Oh, I've thought that for a long time. But everyone seems to be getting the same idea. Why, just yesterday my daughter, who, as you know, baby-sits for the Orsellses [Madame Yvonne knew; actually, she knew quite a bit more about Armance and Julie's activities than their poor old dad], told me that's exactly what Orsells thinks, you know, the Orsells who lives in 53, the bullshit artist [Old Man Sinouls scorned philosophy]."

Obviously Madame Yvonne knew Professor Orsells. He didn't come to the Gudule Bar very often, but he was a nationally respected figure, so she had to know him.

This conversation does not have any great importance in and of itself, but it so happens that it took place (from the verb "to take place"; the conversation takes place, was taking place, took place; that's the way it's said, or the way it should be said) shortly before Inspector Arapède's morning briefing of Blognard and the Narrator on the bench in the square (the middle one, with its back to Saint Gudule's facade), at a time when he had come to resupply himself with Guinness and to order a double Shirley Temple to go for his boss. Arapède did not listen to conversations in cafés absentmindedly, for he knew that café conversations provided the basis for the solutions to eleven percent of all criminal cases. He was acquainted with the two participants, each of whom had merited a chapter in his long book on the case; so he listened to them with

both of his large winglike ears (a detail we may now add to
Arapède's description) and recorded Sinouls's revelation of the link,
established by Orsells, between the case and Poldevia. This was
one of the last clues before the solution of the mystery.

Madame Yvonne and Old Man Sinouls got going on Poldevia:
its history, its geography, and the problem of immigrant Poldevian
workers. Old Man Sinouls whipped out everything he remembered, most of it coming from the article entitled "Poldevia" in the
Great Rationalist Encyclopedia. The Reader is encouraged to have
recourse to it.

CONTINUATION OF CHAPTER 18 (END)

Professor Orsells only allowed his employee Tyucha one trip outside
per day. He would have liked to have entrusted her to his daughters,
Adèle and Idèle, who would have been able to instruct her philo-
sophically while making her trot behind their bicycles, but Madame
Orsells, nee Hénade Jamblique, had taken pity on her, so Tyucha
was under Veronica Bouelles's care. She would take her to the sandbox, where they could both play and piss in tranquillity and se-
renity. Tyucha's fur on those fall days harmonized harmoniously with
the color of the leaves on the chestnut trees, which were turning
redder and redder. "How harmoniously Tyucha's fur harmonizes
with the autumn red of the chestnut trees," Alexander Vladimirovich would think while watching her play in the sandbox.

But at the same time, that same sight was, without Alexander
Vladimirovich realizing it (Love makes even cats careless), piercing
Madame Eusèbe's breast with the red-hot poker of jealousy. Armed
with a pair of binoculars inherited from her late father, she staked
out Professor Orsells's window and soon had no doubt about the
harsh reality of Alexander Vladimirovich's betrayal. She cried a
great deal and decided to get revenge.

And so it came to pass that one fine morning Professor Orsells
received an anonymous letter. The author, who signed it "a friend
who wishes you well," was, as the perceptive Reader has guessed,
Madame Eusèbe! And to further ensure her anonymity she
had written the letter in blue ink (instead of the purple she

most often used) and *without making a single spelling mistake.*
"Your cat is cheating on you," the letter said. "Ask her what she does under your nose and behind your back while she purrs in your employ. Oh, today's youth! Signed: a friend who wishes you well."

(Continuation and conclusion at the end of Chapter 26.)

24

HORTENSE LOSES
HER ILLUSIONS

This, the twenty-fourth chapter, begins with a bit of drama: contrary to the treacherous claims and insinuations of the Author (who put them in a parenthetical remark in Chapter 2, not suspecting that, thanks to a friend of my wife, I would have access to the proofs that were sent chapter by chapter to the director of the series while the book was being printed, and that I would be able to wait with remarkable cool for the best moment to reveal what follows), and contrary to what I myself said in Chapter 16 (but I said it in all sincerity, I really thought as much at that moment, and that idiot of an Author fell headfirst into the trap I had inadvertently set for him, leading him—he thought he was so clever—to claim that I "had lost any chance with Hortense" and to gossip about my very chaste—well, almost chaste—relations with that charming young Poldevian, Magroorska [a real little pony, and what delectable breasts!]), not only had I not stopped thinking about Hortense, but, having been freed by my professional success, I allowed myself to love her; and I did love her; and what is more, I was not unaware of the facts of her life, because my mother (a happy coincidence) was a great friend of Yvette's, meaning that I was invited to her home (all the more frequently since we were neighbors), and Yvette had told me everything; and I, like Yvette but even more so, of course—she had a tendency to take all that too lightly—was worried about Hortense and impatient to see her open her eyes to the true nature of this burglar she had fallen for with such charming spontaneity, owing to her youth and inexperience as well as her being consumed by the study of a philosophical system as complex and intellectually stimulating as that of the great Orsells. (The Author is looking good, don't you think? And that's not all, wait till you hear the rest!)

Everything I am telling you here I have from a reliable source, first Yvette, and then Hortense herself later on.

In the days following the discovery, made with Yvette's help, of the trunk and its contents, Hortense felt reassured and dove back into the delights of her amorous relations. She began by confessing her curiosity to Morgan (he was quite up to date, since Yvette, in opening the trunk, had broken the Poldevian pony hair he attached to the clasp so as to be sure, each time he went out, that no one had been pawing through his things; hence he had known that very night that Hortense had learned of his true profession, and he was ready to disappear if need be). She told him she didn't blame him at all, since everyone should follow his natural inclination, and she was even happier when, as she was skillfully questioning him indirectly and theoretically so as to be able to apply Orsells's Golden Rule of Ontethics, he answered in the most satisfying way by pointing out that he considered everyone perfectly entitled to act this way (his ancient Poldevian bandit heritage was showing itself, but Hortense suspected nothing) and saying that if he, Morgan, encountered someone strong enough to rob him, he would get a good laugh out of it (and thus, by means of his application of the Golden Rule, he proved in Hortense's eyes not only that he was perfectly justified in his actions, but that in fact he necessarily and morally *should* act accordingly, in all possible worlds [including worlds in which there was no Poldevia, but perhaps Hortense could not push the reasoning that far, since she was unaware of his birthright; perhaps he was *necessarily* Poldevian—that is to say, Poldevian in all possible worlds, including those in which there is no Poldevia]).

In short, Hortense was delighted to be in the arms of a burglar, and she allowed him to commit breaking and entering on her in all ways imaginable. It was the Indian summer of their love. They spent deliciously lubricious afternoons together. They ate egg noodles or pizzas lovingly reheated by Hortense, accompanied by macaroons that Madame Crussant had put into various snacks to keep her from wasting away. Toward evening, Morgan would go off to his burglaries, coming back to sleep in the morning. It would have lasted, Hortense thought it was going to last, but it was not to last. I must say that it was all rather hard on me, particularly since Yvette knew nothing of my feelings for Hortense and spared me no detail; had it not been for the excitement and distraction provided by the investigation's nearing conclusion, I don't think I would have been able to stand it (Oh, and just what would you have done, fathead?—*Author's note*) (He's getting pissed!—*Narrator's note*) (Knock it off! Do you think your readers could care less about your little squabbles?—*Series Director's note, passed on to the editor and approved by the editorial board, the secretary, the typesetter, the secretary's lover, and the marketing director*).

It happened in the following way:

The weather continued to be pleasant. The sunny days were like Norwegian omelets surrounding cold but invigorating nights. The first day of classes was drawing near, however, and gloomy weather was being forecast with more and more likelihood and insistence. The *Haute Delicatesserie*'s winter campaign was being designed by its grand strategists, meaning that it was no longer possible for Hortense to put off the essential operation of *putting away her summer clothes and getting out her winter clothes,* for three reasons:

—First, once school began, Hortense would have to take classes. They would use up what little energy she would be able to muster in the wake of Morgan's amorous fervor.

—Second, as soon as the weather got really cold, and especially rainy, it would no longer be possible to wear summer clothes and would then be necessary to move on to winter clothes. Besides, several of her friends had already taken this step, so she couldn't put off the operation for very much longer.

—Last, but definitely not least, was the third person: Hortense could not undertake this wardrobe transformation all alone, because:

First (i.e., first subreason of the third reason), she had a tremendous number of summer as well as winter clothes—everything had to be moved around, and her drawers, bureaus, and closets all had to be reorganized; second, for this project Hortense called on her mother, who decided what should disappear and what was missing and should therefore be filled in through Hortense's father's sadism; third, because of the *Haute Delicatesserie*'s Christmas campaign (choosing varieties of turkey, ordering pâté, truffles . . .), Hortense's father would soon be very nervous and would need his wife's presence at every moment, meaning that she would not be available for the *Rearranging* and the shopping that went with it.

For all of these reasons (one, two, three-one, three-two, and three-three), Hortense phoned her mother, and they set up an early-afternoon get-together for Friday. Hortense sent Morgan away and began taking out her summer clothes.

Hortense's mother took one look at her daughter's wardrobe and immediately saw what should have been apparent to Hortense herself for a long time now, had she not been distracted, naive, young, inexperienced, and in love: to wit, *a huge amount of it was missing;* and what was missing was mostly her most expensive, most elegant, and rarest clothes, which the Reader, unless he too is young (or old, it makes little difference), inexperienced, and distracted by love, suspected from the outset. Hortense's mother grew pale. All the wildest hypotheses raced through her maternal heart (or rather her head, but after a distressing stay in her heart): drugs, a secret vice, abortion, a Man "sponging off her". . . —all the worst hypotheses that fill modern mothers with fright and worry and are associated with prefabricated stock phrases. Hortense did not at first understand her mother's indirect and terrified questions. Then she saw what she was getting at, and her eyes opened wide. She stammered, blushed, and reinforced simultaneously all her mother's most horrible and contradictory hypotheses by refusing to answer, and instead sending her off, with a promise that she would tell her everything, before sitting on her bed and bursting into tears.

She cried for fifty-three minutes. Then she wiped her eyes, took a very hot bath, and began to get angry (Bravo, Hortense! That's what I was waiting for! Dear, oh most dear Hortense—*Narrator's note*). Burglarizing country houses, bra factories, or jewelers was all well and good, that was Morgan's calling, his destiny, the Golden Rule practically forced him to do it, she had nothing against that. But setting upon her very own shoes, stealing from her on the sly and in the silent warmth of the *afterglow* (In *Gone with the Wind* that's what they call those moments when one basks amid the disorder of one's bed in that deliciously languid exhaustion that follows the most intensely passionate encounters)! He had stolen some of the most beautiful and expensive pairs from her shoe collection, it was too much! Suddenly Hortense saw Morgan in a different light, a light not at all flattering to him. She decided to consult Yvette. She phoned her and told her of her *Disillusion*.

Yvette acted immediately. It was 3:06 P.M. Three phone calls later, she convened a Strategy Session for 5:00 P.M. at Old Man Sinouls's place. Those taking part were Sinouls, his wife, his daughters and Balbastre (because of his great experience with the slings and arrows of love ever since Voltige), Yvette herself, and I, your Narrator. I was included in this key meeting because Yvette (aware of nothing) thought I could prove useful, given my ties to Blognard, if it turned out to be necessary to follow up on this little business by calling in the police. Aside from the decisions made there, the Strategy Session at the Sinoulses' resulted in the beginning of the friendship between Hortense and Armance (who thought Hortense was nice, even if she was a bit of a sucker for her age), a friendship that was useful to me later, when Armance did an internship with the Author's publisher.

Under Yvette's direction, the Strategy Session convened at 5:00 P.M. in the Sinoulses' living room, before a substantial plate of Crussant petits fours and cream puffs intended to encourage thought and stimulate the imagination. Hortense was dressed in a manner appropriate to her painful circumstances. She had chosen her most severe summer dress, the one she would have worn during a weekend in Wales, for example, where you can't see the ocean until you've stuck a foot in it, the mix of rain and fog is so dense; you stay in the pub or in your room and eat scones with Cornwall cream. Hortense's dress, however, tried to compensate for its severity by being generous at both the top and the bottom: at the top, by frequently revealing a delightful portion of Hortense's breasts whenever she leaned over to sink her spoon into a cream puff; at the bottom, by coming up, as if under its own power, rather high above her knees, whose involuntary separation, brought on by Hortense's distress, caused me to lose my breath and very nearly my voice as well, placed where I was in relation to her.

Yvette began by briefly explaining the reasons for my presence. Hortense didn't know me, but already I felt that the intensity of the looks I had given her from the Eusèbe grocery for more than a month had left some subliminal trace, for in less than a second she made it clear that she took me for her unconditional admirer (which was perfectly true), and I got the impression that, in spite of her unhappiness, she was not unable to stand me. I was more determined than ever to come to her aid and allow her to rid herself of the criminal who had so shamefully betrayed her.

Yvette then gave a quick summary of events up to that point, stressing Hortense's confident, innocent happiness, her great leniency at the time of the burglar's trunk being opened, and finally the tragic discovery early that very afternoon. She then concluded: "That is why I have called you here today. What is to be done?"

Sinouls offered to bust up the guy's face, provided that we hold his hands and feet. This suggestion was rejected unanimously, save one vote.

Going to the police was tabled for the moment. My inducing Blognard to intervene was seen only as a last resort.

"Now, tell me truthfully," Yvette said, "Have you decided to break up with him once and for all?"

She had. Hortense would not spend another night in the arms of the man who had stolen her shoes.

We talked.

We ate.

We drank tea, hot chocolate, Coca-Cola, and beer.

We put a plan of action into motion: to begin with, Sinouls and I, the Narrator, would go to Hortense's house to add a lock to the front door, since Morgan obviously had a complete set of Hortense's keys. Once that was done, Yvette would go to Hortense's and sleep in her guest room. Together they would wait for the criminal to come back. Then, protected by the door and Yvette, Hortense would say to him:

25

HORTENSE'S FIRST LOVE
FINAL SCENE

"It's no use trying, you're not coming in, Morgan," Hortense was to say firmly through the door when her deposed lover came back to her place at dawn, after a night of illegal activity, expecting to find rest at the deceived innocent's side.

It didn't exactly work out that way. Yvette and Hortense ate dinner in the apartment, Hortense had a bit to drink to drown her sorrows, they watched an old Donen movie on television, and then they went to bed. When they woke up, it was morning, and a piece of paper folded in quarters had been slipped under the door:

"I see that you know everything. Meet me at eleven in the square at the middle bench on the Saint Gudule side. Morgan."

"You're nuts, you can't go," Yvette said at the second Strategy

Session, hastily convened at 9:45 A.M. following the previous night's unexpected developments. "What's to stop him from giving his keys to one of his accomplices, and while he's jawing away in the park, the other guy is driving off with your whole wardrobe and all your shoes! You're nuts, you can't go!"

But Hortense proved intractable. She wanted to hear what he had to say. She certainly didn't love him anymore—he had deceived her too shamefully for that—but she could not deny him this last meeting.

An impasse developed, for Hortense absolutely refused to be accompanied by Sinouls or the Narrator, or even Armance, Julie, or Balbastre.

"Excuse me for just a minute," the Reader says to us, "but if my memory serves, first in Chapter 16 and more recently in Chapter 23, at the time of the conversation between Madame Yvonne and Old Man Sinouls overheard by Inspector Arapède, did you not say that this very bench is occupied every morning, since it is the point from which Inspector Blognard carries out his investigation? Would it not be possible," the Reader adds, "and excuse me for meddling in the creation of a novel, which is really none of my business, but still, I've been reading novels for a long time, I started at the age of seven with *Last of the Mohicans* before moving on, like everybody else, to *Remembrance of Things Past, The Sentimental Education, Pierrot mon ami,* and I don't know what all else, so you see, it's almost as though I had written novels myself, and that's why I'm allowing myself to make this suggestion; after all, wouldn't it be an elegant way to solve the problem of protecting Hortense while respecting her scruples if her conversation with Morgan were to take place on another bench (there are two others—one on each side, if I am not mistaken), and Monsieur Mornacier would most naturally be there as well, so he could not only keep an eye on Hortense, but could also witness the meeting and report it back to us—That's the Narrator's job, isn't it?"

We have let the Reader say what he has been dying to say, without interrupting, but now we must content ourselves with pointing out to him that the Putting away the Summer Clothes scene—which led to the first Strategy Session, and therefore to the second, which we would now be reporting if we were given the chance—took place on a Friday. Fine. After Friday comes Saturday, we all agree on that; Saturday is the weekend; Inspector Blognard is at home; Inspector Arapède is at home; there is no meeting on the bench in Grands-Edredons Square among those investigating the Case of the Hardware-Store Horror. There you have the answer to our Reader's well-meaning suggestion.

Time was growing short, however, for Hortense had to change for her meeting with Morgan.

Yvette proposed the following:

Hortense would go into the square; this was not wise, but since she absolutely insisted, all right. Armance and Julie would take the window in Yvette's office; looking through that window, one has a very clear view of the square; if anything suspicious happened, they were to immediately call Old Man Sinouls, who would be at home with Balbastre, ready to intervene. In any event, they were to call at the moment when, at the end of the meeting, Hortense was to propose to return Morgan's things to him (his burglar's trunk, his razor, and his toothbrush, along with his socks and his change of underwear) in exchange for her keys. This exchange was to be carried out at the foot of Hortense's stairway. Yvette and the Narrator would be in her apartment, where they would have been waiting ever since Hortense had left for her meeting, so as to avoid the possible carting off of her things by one of Morgan's accomplices if the requested encounter turned out to be a trap, as it well could.

This plan was voted in unanimously by those attending, with the exception of Balbastre, who had no desire to return to the square for a possible run-in with Alexander Vladimirovich.

When Hortense reached the square, he was already there. Her heart beat faster under her dress, but it was already a beat of nostalgic farewell. Love had fled, soon there would be nothing left but regret, which the sepia hues of memory would turn little by little into an amused tenderness. Morgan immediately saw that there was nothing to be done, and that is why we can now restore to him his real name and title and say: Prince Gormanskoï, gentleman and burglar, immediately saw that there was no hope left, for Hortense *had put on a fall dress and fall shoes.* This piece of evidence could not escape an eye as practiced as his. One of his life's charming and happy episodes was coming to an end. It could not have lasted much longer anyway, given coming events.

The last scene of Hortense's first love marked the end of a crucial period in her life. The scene's first part was witnessed by no one but Armance and Julie, who saw everything but heard nothing, and Alexander Vladimirovich, on whose testimony we are thus forced to rely for our account. And Alexander Vladimirovich, for reasons of his own, has greatly censored the dialogue between Hortense and her princely lover, so we must apologize for the many lacunae in our reporting of it.

It was a beautiful late morning in October, tinged with melancholy, of course. The slightly lazy sun was mild and cool, the leaves on the chestnut trees were in their red autumn livery, and the gleaming horse chestnuts covered with a fine flour or downy white dust at their base (the part of the nut that is not mahogany like the rest, but paler and grayer), were beginning to emerge from their still green and juicy husks like young breasts from a corsage; they fell on the skulls of passers-by with a joyful precision. I mean it was October. A fluffy little white cloud, shaped like a cloud for an angel in a baroque painting, was hanging over Saint Gudule's steeple, as if still waiting to find out the wind direction. The square was deserted, the sand was sprinkled about everywhere, and the residents were gone for one final picnic while the nice weather lasted.

Gormanskoï stood up when he saw Hortense:

"How are you, my very dearest," he said to her with great aplomb and ceremony.

Hortense was a bit taken aback; she had been expecting an ashamed, servile Morgan who would beg and whimper; his haughty formality caught her off guard.

"Oh, Morgan," she said, "how could you? I was ready to understand anything, to forgive anything, but my shoes! It's just not possible!"

"I do indeed owe you an apology. It is true that I was wrong, and I am not going to aggravate my misdeed by saying that I could not resist the temptation. But before I explain—if you will grant me the few minutes necessary for this operation—permit me to tell you that my name, as you suspected, is not Morgan. I can now reveal my real name to you, if you swear never to pass it on to a third party, *whoever it may be*. The interests of Europe and perhaps even the entire world are at stake."

Hortense swore (and kept her word—*Author's note*).

"My real name," continued the Prince, "is [..........(censored, as is most of what follows, by Alexander Vladimirovich)]. I am a p[..........] and P[..........]. My mother, a woman with the heart of a saint, was born in E[..........]. She is a direct descendant of Q[..........] V[..........]. From my earliest youth, [..] how could I let my aged mother [....................] jewels [............] pawnshop [....................] wage labor [.................................] she didn't [........ ....]. 'A P[............] p[..........] will never work with his h[..........] or in a b[.............] do you desire my d[...........] and my s[...........],' she said to me, what could I do? [...........................
....
...............................(we are summarizing. The conversation went on for fifty-three minutes, which makes almost twenty-three typed pages, carefully erased in all the key places by Alexander Vladimirovich)]. Will you forgive me one day, Hortense, and perhaps when I have regained my r[..........] K[...... ....], come to my c[...........] as my guest? I will introduce you to my mother. I am sure that in spite of the considerable difference in r[.............], you will have a great deal to talk about. My mother is a very simple person at heart. There you have it."

Hortense had listened to the Prince's speech without interrupting. During his story's most heartrending moments, she had wiped a discreet tear from one of her beautiful eyes, the right one, the one Morgan (for it was Morgan and not the Prince who had been her lover, and she would always remember him by that name) preferred. In the end she spontaneously held out her hand to him, and he kissed it. Then they walked off together in the direction of Hortense's apartment.

* * *

As soon as Armance and Julie saw that Hortense and her companion were leaving the square, they rushed to inform their father and especially Yvette, who was waiting with growing concern (mixed, in Sinouls's case, with growing hunger, for it was almost noon).

The building where Hortense lived could not be entered by simply pushing on the door, as could the Sinoulses'. The door to each of the stairways that opened on the vestibule or the courtyard were locked day and night. Each apartment owner (there were no renters, only owners) had his key; for visitors there was an electronically controlled lock system and an intercom. Yvette had planned the exchange (keys for bag) so that the scene would take place in front of the intercom, allowing her to hear the conversation and intervene with the help of Georges (I'm Georges—*Narrator's note*) if the need arose.

A noise could be heard.

GORMANSKOÏ (to us; but to Yvette and Georges, who are listening in on the intercom, the voice is still Morgan's): Here.

HORTENSE: Here.

GORMANSKOÏ: Our affair has come to an end. It was nice.

HORTENSE, with a quiver of emotion: P[. . . . .] (Alexander Vladimirovich is not the one responsible for the disappearance of the title by which Hortense designated her interlocutor this time; rather, in keeping with her promise, Hortense herself put her hand over the intercom at that moment)]. In a month, in a year, how we shall suffer, k[. . . . .] that so many mountains separate me from you. [Bewilderment on the part of Yvette and Georges.]

GORMANSKOÏ: Come, my little Hortense, in a month you will no longer think about it.

HORTENSE, pulling herself together: Oh, Morgan! How could you, for my shoes?

GORMANSKOÏ, formally: I admit that that was a mistake and repeat my earlier apology. I could not foresee the importance you put on putting them on, if I dare express myself in such a way. Unfortunately, I no longer have them in my possession; you know what it's like being weighed down, you have to strike while the iron is hot. As compensation, I am going to have six first-rate potatomashers sent to you, along with a state-of-the-art IBM word processor, it's a real gem.

(There followed a technical discussion about the different models, the presentation of which is not essential.)

HORTENSE: Thank you. Here are your things.

GORMANSKOÏ, after a pause: Everything is here.

HORTENSE, curtly: Of course everything is there!

GORMANSKOÏ: Here are your keys and the four duplicates I had made. Well, we must now part.

HORTENSE, again with tenderness: We must now part. Oh, Morgan, it was so good when you [.......... (here again Hortense put her hand over the intercom).]

GORMANSKOÏ: Farewell, Hortense, farewell.

HORTENSE: Farewell, Morgan, farewell.

Sound of steps moving off. End of the final scene of Hortense's first love.

26
THE DEDICATION

The dedication of Rue de l'Abbé-Migne took place as planned on October 14, the second Sunday of the month. Monsignor Fustiger had a blind and absolute confidence in Providence when it came to the Big Picture but was less certain about how it acted on a daily basis. He had had several difficult weeks, for until Wednesday he remained without news of young Prince Gormanskoï, whose absence, if such was the fate to which he would have to resign himself, would greatly diminish the ceremony's value. Father Domernas, having been driven into a corner, went so far as to speak to one of his three faithful; unfortunately, she was young and ardent but of a faith that was not genuine, and she took advantage of the situation to make him such precise offers that he ran off in a state of extreme confusion.

Finally, on Wednesday, the miracle came to pass. Father Domernas informed Monsignor Fustiger that someone wished to meet with him on behalf of "you know who." The meeting was planned for Grands-Edredons Square; Monsignor Fustiger was to wear street clothes and sit on a bench holding a copy of that day's *Times* (it was no easy matter, obtaining *that day's Times*); he was to wait until he was given a sign. Prince Gormanskoï's envoy would use a password, really a pass-sentence, which was to be: *The sun rises in the west on Sundays.*

Monsignor Fustiger was more than slightly surprised by the identity of the person he encountered early Wednesday afternoon. The man in question was very old, looking to be nearly a hundred (no one knew exactly how old he was), and walked bent over and hunched, his head to one side and sunk into his shoulders, his back practically misshapen by the weight. But all that was not what made him strange; the strange part was that he was dressed like an eighteenth-century fop, what with his three-cornered hat and the gold-handled cane he never stopped twirling in the palm of his hand. His general appearance and the leers he cast around him made him look shockingly like those portraits of old rogues that adorn the walls of the Old Books section of Restif de la Bretonne or Crébillon fils, or those that can be seen in eighteenth-century English novels in which shifty old hags offer up innocent young girls to an "old rake" who looks at them with the basest desire.

Monsignor Fustiger first jumped back but then immediately pulled himself together. The message was simple: Prince Gormanskoï would be present at the ceremony, but only at the ceremony itself. He would be entirely hidden under a black cape and would only show, for the briefest moment, the part of his anatomy bearing the brand of the Poldevian Princes. The current Prince or his envoy would recognize it immediately; it was more valuable than any piece of identification. He would not stay for even a minute after the ceremony, and no one was to inquire after his whereabouts until one year and one day had passed. At that time, if he had not appeared at the court, it was permitted to make inquiries, but it was highly unlikely that that would prove necessary. Prince Gormanskoï requested only the word of Monsignor Fustiger, in whom he had the utmost confidence. His conditions were nonnegotiable. Monsignor Fustiger did not hesitate for a moment.

The old fop given the responsibility for the mission was a well-known figure in the area around Saint Gudule, where he had lived for as long as anyone could remember: he lived in a garret no one had ever entered on Rue Vieille-des-Archives and only went out once a day, at nightfall, for a walk whose route was always the same. No one knew his name or how he fed himself. He walked down the sidewalk taking small steps, his head bent forward, with a grimace on his strangely waxy face that conjured up images of a debauched old man emerging from some frenetic orgy during the time of the Monarchy, all the while mumbling unintelligible words as he twirled his gold-handled cane.

Several principal hypotheses as to his identity and the origin of his get-up had made the neighborhood rounds; according to Madame Eusèbe, who was supported in her belief by Madame Yvonne, he had once been employed by a winemaker, Coachman Wines; at one time, some thirty years earlier, Coachman Wines had put together a somewhat successful advertising campaign, for which they had had a stagecoach with a real horse and a real coachman going around the neighborhood promoting their products; the coachman was supposed to have been the old man, who, unable to accept mandatory retirement, had kept the uniform that had been his during his glory days when all the neighborhood children would follow him on his always identical rounds and applaud him. Another less prosaic hypothesis was defended by Madame Crussant, who had inherited it from her mother, and also got Madame Bouelles's important stamp of approval: according to them, he was supposed to have received a very significant sum of money along with his garret as an inheritance from an English cousin of his who had made a fortune in Poldevia, but with one stipulation: every day until the day he died, he was to make the journey he was seen to make, and wearing the very clothes that were his.

We will not settle the argument.

In giving an overview of this, the novel's grand Sunday, we shall start in the Sinouls household:

Old Man Sinouls woke up very early after a night of very intense "pigmarish" dreams, as he called them. He took a long, hot bath, all the while singing at the top of his lungs: "When most modest dawn / Blushes in a sky so true / Celebration graces nature's lawn / All sings in that purest blue," one of his big hits.

Then he made himself a pot of black coffee, with Balbastre for company.

Next, he walked around the house naked looking for his tuxedo's various components, which had been hidden by malicious hands. He had not gotten out his tuxedo in two years, and he now discovered that he could no longer buckle his belt; he had to have recourse to his two girls' combined efforts:

"Suck in your gut, you old fatty daddy," Armance said to him.

He ended up compromising by leaving the top button on his fly undone and putting his trust in the belt.

The ceremony was to be conducted in three parts.

The Mass was at ten. Monsignor Fustiger's sermon was grave, eloquent, flowery; he traced the history of Poldevia and its Princes, paying particular attention to the branches of the family that had seen the light of conversion shine on them, and that light, he added in a bold transition, is that of the torch whose flame burns on the Poldevian oil fields, bringing not only financial and material well-being but also, and much more importantly, spiritual well-being to those courageous but untamed peoples, for the oil, bred in those stygian, mosquito-ridden regions from the Earth's past, in regions that belong to the Kingdom of the Underworld, by the will of Providence, can become a thing of the pure flame of the spirit, burning moral and hot, ready to transform the ethical landscape of that valiant nation; and how happy we are to have been able, here in Saint Gudule, to work to safeguard the precious chapel dedicated in days of old by our brother Mounezergues to the memory of that unfortunate prince, Luigi Voudzoï, whom God called back to Him prematurely and on horseback, as you all know. Soon, Monsignor Fustiger added as he drew to a close, we will be associating the unfortunate prince, through a joint homage, with one of the Divine Word's finest servants, Abbot Migne, author of the *Patrology,* who will at last have the road he deserves dedicated to him in our City—the only road, furthermore, that would be appropriate for him, as will soon become apparent.

Then came Old Man Sinouls's performance of the thirty-six Telemann variations on that Poldevian folk theme, "Berrichon chon chon." The flowing, moving music, subtle yet simple, filled the Gudulian space into which was packed, in an unusually crowded assemblage, almost the entire population of the area, as well as many of the faithful and numerous officials who had gathered from miles around. In attendance were:

—Monsieur and Madame Crussant, accompanied by the nine little Crussants, each holding a chocolate croissant,

—Monsieur and Madame Yvonne,

—Madame and Monsieur Bouelles, accompaned by Veronica,

—Eusèbe, Madame Eusèbe, and Alexander Vladimirovich,

—Madame and Monsieur Lalamou-Bêlin,

—The widow Anylline, owner of the dry-cleaning establishment on Rue des Grands-Edredons,

—Monsieur Anderthal, antique dealer,

—Yvette,

—Hortense, accompanied by Monsieur Georges Mornacier, Narrator,

—Monsieur Jacques Roubaud, Author,

—the Orsells family: Monsieur Orsells, Madame Orsells—née Hénade Jamblique—Adèle and Idèle Orsells,

—Sir Whiffle, porcine writer,

—Mademoiselle Muche,

—Monsieur Sauconay Vacuman,

—Madame Croche, the concierge of 53,

—Inspector Blognard and his wife,

—Inspector Arapède and his mother,

—a worshiper whose faith was not genuine,

and many, many others.

The Great Ritual Snail Race began in the early afternoon. In Poldevia, everyone attends the great snail races, and especially the ritual races that accompany the succession ceremony, but here attendance was limited to children. The combined efforts of the Crussants, Eusèbes, and Yvonnes had allowed for the organizing of a gigantic snack with ice cream, fruit juice, and cake. The snack was to take place at the end of the race, when the names of the three snails called to mount the podium, in the arms of the boys or girls who had coached them during the ordeal, would be known. The race took place on a huge piece of oilcloth that had been painted white and unfurled at the foot of Saint Gudule. To make it possible for all to follow the scintillating events (for all the snails entered were champions), the race was filmed, enlarged, and projected onto a screen in the square that made the competitors look huge and allowed you to follow, minute by minute, the grimaces brought to their faces by their colossal efforts. The reigning champion was a big, pretentious snail from Burgundy who was attended to by numerous *gregarii*. They crowded in around him and brought him lettuce leaves and blades of fennel in the passes (through a clever arrangement of bricks on the race-course, passes had been set up, along with other obstacles, most notably a river that had to be crossed by means of twigs). The popular favorite was a young, all but unknown little gray snail who had come from the Poldevian chapel's vegetable garden and was full of Poldevian bravery, imagination, and fire; his coach was Veronica Bouelles, and finally, to the crowd's thunderous applause and in spite of the many obvious little pushes given to his rival, the reigning champion, in defiance of fair play (not to mention the rules), he crossed the finish line first and came to receive his prize, a yellow tomato, in the arms of Veronica, who kissed him on his tender muzzle for the television cameras.

At last it was time for the dedication proper:

On the rostrum, the following people encircled Monsignor Fustiger: the members of the assembly, in the process of assembling or disassembling (you know, the authorities); the Poldevian Princes' envoy, the Count of Monte-Cridzoï; Father Domernas and Old Man Sinouls; and, slightly farther back, a mysterious figure in black wearing a black cowl that completely hid his features. All eyes were riveted on this strange apparition; a few wags started a rumor that it was a stripper. In short, everyone was curious.

Night fell. The sun was still loitering around Saint Gudule: it didn't want to miss the climax. The sounds of traffic were distant and weak. A kind of silence developed, made up of solomnity and darkness.

Monsignor Fustiger moved forward: he gestured, and both the Poldevian Princes' envoy and the mysterious apparition in the black cowl stepped forward. Everybody held their breath. With one rapid movement, Monsignor Fustiger lifted the hem of the ample cloak that hid the mystery (wo)man's features. His left buttock appeared, and on that (indisputably masculine) buttock was the brand of the Poldevian Princes, a snail! A shiver ran through the crowd. Then the Poldevian Princes' envoy spoke:

"Prince Gormanskoï, we salute you, First Poldevian Prince, we salute you! Defender of the sacred snail, we salute you, protector of our mountains, we salute you, should you rob one thousand stagecoaches, we salute you, should you seduce one thousand and three beautiful Poldevian maidens, we salute you!"

The sextuple salutation (in Poldevian, but simultaneouly translated by Monsignor Fustiger himself) echoed through the square. A great ovation hailed the new First Prince of Poldevia, Prince Gormanskoï.

"We want to see him, we want to see him," shouted the predominantly female crowd.

But the cowl stayed stubbornly in place. With one wave of his hand, the Monsignor restored calm; he explained that the most pressing reasons of security required Prince Gormanskoï to maintain his cover, but that this situation would not last for more than a year, and that he could then be visited in Poldevia. There were a few catcalls, but in the end everyone accepted this state of affairs.

Through an immense effort of will, Hortense remained impassive and faithful to her promise, since she did not wish, through an over-violent reaction to this spectacle, to betray her knowledge of the dangerous equation she was seeing for the last time: Morgan equals Gormanskoï. She did, however, turn quite pale, and the Narrator, who was sitting next to her, offered to escort her home, an offer she happily accepted.

In the meantime, 366 little cardboard boxes stacked in the shape of a hexagonal-based pyramid had been carried onto the rostrum and placed on Monsignor Fustiger's right. He then took the floor again for the surprise of the day:

"My dear friends," he said, "you are aware that today we are honoring, along with Poldevia, the memory of a great man, Abbot Migne, author of the *Patrology,* that magnificient work which, in 366 volumes, enumerates all the works of the Church Fathers. Now then, and this is the reason for our being here today, the street that now bears his name is the only one whose length is exactly such that a display window like the one you see here on the wall to my left [refer to the map on page 49] can hold an *entire bound set of the Patrology*! And that is what it shall hold from now on. The boxes [he pointed to the pyramid of boxes] each contain one volume of the extremely rare first edition of the *Bound-Thus-Massive-Patrology,* thanks to the generosity of the Poldevian Princes, may they have our thanks for it. And now," continued Monsignor Fustiger, "I am going to open these boxes one by one, each time pulling out one volume that will then be placed in the window."

And, uniting word and deed, he opened the box that was sitting on top of the pyramid and was numbered 1, in Roman, Arabic, and Poldevian numerals.

Monsignor Fustiger opened the box, and his face showed intense bewilderment. His hand appeared in the air and

it held a brick!

He began frantically opening the other boxes one by one with the help of the Poldevian Princes' envoy and the assemblymen— both assembled and disassembled. It soon became necessary to face the facts: each of the 366 boxes contained a brick.

The Patrology had been stolen!

Prince Gormanskoï had slipped away.

CONTINUATION OF CHAPTER 23 (END)

Caught up in their passion for one another, Tyucha and Alexander Vladimirovich had grown careless. As soon as Orsells's philosophical snoring could be heard, Alexander Vladimirovich would come into the room, jump lithely onto the desk, and give himself over with transports of joy to a long paw-holding session with Tyucha: their muzzles would rub up against each other's, their whiskers would intertwine, their coats would electrify one another's; their souls would purr to the beat of the same drummer.

Orsells acted immediately and boldly, guided by the Golden Rule of Ontethics: he went to a department store and bought a snore-synthesizer and a miniature tape recorder that he put in the back pocket of his mauve silk dressing gown. He hooked it all up and waited.

Tyucha purred, Alexander Vladimirovich came and loved. The taped philosophical snoring ceased. Alexander Vladimirovich and Tyucha disentangled their paws and whiskers.

Professor Orsells waited until Alexander Vladimirovich had diappeared (he was very much afraid of his claws) before unmasking poor little unsuspecting Tyucha. Then he brought in his wife and daughters, turned on the spying tape recorder, crossed his arms, and looked at Tyucha while maintaining a stony silence. Tyucha's front and back paws were all aquiver.

"You are a hussy, mademoiselle," Orsells said. "Consider yourself fired!"

And the next day at dawn, comforted by a saucer of milk given her on the sly by Madame Orsells and carrying her little knapsack on her shoulder, a shivering Tyucha crossed the deserted Grands-Edredons Square, where a breeze heralding the coming of fall shook the leaves on the chestnut tree in front of the Poldevian Chapel. Where was she to go, alone in this cold, cruel world? What was to become of her?

What do you think?

27

THE ARREST

It was raining the next day, Monday, October 15. Since ten o'clock, Inspector Blognard had been in charge of the Case of the *Patrology* (to which the likely related case of Prince Gormanskoï's second disappearance had been attached). The big boss made himself very clear:

"Blognard, this case is very, very serious. It seems the Holy Father has called the president himself on the purple line. The Swiss navy has called up its reserve. Poldevia is very, very displeased; our treaty of petroleum friendship hangs in the balance. If you stop and think that each volume contained six times twenty-six ounces of gold, nine emeralds, eleven rubies, and fourteen diamonds of eighteen carats each, you'll see that it comes to a tidy little sum! We have to act quickly, otherwise I get the ax, and if I get the ax, my dear Blognard, you get the ax too!"

So it was now essential to solve the case of the Hardware-Store Horror even faster. Blognard had doubled the size of his swallows, concentrated even more intensely (if that was possible), and doubled his consumption of Callard and Bowser's. And finally, on Thursday the eighteenth, the solution was found.

The Inspector received us—Arapède and myself, that is—sitting on his bench, but not in the beggar outfit he had worn every other day. He had put on his *arrest uniform,* and I understood that the climax was to come that very day.

"During this entire case," Blognard said, "I have had to go against what experience has taught me and throw out the most established procedures at every turn. For the first time ever, someone has found a lead before me [he pointed to me], and, without wanting to put down your efforts or belittle your talents, I can simply tell you: that isn't normal. I tell you this not to excuse my weaknesses nor out of wounded vanity, but because it was only when I accepted this mystery's exceptional nature that I was able to draw nearer to its solution. And that's not all. Isn't it paradoxical that the novel in which we find ourselves—a mystery novel, since there is a detective (two, in fact), a Narrator who follows the investigation, a criminal, and crimes—*has no murder?* Not the least drop of spilled blood? In all honesty I tell you that this case's atmosphere has something strange, unusual, and I would even say *foreign* about it.

"Now that I have presented this necessary preface, let us move on to the mystery itself. Since I could not solve it in the ordinary way, I headed off in an extraordinary direction. Instead of building my house from bottom to top, from the foundations to the ground floor, from the ground to the second story, and so forth, I began, in some sense, in the middle, hanging in midair. But rest assured, I quickly had my feet on the ground.

"What should the *Solution* give us to be considered acceptable? It should answer the following questions:

"Who is the Hardware-Store Horror?

"Why does he attack hardware stores and not train depots or drug stores?

"Was he in a position to conduct the attacks?

"Last, but not least, is this *who* the only person to fulfill the three other conditions?

"I call this the solution's counterproof."

"But if there are several possibilities, how does one choose?" asked Arapède.

"If there are several possibilities, Arapède, there is one possibility that is better than all the others; if not, there is no available guilty party. Let us go back over everything from the beginning."

"For goodness' sake, boss," said Arapède, "think of the Readers. If you want to go over everything from the beginning, you'll have to tell everything that has already been told *and more to boot,* since for each element of the story it will be necessary to add a commentary of sufficient length to clarify its position within the entire investigation. No novelist in the world would agree to take such a risk, and I am not even sure you would be able to stop there, that you would not be forced, upon reaching for the second time the point where we are now, to go back to explain how your explication of the telling of the story's elements coincides at each moment with those elements themselves, and the novel, having already grown to three times its original size upon your first return to where we are now, would, upon your second return, have grown to seven times its planned length; and I should say, to be completely scrupulous, that it is not apparent to me that you could stop there, making it, I fear, a geometric series with a ratio greater than one, which therefore does not converge, meaning that *the novel could never end* and, what is more serious yet, since the criminal is to be arrested *after* the point we are at now—I don't think he has already been arrested, correct me if I am wrong—the *criminal would escape arrest*! Boss, you cannot be contemplating such an end to our investigation! That is why I implore you, boss, do not go back over everything from the beginning, but summarize, boss, summarize!"

Blognard remained silent for a moment, mechanically searching for a candy in his pocket. There was no candy, however, for Madame Blognard forbade his carrying candy when he wore his arrest uniform, lest he sully it in any way *before* the arrest. He seemed to be ruminating about Arapède's argument and following

198

its progression. It must have struck him, at first glance, as
irrefutable, for he told us with a sigh:

"Fine, I will summarize."

"Let me then start with the moment when, thanks to our combined efforts, we had tracked the criminal back to his lair, 53 Rue
des Citoyens—in other words, here [and he pointed to the building].
In a short time, thanks to my questioning of Veronica Bouelles, we
narrowed down the possible locations of the criminal's hideout to
ten apartments, which number soon fell to eight since one of the
apartments was empty and the other was occupied by a certain
Mademoiselle Muche, an old lady who is practically an invalid and
a whiner on top of that. Careful! Contrary to what you thought
and what I have let you think so as not to complicate matters, we
are still not talking about *suspects:* a suspect must have a motive
and we still hadn't gotten to the motives! No, we were still just
talking about not-impossible entities. And then the great storm on
the equinox reduced the number of such entities (I am counting in
apartments, which makes more than three people) to three in one
fell swoop."

"What!" Arapède and I shouted at the same time.

"Three," Blognard said firmly, "and I will prove it!"

He violently furrowed his dark brow, and a wild flame of energy
gleamed in his eyes. At that moment I am sure the criminal must
have been pierced by a dagger of terror.

"Take out your maps from Chapter 7."

We took them out.

"At the foot of 53, slightly to the left of the D stairway as you
go toward the C stairway, are six little x's, see them there?"

We saw.

"On the morning following the great storm on the equinox, as
on every other morning, before sitting on this bench, which you
can also see on the map, 'Inspector Blognard's bench'—not half
bad, eh, Old Man Sinouls drew it for me, helped me a lot during
the investigation—so every morning I would take a little walk
around the building along the side facing the square, in an effort to
get some intuitive sense of the place where, behind his closed
shutters, the criminal's soul attempted to find some rest (I know

he's a nocturnal beast). On that particular morning, there were some pottery fragments there at the foot of the building where I put the six crosses on the map. *They were the fragments of a Poldevian statuette!*"

"They could only have come from the criminal's apartment," Arapède and I said simultaneously.

"You're right."

"But how are you further along?" asked Arapède.

"Quite simply because in no way could they have fallen from an apartment on the *left* side of the stairway, unless you figure they had wings!" the Inspector said triumphantly.

We silently contemplated this irrefutable reasoning.

"But in that case," I said, "there are still five remaining possibilities, I mean four [I had almost forgotten Mademoiselle Muche]."

"No," said Blognard. "Arapède?"

"Yes boss, only three indeed, since the ground-floor window is too low to have caused the statuette to break into fifty-three pieces. To my great regret, we must indeed eliminate Monsieur Anderthal, the antique dealer."

"You had him in your sights, eh?"

"Yes, I did, and I will tell you why later."

"So that left three possibilities," Blognard went on, "and I am not going to say which one is the right one just yet. We must first eliminate one. For it must not be forgotten that the statuette, a mediocre copy of one of the original casts of the famed Poldevian Venus, Venus with Snail, shows very clearly that the criminal had a tie to Poldevia. *Poldevia is at the heart of this case.* Now, of the three remaining apartments, only two contain someone having any strong ties to Poldevia. Madame and Monsieur Yvonne can be crossed off the list without any hesitation."

"So much the better," we said.

And Arapède added:

"'And then there were two,' I hope it's not going to be like in the song: 'and then there were none'! When you get right down to it," Arapède added, "a detective is like a serial killer—he eliminates the suspects one after the other."

This idea seemed to bring him a great deal of pleasure.

"Ah yes," Inspector Blognard went on, "before even considering the motive, I knew that there were only two possible suspects: Professor Orsells and Monsieur Sauconay Vacuman!"

We stopped for a moment to consider the enormity of what he had just said.

"Each of them immediately turned into a suspect, since neither of them has an alibi. Monsieur Vacuman lives alone and is always out traveling. Professor Orsells works nights in his locked study and has a way of getting out of his apartment without being seen by his wife, daughters, or anyone else, save the cat. They have both been to Poldevia; Monsieur Vacuman represented his company there for three years. Monsieur Orsells lectured there, and what is more, his wife, nee Hénade Jamblique, is Poldevian by birth.

"They both have a powerful motive:

"Monsieur Vacuman lost the hardware-store frying-pan market to a Poldevian company, the very one that offered the statuettes to the unfortunate hardware-store owners. Hence his motive is revenge.

"Orsells's motive is just as powerful, if more subtle: envy. Envy of those who take up more space in the newspapers, all those people who are talked about in columns and who don't come up to his ankle. By becoming the Hardware-Store Horror, even if in an indirect way, he got to be the star, the one whose deeds take up the whole front page, the one about whom you frantically search for more information inside the *Paper.*

"Each of them, if either of them is the criminal, needed to draw attention to himself, both as a challenge and because of the secret desire, shared by all criminals, to be arrested, and *arrested by me,* of course. Or, if not, to defeat me.

"A quick glance at Monsieur Vacuman's dossier revealed his link to Poldevia. It was harder with Orsells, since *the evidence had been covered up.* Old Man Sinouls's remark, passed on to me by Arapède after he happened to overhear it in the Gudule Bar, was what put me on the right track, because it forced me to go back through the dossier; otherwise I would have had only one suspect left, the most obvious one.

"There, now you have all the evidence in hand."

There was still one last customary, solemn, unavoidable duty to carry out. Both suspects were at home. The neighborhood had been discreetly cordoned off since dawn, and the border patrols had been reinforced.

Upon reaching the foot of Stairway D, Arapède pushed a button. The door opened. We walked up behind Inspector Blognard. There was the sound of a doorbell, and the door opened:

"I'm sorry to bother you, madame," Blognard said. "I'm Inspector Blognard. I'd like to talk to your husband, Professor Orsells."

That moment will be forever etched upon my memory. Tall, lovely, pale Madame Orsells standing there with her long blond braid of hair tumbling down her back, her one shoe on her left foot. Behind her, holding hands and wearing somber dresses, stood the two little girls, Adèle and Idèle, the very picture of innocence. It was the last happy moment for a family that was about to be turned upside down by the inexorable march of justice.

Orsells appeared, no doubt emerging from his study. He and Blognard looked each other over for a moment like two fencers before the first touch; Orsells's eyes, with their look of feigned surprise and hypocritical confusion, seemed to be saying: "I may have lost a set, but I haven't lost the match!"

For a moment nobody moved, then Blognard spoke:

"Philibert Jules Orsells, alias the Hardware-Store Horror, I arrest you in the name of the law."

28

THE LAST CHAPTER

This is the last chapter, meaning that I am, at this very moment, in the process of writing it in my study on a pretty spring morning. Before writing my last chapter, I did some research; I read the last chapters of three-hundred sixty-six novels, from which I derived a few rules I am going to try to put to use.

First of all, you must have a last chapter. Reading all the last novel chapters I read made me want to dispense with this chore, for I have the sense that, for the vast majority of my brethren, it *is* a chore; the novel's climax is almost always to be found at the end of the second-to-last chapter, and what comes next is thus necessarily an anticlimax.

Only, the problem is that it is very difficult to do without a last chapter: for if you do away with the last chapter, thereby ending the novel with the second-to-last chapter, then the second-to-last chapter becomes ipso facto the last chapter, with the major drawback being that the final drama, the concluding symphonic cadence, the emotional climax you have planned is now to be found at the end of the last chapter, meaning that the second-to-last chapter falls flat, and the last as well, since the reader can only allow himself to be filled with surprise and wonder if he knows that what he is reading is not the last chapter, which he certainly has no intention of reading but which he expects to be there, all the same, right before the index or, failing that, the words THE END. And if, taking this fact into account, you decide to move back another notch, you still make no progress unless you continue in this fashion until you find yourself with zero chapters, which is not very many at all. Then you have no last chapter, but look at the price you pay.

Which reminds me that at one point I had thought of putting a *summary of the preceding chapters,* as can be found in some excellent novels I have read, into the novel under the chapter number and title. But I gave up this idea for the following reason, which is not unrelated to the one that made me give up the idea of doing without a last chapter—the problem in this case being the *first chapter.* Indeed, what do you put at the beginning of the first chapter under the heading *summary of the preceding chapters*? Nothing? Then the work has an unfortunate dissymmetry that will be judged most harshly by the critics and the Ph.D. students at the University of Nebraska. My colleague Stephen Leacock, in his wonderful novel *Gertrude the Governess* if I am not mistaken, thought he had found a solution to the problem of the first-chapter summary by simply writing: "Chapter One: summary of preceding chapters: There are no preceding chapters."

The solution is ingenious and elegant but too sophisticated, I fear.

One of my friends, the avant-garde novelist Denis Duabuor, pushing Leacock's idea to the limit, wrote a beautiful novel based on this principle. The text of the first chapter, whose summary is "There is no preceding chapter," is: "There is no preceding chapter." Then comes Chapter 2. The summary of Chapter 1, put at the beginning of Chapter 2, is: "In Chapter 1, it was said that there was no preceding chapter." The text of Chapter 2 itself is: "There is no chapter preceding the preceding chapter." It's very beautiful. Unfortunately, having been unable to obtain either a contract or an advance, Duabuor evidently gave up, meaning that I do not know how he would have solved the problem of the last chapter, a problem he would not have been able to avoid running into at some time or another.

But let us get back to the subject at hand, I mean our own paradoxical subject, the current novel's last chapter, which will be traditional in its conception.

The last chapter is written in the present tense, for it is at this moment that the novelist and the Reader are together in the same narrative time. All the passion, all the crime, happiness, and despair have come and gone, the mundane has reasserted its rights; the Reader reads and the novelist writes his last chapter, in which he takes his leave of his characters and explains what has become of them since the second-to-last chapter, the one in which the main issues were resolved. The time that has passed is exactly that which was necessary for the novelist to write his novel, and now he has come to the last chapter.

Inspector Blognard, accompanied by his faithful assistant Arapède, is up to his neck in the Case of the *Patrology*. If the case of the Hardware-Store Horror ended in victory, the victory was only partial. Orsells was found guilty of a lesser charge; a certain doubt remained in the jurors' minds. Finally, as a result of a massive public-opinion campaign in which Hortense participated, he was freed. The reason for this turn of events was the failure on the part of the District Attorney, an oaf, to accurately reproduce the reasoning by which Blognard proved that Orsells's own philosophy, The Golden Rule of Ontethics, made his guilt inevitable. The D.A. got all tangled up, and Orsells's lawyer had no trouble using the same rule, not to prove Orsells's innocence, but to raise at least a shadow of a doubt in the minds of the jurors, who extricated themselves from their predicament by using the clumsy solution of convicting the accused on a lesser charge than that brought by the prosecution.

It must be admitted that Arapède was not entirely convinced by Blognard:

"It looks like a proof," he would say of the argument drawn from the Golden Rule, "it tastes like a proof, it's dressed like a proof, but is it really and fully a proof?"

Blognard, who dismissed these reservations as yet another manifestation of Arapède's well-known skepticism, did not hold it against him. He also did not hold the Narrator's neutrality (better than an outright defection, anyway) against him, because its cause was perfectly understandable in his eyes; but the best part is that I can give you a chance to read a letter from the narrator himself, sent at a time when our relations were still excellent (that is to say, before the vulgar and unmerited success of his mediocre book about the case):

"As you will easily understand [the letter was accompanied by an invitation to his and Hortense's wedding], I have remained strictly neutral during the trial, since Hortense has taken up Orsells's cause and I myself am linked to Blognard (he apparently doesn't hold it against me). And I must say that the open, passionate discussions we have had concerning the application of the Golden Rule of Ontethics to the problem have shaken me a bit. I am sure, however, that Orsells is guilty."

So the Narrator married Hortense. He patched things up between her and her family; Hortense mellowed to the point of allowing a respectable number of Poldevian hams (the best in the world) to be converted into a pleasant house in Normandy to which the couple retired after Orsells was freed—she to finally finish her thesis, he to write a best-seller about the case of the Hardware-Store Horror.

Madame and Monsieur Yvonne are fine. The Crussants, the Bouelleses, the Sinoulses, and Yvette are all fine. Madame Eusèbe has apparently gotten over the disappearance of Alexander Vladimirovich, who was never seen again after the Sunday of the dedication. Eusèbe resumed his life's work observing the Tourists (female only, of course), but occasionally his gaze drifts and wavers, and he catches himself contemplating a passing dog.

Saint Gudule is fine.

Everything is fine.

THE END

THE POSTULTIMATE
CHAPTER

About three months after the events reported in chapters 26 and 27—that is to say, the day after the sixth attack by the criminal dubbed the Dry-Cleaner Debater (the victim was the widow Anylline, still living at 53 Rue des Citoyens, Stairway D. Following his m.o., the criminal, possessed of a heretofore unheard-of audacity, had slipped into the dry-cleaner's just before closing and demanded that a disgustingly dirty pair of pants be perfectly and immediately cleaned. Upon receiving Madame Anylline's refusal, he had started an argument with her and, in a fit of most likely simulated rage, had begun pouring out a highly intricate trail of [smoking] nitric acid that had a catastrophic effect on the store's contents. He had then disappeared, once again undescribed and therefore unapprehensible)—Carole, an Aerial Paleontology student, boarded the Q-line bus at the Vieille-des-Archives stop. The Q line, as everyone knows, runs perpendicular to the T line, which it crosses at the intersection of Rue des Citoyens and Rue Vieille-des-Archives.

Carole, a beautiful young brunette, was dressed warmly (it was freezing outside). She put her things down on the empty seat facing her. As the bus was pulling away from the stop, she noticed a white silhouette of a woman with a blue bra painted on the wall of the building facing 53 Rue des Citoyens. The silhouette was standing up *and pissing*. At the third stop (she was going to the Museum of Natural History), a young man moved down the central aisle and showed his intention of taking the place facing her. Carole immediately picked up her things and put them on her knees. The young man sat down.

As he sat down, he looked at Carole and said:
"You have beautiful eyes, mademoiselle, especially your left."
It was true.